TAINTED

RILEY EDWARDS

BE A REBEL
Riley Edwards Romance

Tainted

Triple Canopy Book 5

Cover design: Lori Jackson Designs

Cover Image by: Wander Agular

Written by: Riley Edwards

Published by: Riley Edwards/Rebels Romance

Edited by: Rebecca Hodgkins

Proofreader: Julie Deaton, Rebecca Kendall

TAINTED

Print ISBN: 978-1-951567-22-4

First edition: November 30, 2021

To my family - my team – my tribe.
This is for you.

1

Chelsea rolled off me, then without missing a beat, rolled off the bed. My gaze zeroed in on her bare heart-shaped ass and I caught sight of the marks my fingertips had left. That made me think about why she was wearing my marks and how good she'd felt while I'd given them to her.

"Where are you going?" I asked and looked at the clock.

It was barely four in the morning, and by my way of thinking, we could get round three in before I had to leave for work.

"Home," she answered and bent to pick up something off the floor.

When she straightened, she pulled her shirt over her head and her response hit me. She was leaving. I tried to remember the last time a woman rolled off me, then seconds later, out of my bed. *That would be never.* Then I tried to remember a time when a woman hadn't attempted cuddling. *Again, that would be never.* Finally, I tried to think of a time a woman hadn't tried to angle to spend the night. I fell short of finding an answer to that, too, because women always wanted to stay.

Chelsea's exit should've been refreshing; instead, it was irritating.

Therefore, I didn't hide my contempt and grunted, "Home?"

She craned her neck and looked over her shoulder at me. She didn't hide her displeasure at my tone.

"Yes, Matt. *Home*. I have training at seven."

"Skip your..."

Her eyes narrowed and her perfectly sculpted eyebrows pulled together, I clamped my mouth shut.

I'd spent months watching Chelsea—more like studiously scrutinizing her. She was a study of opposites. Everything about her was contradictory. The woman was a bona fide cowgirl. She rode in rough stock events—bull riding and bareback broncs. A tomboy, yet all woman. Work-rough hands, yet manicured nails. Her body was hard and angled and shredded to perfection, yet she still managed to be soft. She was fun-loving and funny yet closed off. She was friendly with all the women at Triple Canopy, especially Adalynn, yet she held herself remote.

Now I could add hardworking despite being up all night. And quick-tempered despite multiple orgasms, the last one happening less than ten minutes ago. The hours she spent in the gym strengthening her body did not go unnoticed or unappreciated. Her thick muscular thighs, her strong core, her pussy snug and wet. She rode me fast and wild—all I'd needed to do was hold on and she brought it home. both of us crying out in pleasure. Her not breaking a sweat, me in awe of the woman who'd spent all night drinking and laughing with friends, yet still had it in her to let loose and fuck all night.

"Tell me, Matt, *you* ever skip on training?"

That would be a fuck no.

Apparently, Chelsea didn't either.

"Nope," I answered.

"So, what makes you think I'd skip mine?"

I obviously hit a sore spot and shuffled through what I knew about her. Last night when I caught her in the backroom of my new pool hall crying, she'd mentioned her ex-boyfriend and needing to move her horses from his property because his new woman didn't like the smell of horse shit—which I was almost certain was code for the new girlfriend was jealous.

"Did your ex have an issue with how much you train?"

"What?" she asked and bent to pick up another article of clothing. "Why would you ask that?"

I watched as she stepped into her panties and settled them on her hips, wondering why in the hell I was talking about the ex and the apparent hang-up she had about being asked to skip out on a workout.

That was not what this was.

I had no right to ask her personal questions.

"No reason."

I'd avoided Chelsea for months, not wanting the entanglement. And seeing as now, I was curious about her life when I shouldn't have been made this all a mistake. I'd been so worried about how Chelsea would react if we ever casually hooked up, I'd never contemplated my feelings. That thought in itself was laughable. I didn't form emotional attachments to women. I'd learned the hard way that when a woman found out I had money, I ceased being a man and started being a sugar daddy. Now don't get me wrong; I was all for spicing things up in the sack, and if a woman was the type who liked a little kink, I was down to play. But outside of the bedroom, I had a serious fucking issue with women using me as their personal ATM. Or worse, asking me to buy her expensive shit just because she thought I was rollin' in it.

Unfortunately, when I was young and dumb—before I'd learned—I fell for the shit women said. But when I learned, I *learned,* and the way I learned was punctuated with a capital L, an exclamation point, and two thick lines underlining the word. After that, I shut down my emotions and kept my relationships casual.

No one got hurt when there wasn't the promise of a tomorrow.

"Matt—"

"Straight up, Chelsea, I shouldn't have asked. This isn't that. You need to roll out of here in the middle of the night, it's not my business why. Now the real question, the one I shoulda asked is, do you have plans tonight?"

Chelsea looked completely unfazed, and for some unknown reason, her non-reaction annoyed me. If any other woman would've looked at me with a blank expression after I reminded her that her personal life wasn't a topic I wanted to discuss, I would've said she was a keeper. But Chelsea doing it irritated me.

This wasn't a good idea.

But damn if I could stop myself from wanting to see her again.

"Eleven work for you?" My face must've registered alarm because Chelsea grinned and shook her head. "Eleven *p.m.,*" she clarified.

Yep, she was perfect.

By my calculations, ninety-five percent of women still angled for dinner the next night even after they swore they understood dinner dates, spending the night, and home-cooked meals weren't up for discussion. Clearly, Chelsea was one of the rare five percent.

"Do you want me to come to you?" I asked.

I could be a gentleman.

Chelsea bent again and picked up the rest of her clothes, tossing her bra on the bed before she put on her jeans. She was buttoning them up when she answered.

"No. I'll come here."

"Afraid you won't be able to kick me out of your bed?" I quipped.

But I was actually interested in why she wanted to come back to my place.

"I like to be able to leave when I'm ready to go."

So, totally fucking perfect.

Then why do I feel like I've been punched in the gut?

"A woman after my own heart," I swooned to cover up my aggravation.

I had no reason to be frustrated, yet I was.

Chelsea tagged her bra off my bed, tucked it into her back pocket, then moved to my nightstand. After shoving aside condom wrappers, she nabbed her keys, hair band, and turned to leave but paused.

"Thanks for a good night," she muttered.

A good night?

What the fuck?

I shoved the anger down and plastered a smile on my face.

"Anytime, babe. See you later."

"Yeah, Matt, later."

I stayed in bed, naked as the day I was born, spent condom still on my cock, and watched Chelsea walk out of my room.

What the fuck just happened?

The front door slammed.

With no answers to be had, I got up to flush the rubber and take a shower.

By the time I was back in my bed, with the faint smell of sex still in the air and Chelsea's musky perfume lingering, it hit me she hadn't even left her hair tie on my nightstand.

Women liked to leave shit behind as an excuse to come back. But not Chelsea—not even a rubber band.

She'd dressed, grabbed her shit, and bolted.

My irritation grew—not at Chelsea's behavior but at my own.

Why the hell was I thinking about a hair tie?

Why did I care if Chelsea got off and took off?

I tossed and turned and tried to convince myself I didn't give a fuck if all she wanted was a few more orgasms.

Simultaneous pounding on my door and the shrill ring of my phone jolted me awake. The life I'd led, the job I had, meant a wake-up call that included both a personal visit and a phone call could mean anything—and that anything could mean mayhem and blood. It was with that in mind, I quickly jumped out of bed, tagged a pair of sweats off the floor, and ignored the phone in favor of making the knocking stop. By the time I made it to the door, I was unhappily tying the drawstring of my sweats and plotting somebody's murder unless the six in the morning visit was to inform me someone was bleeding out.

When I opened the door, three men in suits were staring at me. My heartbeat thumped faster.

"Can I help you?"

"Are you Matthew Kessler?" one of the suits asked.

"I am."

As if they'd practiced in perfect synchronicity, they flashed their badges and, just as coordinated, flipped the wallet so I could see their IDs.

"Mr. Kessler, I'm Agent Weaden," suit number one introduced himself, then jerked his head to the right and said, "That's Agent Ewing." A jerk to the left. "And that's Agent Moody. May we come in?"

Three FBI agents at my door first thing in the morning. Well, that's not fucking good.

"Is someone hurt?" I asked instead of extending an invitation to enter.

"No, Mr. Kessler. We just have a few questions."

"About?"

"Perhaps—" Agent Weaden started but stopped when my phone started ringing again.

Since I had not one thing to hide and needed to get work, I stepped back and swept my arm in a wide arc as a silent welcome to enter.

"Excuse me a moment." On my way to the kitchen, I pointed to the living room. "Have a seat."

I grabbed my phone off the wireless charging pad and my body instantly started humming with dread.

Roland Huston, my father's longtime attorney, calling me before normal office hours, coupled with the FBI at my door, couldn't be a coincidence.

I slid my thumb across the screen and brought the phone to my ear.

"Mr. Huston. Everything okay?"

I heard the deep inhale and I should've braced. At the very least, I should've sat my ass down.

I did neither; therefore, I was ill-prepared.

Not that there was a proper way for a man to ready himself for his world to crumble.

"Your father's been arrested."

My gaze shot to the three men standing in my living room, and I asked, "Come again?"

"It is very likely you'll receive a visit from the FBI today. It is imperative you do not speak to them."

"Arrested?" I spat. "What for?"

"The charges are not what's important at the—"

Was Roland insane? The charges damn well did matter.

"What are the charges?"

"Racketeering, money laundering, and tax evasion. Though, the tax charges look like they'll be dropped."

My head was still spinning when I sarcastically spat, "Well, thank fuck for that."

"This is serious, Matthew," Roland chided.

Was he high?

"The three FBI agents in my living room was my first clue, Roland."

"Already," he mumbled. "Ask them to leave. You do not have to speak to them. They don't have a warrant, and you're not named in the charges."

I wasn't named in the charges?

What the fuck?

I felt the muscles in my neck tighten and the beginning of a massive headache coming on.

"Get rid of the feds and call me back," Roland clipped. "I'll send my company jet down to Georgia. This is something that should be discussed in person."

Roland would send his jet, not my father's.

Vern and Ginny Kessler didn't fly commercial, and neither did my older sister, so, naturally, my old man had his own private jet.

Fuck.

"What about Alessandra and my mother?"

"Matthew, I think it is best if you come up to Connecticut so we can speak about this in person. There are other matters, including your obligations to your sister and mother."

"And I think it's best for you, *right now*, to explain to me what's going on and why my father would be arrested on these ridiculous charges."

"Matthew—"

"Now, Roland!"

"This is a face-to-face—"

"Never mind. I'll call you back."

I disconnected the call and looked at the three men, who I knew would be all too happy to share. Then I could explain they had the wrong man; my father would never engage in any sort of illegal activity, and I certainly had no ties to whatever they were investigating.

"Would one of you like to explain why my father's been arrested?"

Agent Weaden gave me what I reckoned was supposed to be a grim look, but the excitement in his eyes negated the sentiment.

"Do you know Arnie Mancini?"

My insides churned and apprehension crawled up my spine.

I knew Arnie Mancini well. He and his wife migrated to the States from central Italy to open a restaurant. I'd known him and his family practically my whole life. I'd spent summers with my mother and sister at his home in Ancona. The house was not palatial, nor was it the size of the other homes in the hills overlooking the Adriatic. It was bigger than most and had the best view of the sea. The Mancinis also had quite a bit of land and a full-time caretaker. Arnie had come to America poor, and he was currently living the dream of owning one of Greenwich's premier hot spots. His restaurant, Mancini's, had a months-long waitlist. Not even celebrities could use their status to cut the line.

Except for a Kessler.

There was always a table available for my father. And while I'd never tested the theory, I bet if I'd walked into Mancini's without a reservation, *Zio* Arnie would have a table ready.

Fuck.

The Mancini home in Greenwich was palatial. It was also over-the-top ostentatious. *Zia* Sophia decorated in gold with a heavy bent toward velvet and silk.

They were wealthy, extremely so my father managed their money.

Too wealthy for restaurateurs?

"Yes, I know Arnie Mancini. What does he have to do with my father?"

"How well do you know Mancini?" Agent Ewing asked.

"Well enough. I call him *Zio* and his wife *Zia* and spent a fair amount of my childhood in their home."

"You know we looked into you," Agent Moody entered the conversation. "You forfeited your place at Kessler Management and the salary that would've come with it. Instead, you joined the Navy as an enlisted sailor, making less in a year than what you could've made in a month with the company your grandfather founded. You spend fourteen years in the Navy, ten of those as a SEAL, eight of those as a SEAL sniper, and when you left the military, you still weren't making near what your investments were paying out."

As annoying as it was, the FBI had looked into me. My military service and salary were public record. My missions were not. However, any idiot could find me on Military

Buddy Finder. But what had me curious was why Moody was so interested in money.

"Is there a reason you're wasting my time explaining to me shit I very well know instead of, say, enlightening me as to why the hell my father has been arrested?"

"I just find it interesting that you had everything a man could want laid out for you from the time you were born and turned your back on it to join the service."

Moody said the word "service" like it tasted bad on his tongue, and his tone was tinged with more than a little jealousy.

"A man who values money over country might find it interesting. But a man who values integrity and honor over the almighty dollar would not. Which I have to say, says a lot about the type of man you are but has fuck all to do with my father." I glanced back to Weaden and said, "You've got two minutes to tell me why you're here and what's happening with my dad, or I'll show you the door."

"Arnie Mancini's been under investigation for years," Weaden started. "Your father almost as long."

"For what?" I cut in.

Weaden stared at me, he even tilted his head and squinted his eyes. The look conveyed disbelief and not a little of it.

The man thought I was a liar.

What the fuck?

"I didn't take you as the type," Weaden mumbled.

My back shot straight.

"Come again?"

"Nothing in our investigation pointed to you directly. But there are many ways a man can be complicit without being openly involved. You either knew about Mancini's ties to organized crime and through him, your father's, and you turned a blind eye, or you're—"

"Organized crime?" I seethed. "No fucking way."

Once again, Weaden eyed me skeptically, and it was then my perfect life started to crumble. It wouldn't be until later when it completely shattered. But the first crack in the foundation had been made.

2

"Mr. Kessler, why don't you take a minute and get dressed. We'll wait here," Agent Ewing suggested.

I wanted to suggest he and his cohorts get the fuck out of my house, but unfortunately, I needed answers and not the kind that Roland Huston would feed me. I wanted to know why the FBI would think Arnie had mob ties, but more than that, I needed to know how my father fit into their investigation.

"Make yourselves at home," I invited. "I haven't made coffee, but help yourselves to the kitchen."

Weaden was still eyeing me up like I was a liar, and he was gauging my performance.

"You're looking at me like I'm crazy," I said to Weaden. "I've got nothing to hide, so I've got no issue leaving you alone in my living room. And just to put your mind at ease, I'm not going to call my father's attorney back while I'm getting dressed, but I am going to call my boss. And since you've looked into me, I don't have to inform you that Nick Clark's former FBI. I'm going to ask him to come over. If you don't like that, I suggest you use the door."

With that, I left the living room, dialing Nick's number on the way to my room. My bedroom door barely clicked shut when Nick picked up.

"Everything all right?"

"Three FBI agents are in my living room," I told him and rummaged through my closet for pants. "My father's been arrested. Racketeering and money laundering."

I heard Nick's low whistle, then he said, "You sound oddly calm."

"That's because the shock hasn't worn off yet, and I'm still trying to wrap my head around how in the hell my father could possibly be involved in this. And they said a man who I grew up thinking as an uncle is involved in organized crime."

"Shit," Nick muttered. "I'll be there in fifteen minutes. Until I get there, keep your mouth shut."

"Why? I have nothing to hide."

There was a weighted pause before he said, "Right now, brother, you have everything to hide."

Fucking hell.

Two hours later, Moody, Ewing, and Weaden were standing at my front door. Nick was showing them out while my ass was rooted to the chair with my eyes glued to the charging documents in front of me. This after the three FBI agents had produced a stack of pictures of my father with a man I recognized, a man that anyone over the age of thirty would know, and anyone who lived in or near New York would absolutely have heard of—Lorenzo "Angel Face" Zanetti.

Zanetti was unmistakable. At seventy, he was still a good-looking man. The paparazzi loved him, and every gold-digger in the city flocked to the old man who was never pictured in anything other than his signature Brioni suit. He was also the head of the Zanetti crime family. One of the five families that still had a stronghold in New York. Unlike the other four families whose origins stem from the original and most recognizable *Cosa Nostra,* Zanetti ties were with the *Camorra* out of Naples.

Zanetti was a modern-day mobster.

What the hell was my father doing with him?

No, scratch that—how the hell did my father even know him?

The FBI had given me their version. They'd shown me their evidence. They'd asked about my involvement in my father's alleged affairs. They'd produced bank documents, investment portfolios, deeds to land, contracts, audio recordings, and still images. A slew of damning evidence that my father not only had Lorenzo Zanetti as a client but a business partner. And further from that, my father owned a plethora of businesses I knew nothing about.

I sat back in my chair and pressed the heels of my palms to my eye sockets, wishing I could rewind to last night.

How was this possible?

If this was true, my whole life had been a lie.

My father's association with Zanetti went back three decades.

How was it possible I didn't know my father was in the fucking mob?

"Matt?" Nick called.

I dropped my hands to find Nick standing across the table from me.

"What's your take?" I asked.

My boss eyed me cautiously. What he didn't do was answer my question.

"If I wasn't your friend and employee. If this wasn't my father. What's your take?" I prompted.

"Vern Kessler's fucked," Nick declared. "The feds have years' worth of surveillance which yielded enough evidence to prove Vern was not a victim of blackmail. He wasn't strong-armed or terrorized or intimidated. Which would give him and his attorney a defense to present to the court. He was a willing and active participant. As Weaden pointed out, your father's a small piece of the puzzle. They want Zanetti and Mancini. That gives your father a bargaining chip. Though if he was smart, he'd take what he knows to the grave and serve his time. He talks, he puts you, your mom, and your sister at risk."

Jesus Christ.

At risk.

That was a goddamn understatement. What Nick actually meant was if my father turned on the mob and talked, they'd turn on him and kill me, Alessandra, and my mom.

In the blink of an eye. A single beat of my heart. One breath.

Everything I thought I knew about Vern Kessler—a loving father, a devoted husband, a smart businessman—changed.

Now the question was, what was I going to do with the information I'd learned?

"You haven't asked me if I knew," I pointed out.

"Don't be an asshole."

Nick shook his head and pulled out a chair.

"I'm not, Nick, but the evidence is suggesting my dad's a fuckin' criminal. I'm close to him, to my mom. I know Mancini and his wife well. My dad handles my investments..." I trailed off, and sour hit my gut.

"Obviously, your investments and money are clean, or

the feds would've seized your assets as well."

"Money that came from him."

"Money that came from an inheritance that your grandfather left for you," Nick corrected.

Money that was now tainted.

"I'm a shareholder in Kessler Management," I reminded Nick. "My earnings get rolled into my portfolio."

Nick had nothing to say to that. All of my father's personal accounts had been frozen. Same with the Mancini and Zanetti accounts my father managed. But the hundreds of other clients Kessler managed were left untouched, including mine. It was true the bulk of my personal wealth was funded by my sizable inheritance. But, I still received dividends from Kessler, which meant I'd received dirty money and profited from my father's mob ties.

The thought made me sick to my stomach.

My phone rang and my heart jumped in my chest. The shock of the situation was wearing off, and anger and shame had started to creep in.

Family was everything.

But was that still true when it was all an illusion?

I glanced at the screen and saw my mother's name. Shit, she must've been freaking out. Weaden had told me a tactical team had raided my parents' home just after midnight. My father had been immediately taken into custody while my mother had watched. They'd even gone out to the guest house, where my sister lived, and had woken her up to bring Alessandra into the main house. Since the guest house was on the property, the feds had searched her home as well.

In my misery, I'd selfishly only thought about myself, barely giving a passing thought to my mom and sister and how they were feeling.

I snagged my phone off the table and answered the call.

"Mom? Are you all right?"

"It's Alessandra," my sister snapped. "And no, mother's not doing *all right*. She had to be sedated. When are you coming home?"

It could be said I was not close to my sister. She was older than me by five years, putting her in her forties, and she still lived with mommy and daddy. Sure she had her own four-thousand-foot residence, but it was on our parents' estate. Alessandra was also as stuck up and entitled as they came. The cost of the designer gear that hung in one of her many closets was whacked. The vacations she took on our father's dime, extravagant. She held an honorary position at Kessler Management, but she didn't actually work. She entertained clients. I wasn't fond of her, and she returned the sentiment and didn't like me much. We were cordial to one another because that was what was demanded of us—we were Kesslers, after all.

"I haven't made plans yet."

"Mr. Huston called and informed me he offered you his jet. You don't need to plan anything. It's been done for you."

In an attempt to cool my temper, I took in a deep breath. Unfortunately, it did nothing to calm my flaring anger.

"I don't need Roland's jet," I snarled. "I have things I need to take care of here before I come home."

Home.

Did I actually have a home, or did I have a mansion built with lies?

"Of course, you do." Contempt and indignation laced her catty statement.

"What does that mean?"

"It means you always have something else to do. Why would this be any different? Matthew, the golden child, off doing whatever the hell it is you do, uncaring you abandoned this family and turned your back on your birthright."

My birthright? Was she serious? What were we, catapulted back to the sixteenth century?

"Well, dear sister, since you're the first-born, Kessler Management is *your* birthright, not mine. Consider me stepping aside as doing you a favor, giving you what you never hid you wanted—your place at the head of the table. Now's your time to shine, Alessandra. Step up and steer the ship. I hear it's sinking."

"God, do you always have to be a dick?"

"Typical. I'm a dick when I'm not bowing to your attitude like everyone else seems to do."

"I don't have time for this nonsense. We have real issues to discuss, and you're needed here. So, if you'd please clear your busy schedule playing cops and robbers and come home, Mother would appreciate it."

She was so full of shit. My mother was currently sedated. It was my sister who needed me to come home to deal with our father's arrest. Alessandra didn't have the first clue how to deal with a hangnail—forget dealing with a hysterical mother and a father in lockup.

"What's Roland doing to get Dad out on bail?" I asked.

"What's needed."

That was vague.

"After Dad was arrested, did the FBI talk to you?"

"Yes," she hissed. "They didn't leave until after five. They also ransacked the house."

"Did they ransack it or search it?"

"Same thing."

I sighed and focused on Nick's solemn face.

"Did you know?" I asked.

"Do you think I'm stupid, Matthew?"

What the hell did that mean?

"Seriously? You knew?"

"I'm not stupid enough to answer that after our father's been arrested and our phones have been tapped for the last year."

She knew.

My fucking sister *knew*.

Holy shit.

She wasn't freaking out that our father had been wrongly arrested. She wasn't furious with righteous anger that our father had been removed from his home in cuffs. She wasn't defending our father's integrity and morality.

Alessandra goddamn *knew*.

"What the fuck is wrong with you?" I growled. "Jesus, Ally, do you have any idea how fucked we all are?"

"It's like you're not even a Kessler," she weirdly returned. "I see all these years away from the family have made you a holier than thou twit. The board is convening tomorrow morning at nine. Your presence is non-negotiable. In Father's absence, you're the proxy figurehead. We need to present a united front and assure the employees and shareholders this is all a misunderstanding, and it is business as usual."

My sister must've fallen down in a pair of her Jimmy Choos while prancing around at one of the many expensive dinners she attended and bumped her hard head, causing her to have a momentary lapse in sanity if she thought she was going to summon me up to Connecticut.

"I am many things, Alessandra. One of them used to be a Kessler. What I am not now, nor have I ever been, is a goddamn liar. You know this. So why you'd think I'd stand in for Dad and lie is beyond me."

"I suggest you find a pair of balls in the next few hours, little brother, unless you want your mother to be homeless."

Translation: I won't have a place to live and money to spend, and I don't know how to function as an adult. So, please, little brother, come to my rescue and perjure yourself.

I didn't get the pleasure of telling my sister where she could shove her guilt trip before she hung up on me.

"I take it that didn't go well," Nick stated the obvious.

"My sister knew about what my father was doing."

"Christ, did she tell you that?"

No. Apparently, my big sis was wise to evading the law and unsecured lines.

"She didn't have to. She was not surprised our father had been arrested. She wasn't upset, shocked, or crying. She's more concerned with Kessler Management and had the nerve to tell me to grow a pair of balls and fly to Connecticut so I can lie to the board and keep harmony in the company. Her priority is the continuation of money flow, not our dad being wrongfully accused of crimes he didn't commit. And I know Alessandra. She's a bitch who cares a great deal about her reputation and the Kessler name. If my father was innocent, she'd have already called the media."

"How do you wanna play this?" Nick asked.

"Play what?"

Nick leaned back and crossed his arms over his chest, leveling me with a scowl.

"We can keep this between you and me, and I'll do what I can to work my old connections at the FBI, or we can bring the team on board. I suggest having the power of the team behind you on this, but it's your family and I understand if you don't want everyone to know."

"My team's my family."

And at that moment, I realized how true that statement was. Drake, Carter, Logan, Luke, and Trey had been my family from the moment we ended up in the same SEAL platoon. Drake, my LPO, Logan, his second in command. We'd been through hell and back together. When Drake was discharged and Trey was facing medical retirement, it was a no-brainer to follow them into the civilian sector. Thankfully that led us all to Triple Canopy. Since I'd started at TC, Brady, Dylan, Nick, and Jason had become like brothers to me. Not the kind who were forged by blood and war but brothers, nonetheless. Along with Nick came his father, Nolan Clark. Jason Walker's father, Jasper, was a great mentor, as was Carter's father, Lenox. And then there was Levi McCoy. He was quieter than the other men. His wisdom was passed down in deed, which was no less impactful.

The four original principles of Triple Canopy were brothers forged by blood and war. Their bond so strong they'd formed an unbreakable family. Unlike mine with my father, which was so fragile, it had been irrevocably severed.

If nothing else, I had honor.

I had integrity.

I didn't bleed on the battlefield, standing for all that is good and just in this world, for my own goddamn father to be a fucking mobster.

Nick's palms slapped on the table, bringing me back to our conversation.

"Then let's set Dylan on this and get to work."

"I appreciate—"

"Family, brother. It's what we do."

The irony wasn't lost on me.

My family had betrayed everything I value, but my brothers would have my back.

3

"Off your pockets," Ty barked. "Tuck your chin and lift up on your rope."

Sweat trickled down my temple and my left leg cramped as I rolled to the front of my thighs like Ty demanded. The practice barrel dropped forward to mimic a kick, and I transferred my weight from being on my legs to thrusting my hips forward and lifting on my rope.

"How's your leg?"

"Great."

Ty tipped the barrel back to center and I dropped my arm.

"You know, your body doesn't lie."

I clenched my jaw and semi-lied, "I feel great."

"Your shoulder?"

"Jeez, Ty, you wanna go through all my injuries?"

My trainer stepped around the barrel and put his hands on his hips.

"At some point, you're gonna have to ask yourself what it's worth."

"Ty—"

His hand shot up to silence me, and he went on. "Fact of life, cowboy. We all want to go the distance, realize our dreams, be remembered. But, darlin', we all gotta ask ourselves what it's worth."

Without meaning to, my gaze dropped to Ty's right leg. His prosthetic was covered by his jeans and cowboy boot.

"We all know there's a risk of a two-thousand-pound bull stomping on one of our chests, and it's lights out. We all take that risk every time we enter the chute. It's the toll on the rest of your body. How many injuries are you willing to sustain? How many can your body handle before you're using a cane or a wheelchair? How many before you can't lift your arm to brush your teeth? The choice is yours, Chelsea. But you best be asking yourself how much you're willing to give."

Everything.

I was willing to give everything to prove I wasn't what my daddy called me when he kicked me out. I wasn't what the people back in Nebraska thought I was. I should've been long over it, but I wasn't. Maybe I was willing to give it just enough to make it to an event near my hometown to show my brothers I was just as good as they were. If my body would cooperate and I could ride in Omaha, I'd consider slowing down.

But not until then.

Not until I could compete roughstock in a PBR event with my daddy and brothers watching.

Not until the old man eats his words and my brothers have to acknowledge I'm just as good as they are and I'm not a silly girl with a stupid notion.

"You've made your point."

Ty shook his head and changed the subject.

"I heard Todd's being a jackass."

Of course, Ty heard about my ex, Todd.

"Kami doesn't like the smell of horse shit, so he told me I have to move Gypsy and Rebel."

"His asshole ways never cease to surprise me. I'll make you a deal. Saige's niece wants to learn how to ride. She's five, and I don't have a pony here I'd put her on. If you let me use Gypsy, I'll board them both."

That sounded fantastic.

"What if the girl doesn't take to riding?"

"You ever hear the expression, don't look a gift horse in the mouth?" Ty deadpanned.

"Ty, you've got sixteen—"

"Exactly, Chelsea, I have sixteen horses on my ranch. What the hell difference does it make if I've got two more? They should've been here all along. Keeping them at Todd's place was stupid from the start."

What Ty meant was, me getting involved with Todd was stupid. And it was. I knew before I agreed to our first date he was a jerk, yet I still went out with him. Six months later, when he went from jerk to pure asshole, I broke up with him. Not that he cared; I was replaced within a week.

"I'd appreciate you taking them in. I'll pay—"

"You'll pay for their hay and oats."

"Ty, I have to pay for boarding."

He ignored my comment and moved the conversation back to training. "Are we gonna stand here and jabber all damn morning, or are you gonna get your ass on Mr. T?"

"Mr. T?"

The bull was almost docile. Ty used him to train his youth riders.

"First ride back after injury. I'll give five sweet bulls today. Two days' rest, then we'll get you on Monster."

Monster was just that, a monster. He was the biggest bull

Ty had. He was also old and grumpy, so he did his best to spin you off because he was too lazy to kick and jump.

There was no point arguing with Ty; I'd tried in the past and he never gave in. One of the reasons he was a great trainer—rider safety was his number one priority.

I had two months before I needed to be in Athens for my first rodeo. Two months to get my shit straight and my body at a hundred percent if I wanted to start the season with points on my card.

"Let's do this."

I threw my right leg over the barrel and jumped down.

Ty didn't miss my less than graceful dismount, nor did he miss me wince when my boots hit the dirt.

"Chelsea!" Todd shouted. "I'm glad I caught you."

I wasn't glad.

I'd purposefully planned my arrival before he was supposed to be home from work. I even cut my training short so I wouldn't have to do this...whatever this was. It was a crapshoot. Either Todd would be happy, therefore pleasant, or he'd be in the mood to be a dick.

I didn't have the desire to deal with any of his multiple personalities. Thankfully, I hadn't seen Kami's car when I passed their house on my way to the stables. But then I hadn't seen Todd's truck either.

"I'm almost done, then I'll be out of your hair."

I dropped the last bag of oats in the bed of my truck and turned. I didn't want to face Todd, but I couldn't very well keep my back to him. As soon as I did, his gaze did a sweep of my person. There had been a time when I liked the way Todd looked at me, but now it just felt creepy.

"You're training."

It wasn't a question and since I no longer owed him an explanation—not that I ever did, yet when we were together, I'd still felt compelled to share with him my reasons for not quitting when he'd beg me to give up riding bulls and bronc and go back to barrel racing. Which, in his mind, was a perfectly acceptable event for a woman.

"Goddamn, Chels! Is your shoulder even healed?"

Todd had been there when my spur had gotten tangled in the flank strap during a dismount after an eight-second ride in Bristol. The bull, Twisted Fist, violently dragged me around the arena. The beast was spitting mad, twisting, and bucking. The bullfighters did their best to contain the animal, but I still broke my right shoulder and all twelve ribs on my right side. The recovery was painful, the rehab was worse. The only part about PT I'd enjoyed was getting to know Adalynn Walker, my physical therapist. And when she moved her practice to Triple Canopy, a training center her father and his friends had started, PT had become a whole lot more enjoyable.

TC didn't train cowboys. They trained commandos. I used to think my weakness was a man in a pair of chaps with scuffed up boots and a broken-in Stetson. That was until I met the men who worked at TC, and I promptly learned a man in cargos, combat boots, and a baseball hat was just as appealing. Then I saw Matt Kessler waltzing through the gym at TC, and I decided there wasn't a man alive—not one in a cowboy hat or combat boots—who was sexier.

"Since I'm paid up for the month—"

"Jesus, Chelsea!" Todd exploded. "Even now, you can't be fuckin' reasonable."

"My life is none of your business," I returned just as

heated. "I'm here because you wanted my girls gone. They're loaded up and I'm ready to leave. So unless you got something to say about the contract you're breaking, or you want to inspect the stalls to make sure they're mucked to your satisfaction, we got nothing to talk about."

I watched Todd clench his jaw. It was too bad he was just an asshole because he was good-looking. Not nearly as hot as Matt. Todd lacked a certain something that Matt had. I couldn't put my finger on what it was—maybe confidence or just straight-up sex appeal. Whatever it was, Todd didn't have it. He also didn't have a great personality, or manners, or a friendly disposition.

"Was your life my business when we were together? Was your well-being?" he snapped.

"Nope," I answered honestly. "My life is my business and no one else's."

"And that right there is why I dumped your ass. When you drop that huge fuckin' wall, and you check the attitude, you're sweet and funny. But goddamn, woman, the rest of the time, you got no sense. You're so worried about Trevor, TJ, and Russ you won't free the stick from your ass long enough to enjoy life. Do you even like riding bulls, or is it all about showing TJ up? You're reckless, and you're gonna kill yourself. But, then that'd show Trevor, wouldn't it? Having his *daughter* be on the list of dead bull riders."

Todd was dangerously close to getting it right.

"I'd rather my name be on the silver cup than a tombstone. Can't prove my worth if I'm dead, now can I?" I smiled.

"This isn't a joke!" he shouted.

"No, you're right, it isn't. But what it is, is none of your business since *I* dumped your ass for being a monumental prick."

"Right. I'm a prick because I didn't wanna see my woman mangled by a bull."

For the first time since I'd met Todd, he actually looked sincere. Gone was all the arrogance and swagger and instead, he looked hurt.

"No, you're a prick because you were never very nice to me. You're a prick because you demanded I quit riding. You're a prick because you have wandering eyes and would check out other women while we were together. And obviously, one caught your eye because she's now living with you."

"Jealous?"

And, we're back to Dickhead Todd.

"Not even a little bit."

Todd stomped away like the man-child he was. I checked that the gate on the back of my trailer was locked and got into my truck. It took more self-control than I wanted to admit not to spin my tires and leave ruts in front of his barn. I wasn't that immature. Besides, I was hauling my girls and loved them more than anything. I'd never do something that would scare or jar them.

By the time I drove back to Ty's, unloaded Gypsy and Rebel, got them settled, and parked my trailer where Ty said I could store it, I was running late. I still needed to get a yoga class in before I had to go to work.

Slinging drinks after a full day of training was not my idea of a good time.

But after work, I was going to Matt's, and that was the very definition of a great time.

Suck it up, buttercup, you need money. Especially since you don't have a sponsor.

The icing on the shit sundae that was my day happened when I knocked on Matt's door at eleven fifteen and he didn't answer.

I walked back to my truck, pretending I didn't care.

I stupidly did.

4

I woke up with a start when I felt something smack me in the face.

"Rise and shine, sleeping beauty." Logan laughed.

I pried my eyes open and saw my friend standing in the doorway to my office. The first thing I noticed was his smile. The second was the rubber band he was holding up with a paper dart already loaded.

It was the smile that was jarring. I still wasn't used to this new and improved model of Logan the Grouchy. It must be noted that Lauren, our sweet receptionist, had magical powers. Sure, it had taken her months and months of trying, but she'd finally wrought miracles and turned Logan into Mr. Happy-Go-Lucky.

Happiness looked good on my friend.

It sucked for me because I lost my wingman, but I was pleased for the surly fucker.

"What time is it?" I asked.

"Eight fifteen."

That was impossible. The last time I looked at the clock, it was creeping up on ten P.M.

"In the morning?"

"Yes, idiot." He laughed. "In the morning."

Fuck!

Chelsea.

"Shit."

I sat up and scrubbed my face. I hadn't meant to fall asleep. I moved from my desk to the couch I had in my office because after hours of sitting in a chair, my back had been sore.

I spied my phone on my desk. Regrettably, it would do me no good since I didn't have Chelsea's phone number.

"Do you happen to have Chelsea's number?" I asked Logan.

"Um...negative," he drawled. "Is there a reason why after the day you had yesterday, the first thing you ask me is if I have Chelsea's number and not if Dylan found the info you asked him for? Which by the way, he did."

That was good news. But I could wait to read through a report that would tell me just how big of a lie my whole freaking life was.

Chelsea couldn't wait.

I had to explain why I'd stood her up.

Sex was sex. But also, plans were plans, and we didn't have to be in a relationship to show the other person consideration and respect. I'd screwed up, and now I needed to rectify that as soon as possible.

Before I could come up with a good excuse as to why I'd want Chelsea's number, Logan asked, "Why do you want her number anyway?" There was a beat of silence before Logan figured it out, "Oh, shit."

"Bad timing," I started. "We had plans last night. I fell asleep here, and I don't have her number."

"You had a date?"

I raised my eyebrow and shook my head.

"Right," he muttered. "Advice: do not ask one of the women for her number. They'll be up your shit so fast your head will spin."

Damn, Logan was right.

That was one of the many reasons I'd kept my distance from Chelsea. She was close to all the women around Triple Canopy. I loved them all like sisters, but they were in-your-face nosy with the best of intentions.

I didn't need them poking around my life, and I didn't think Chelsea would appreciate them knowing her business unless she made it their business.

Which meant I'd have to do it to Dylan and ask him to get into Addy's patient files and get me her number. He'd give me a good amount of razzing, but he'd do it.

With that, I changed the subject.

"I take it you read Dylan's report. So, tell me, was my grandfather caught up with the mob, too?"

"Nope." Logan added a shake of his head. "Your granddad was as clean as a whistle."

Well, that was good news. It meant the corruption and dirty money had started with my father, and every dollar of my family's money wasn't tainted.

The bad news was my father was guilty as fuck. Once Dylan started digging, he'd found more the FBI hadn't told me about.

I nodded my acknowledgment and struggled to find something to say.

Yesterday when Nick and I got to the office and laid out all the information about my father, not a single man asked me if I knew my dad had been working with the mob. Not one of them had asked if I was somehow involved. I was ashamed to admit I'd been prepared for their questions. I wouldn't have blamed them if they had asked. It was pretty unbelievable that I didn't know. That I hadn't seen or suspected anything throughout the years. Maybe if I'd visited my family more than a couple weeks a year, I would've picked up on something. But when I went home to visit, it was just that—a visit. I didn't pry into my father's business dealings. I didn't question the money he made or how he made it. Why the hell would I? Kessler Management was thriving. It had always been thriving. It had been highly profitable when my grandfather was at the helm, and that did not change when my father had taken over.

From the time I was a teenager, I'd known I wasn't going to work for the family business. The mere thought of sitting behind a desk all day had given me the shakes. I always thought it was cool that my dad hadn't been pissed. He didn't push me to go to work at Kessler. He hadn't complained once. Not even when I told him I was joining the Navy. He'd been supportive and had bragged to all his friends about how proud he was of me.

Knowing what I know now, I wondered if he didn't want me to work for Kessler. It had been all too easy. Growing up the way I did, it was a given my friends would follow in their parents' footsteps. Whether it be a doctor or lawyer or joining their family's business. It was expected. But my dad hadn't even attempted to talk me around.

Was he protecting me?

Was he protecting himself?

It was a total mind fuck.

But what had eaten at me last night as I went through all the evidence was how quickly I came to believe my father was guilty. I'd given up the idea that somehow my dad was innocent.

Maybe he'd been set up.

Maybe he was being blackmailed.

Or maybe he was a greedy bastard who didn't care about the family he proclaimed to love.

My phone rang and I hopped up from the couch, hoping it would be Chelsea. When I reached my desk and saw who was calling, all of yesterday's anger came back tenfold.

My sister had some nerve.

"What can I do for you, Ally?" I greeted, using the nickname she hated.

Ally was too common. Alessandra was a proper name.

"Where are you?"

Snappy right off the bat.

"In my office."

"Unbelievable," she seethed. "I should've known you'd turn your back on the family."

"What's unbelievable is that you thought I'd come to Connecticut and lie for you. It's becoming clearer by the hour just how deep Dad's—"

"The phones are tapped, you idiot," my sister cut me off.

I couldn't stop myself from laughing at my poor naïve sister.

"They've got him dead to rights. And I don't give the first fuck if the FBI is still listening. I've got nothing to hide. But I'm getting the feeling you do. Which wouldn't be as shocking as finding out my father's been involved with mobsters for the last thirty fucking years."

"I don't know what you're talking about."

Yeah, she knew exactly what I was talking about. My sister was a lot of things: spoiled, stuck-up, conceited. But stupid she was not. She was also conniving and money-hungry. If she hadn't only been ten when my father first got in bed with Mancini, I would've said this mess was all my sister's idea.

But, hey, what did I know? Maybe she was cunning enough to run a racket at ten.

At that point, nothing would surprise me.

"The board is going to move to—"

"Newsflash," I growled. "I don't give a rat's ass what the board does."

"You should. Your livelihood is on the line."

Was she high?

"No, it's not. I have a job. You know, a place I go to five days a week to earn money? You should try it sometime, big sis. It's rewarding making your own money and not mooching off mommy and daddy."

"Oh, please. The only reason you get to play super-soldier is because of the money Grandfather left you. If it wasn't for that, you'd be living in a one-bedroom apartment driving a Toyota."

Alessandra said apartment like the thought of not living in a sprawling mansion was so far beneath her she couldn't even stomach the word.

God, she was a bitch.

"How is it possible we're even related?"

"I've asked myself that since the day you were born and Mother and Father brought home a sniveling, crying baby. At five, I knew you didn't have it in you to be a Kessler."

"Thank fuck for that."

"Your language is appalling."

"Better my language be appalling than my morals."

With that, I disconnected the call. I'd had all the verbal sparring with my sister I could take. There was a reason I avoided her when I went home. Sometimes the time between visits, I forgot how horrendous she was, and I'd sit down at the dinner table expecting pleasant conversation.

Then she'd open her mouth, and something pretentious and shallow would come out, and I'd remember.

"The she-devil?" Logan asked.

"Yep."

I wasn't close to Alessandra, but that didn't mean my team didn't know about her. Over the years, they'd heard me complain about her.

"You think she was in on it?"

"I'm not sure she was involved, but she knew my dad was."

"Greedy."

"Got that right. I still haven't talked to my mom. I tried calling her last night, but I got her voice mail."

"I'd find it hard to believe Ginny knew," Logan said quietly.

I wish I could say the same. My mother had a soft disposition. She wasn't a pushover, but neither was she strong.

"Never thought much about it," I started. "But now, thinking on everything, wondering how much I missed, I'm questioning everything. It's an uncomfortable feeling scrutinizing your relationship with your parents. Examining theirs and coming up with answers you don't like."

As soon as the words left my mouth, I regretted them.

"Shit, brother, I wasn't—"

"Not the same thing," Logan interrupted my apology. "My dad was a wife-beater and child abuser. After he died, I didn't have to search my feelings to know how I felt. I was happy he was dead. Totally different." Logan's gaze went over my shoulder, and when his eyes came back to me, I braced. "You need to take a few days and stop dissecting every minute of your life. I've heard you talk about your dad, your mom, how they supported your decision to join the Navy. How your dad never missed a high school lacrosse game. How your mom went all out with fundraisers for your team. They were good parents to you growing up."

I hadn't been prepared for Logan to defend my father, therefore, my response was unchecked and full of irritation.

"So, that makes it okay? He gets a free pass because he was a good dad? What the fuck?"

"Not everything is black and white. There are shades of gray in there, too. I'm not excusing what your dad has done, Matt. All I'm saying is, he can be both—the supportive, attentive, loving father you had growing up *and* the corrupt businessman."

What in the actual hell?

"He lied," I spat. "Everything is a damn lie."

"The way he loves you isn't a lie."

Logan's words sliced through me, leaving me winded and emotionally bloody.

"I can't—"

"Brother, take a breath and take some time before you decide what you can't do. It fucks me to say this, but from everything we went over yesterday, your dad's going down. He's guilty, and his attorney can present whatever defense he comes up with, but the Feds have your dad red-handed. But again, that doesn't negate who he is to you. His criminal activity doesn't erase your life. It doesn't make it a lie. It doesn't change a damn thing, except your father made some piss-poor choices and got involved with people he shouldn't have."

Jesus.

Who was this man, and where did my old friend Logan go?

It wasn't too long ago he was a jaded, cynical bastard who didn't believe love existed.

"I don't think I can separate the man who raised me and

the man I now know laundered money for the mob. I don't think I'll ever be able to reconcile the double life he's led."

Logan huffed an exaggerated sigh.

"That's not you taking time," he chided. "It's been twenty-four hours. Your sister's breathing down your neck, you got the Feds feeding you information from a firehose, Dylan's throwing more information at you. You're not in the right frame of mind to make any decisions, and you damn well know it."

Logan was right about one thing; I wasn't in the right frame of mind to think rationally. Something I learned long ago was never to make a decision in the heat of the moment. I didn't think my anger was temporary or out of place, but that didn't mean I didn't need to get my shit together before I blew up bridges in a very permanent way.

"I'll take some time," I acquiesced.

Logan nodded then changed the subject.

"Ready for Trey's wedding this weekend?"

Shit. I needed to pick my tux up from the dry cleaners and pick up their gift from the travel agent. Without meaning to, my mind wandered back to my father's illicit activities, and I couldn't help wondering if the expensive gift I'd purchased for Trey and Addy was bought with dirty money.

I was sending my friends on a first-class all-inclusive trip with filthy, tainted mob money. Fucking perfect.

"Jesus, Matt, you look like you swallowed something nasty."

I felt like it, too.

I ignored his comment in favor of answering his question. "Yeah, I'm ready. What about you?"

"I've been ready. But Lauren's another story. She still has to pick up her dress from the seamstress. And Emily enlisted all the bridesmaids to help her with some top-secret thing she's planning, so now they're all running around doing her bidding."

Emily Walker was a force to be reckoned with.

"Trey seems awfully calm for a man who's about to have Jasper as a father-in-law," I noted.

Logan's lip twitched, but before he could comment, my phone rang again.

I glanced at the screen and quickly declined the call.

"Alessandra?"

"No, my father's attorney."

I couldn't talk to Roland until I had a plan. He'd already expressed his desire to have me fly to Connecticut, which I would have to do eventually, but the trip would happen after Trey and Addy's wedding. And after I figured out what I was going to do with my shares in Kessler Management. Going back to Logan's point, I needed to understand the full picture, and I couldn't do that until I had more information.

"I'll let you get to it." Logan moved to the door but stopped. "Hope you know we all have your back on this, Matt. *I* have your back. Whatever you need, you just say the word."

"I know, and I appreciate it."

Logan took his leave, and now that I was alone in my office, I debated the merits of going home and showering, but before I could make my decision, my office phone rang.

The next five hours were thankfully filled with actual Triple Canopy work, and by the time I made it to the locker rooms behind the gym to shower and change, it was after lunch. On the way back to my office, I spotted Chelsea kitted out in workout gear coming out of the gym with the strap of her bag over her shoulder. She winced and quickly moved the bag to her left side. She looked up, and when our eyes caught, hers registered surprise. The speed at which she schooled her features and plastered a fake smile on her pretty face was maddening.

"Hey, Matt," she breezily said and continued on her way.

What the hell?

"Yo!" I barked.

Chelsea's steps faltered. Once she came to a complete stop, she turned and scowled at me.

"Did you just *yo* me?"

Indignation was practically seeping from her pores. And for some reason, I didn't want to give headspace to; I liked her all riled up. I liked seeing some flicker of emotion coming from her. It was much better than the way she'd left last night.

"What the fuck was that?"

The creases between her brows deepened, and I liked that, too.

"What was what?"

"'Hey, Matt?' That's it?"

She stayed where she was but turned fully to face me. For months, I'd watched her strut around TC in her tight-fitting yoga pants and equally tight top. She'd likely have my balls if she knew how much time I'd spent watching her, which was somewhere between unhealthy and stalker. But damn if something hadn't drawn me to her—and it was more than the way she looked. I'd never seen her not in a rush. The woman was always active. Even when she was sitting, she was moving—her knee was bouncing, her hands were in motion as she told a story, her gaze darted around.

But right then, her body was statue-still, and her eyes were glued to mine.

"I'm sorry, what did you expect? A curtsy?"

Smartass.

I liked that about her, too. She took no shit from anyone, and she always had a quick comeback.

"I stood you up—"

Her hand shot up, and she shook her head.

"No need to explain. We're not *that*, remember?"

"We're not what? Friends? We had plans, and I accidentally broke them. I owe you an explanation and an apology."

"Don't worry about it." She waved me off and shifted to make her exit.

That would be a hell to the no.

"I am worried about it. But more, you should be worried about it. While I didn't mean to fuck off our plans, I still did. And I hafta say, it's a little concerning you don't seem to mind that you went to my house last night and I wasn't there."

Chelsea's shoulders snapped back, and her eyes narrowed on me until I could only see a sliver of her irises.

"I don't mind because we are not *that*, Matt. We spent a few hours together. It was good. I didn't mind a repeat. You obviously changed your mind. Not a big deal. No need to apologize."

She was speaking in short, dismissive sentences that had my blood boiling.

That's new.

"It was good?" I spat.

Chelsea's gaze unlocked from mine, and she glanced around the small hallway. There were only a few people in the building, and no one was close enough to hear our conversation.

"What do you want from me, Matt?"

Nothing.

Everything.

More.

"Come over tonight. Let me make you dinner and give me a chance to explain."

Make dinner?

Was I crazy? I didn't cook for women, nor did I allow them to cook for me. Cooking said playing house. Dinner at a restaurant communicated something far less familiar.

"Not necessary."

"Please come over."

"I have to work tonight, and even if I didn't, that ship's sailed."

Unfortunately, my brain wasn't functioning fast enough, and before I could process her brush-off, Chelsea was almost to the door. I took a step in her direction but immediately stopped.

What was I doing?

My life was in shambles.

I had nothing to offer the woman, and I'd be doing her no favors getting involved with her on any level.

I forced myself to stay rooted in place even though every muscle in my body was screaming at me to go after her.

I watched the door close behind her, and my chest tightened.

That felt an awful lot like a mistake.

5

I was late.

Though that seemed to be the reoccurring theme of my life. When I was a kid, it pissed my dad off something fierce. My mom didn't pay much mind to my tardiness, though she didn't pay much mind to much. And my brothers liked that I was always late for my chores because if our dad was focused on me, he wasn't focused on them.

I thought I'd have time to sneak in an early morning nail appointment before I headed to the church to get ready with Addy and the rest of her bridesmaids. The nail appointment was an absolute must since it went against every rule in the Woman Handbook to wear a beautiful, peachy-colored dress with blood-red nails. And I would've had plenty of time if Ty hadn't called to tell me Rebel was being stubborn and wouldn't allow Daisy, Ty's ranch hand, to bring her back to the barn. There was a reason I renamed my girl from Breeze to Rebel. First, who named their mare Breeze? But more importantly, Rebel was not a breeze. She was rebellious and ornery. Hence not letting Daisy bring her in, and Ty wasn't at the ranch to help, which meant I had to go. That took nearly an hour. Consequently, I was now late.

I parked my dusty old Ram pickup truck next to Matt's shiny black Chevy and I sighed. It was stupid that my heart rate sped up just seeing his truck, but there was no denying that was the case. Last night at the rehearsal and during the subsequent dinner, I'd managed to successfully play it cool when really, I wanted to ask him why he'd stood me up. When he'd cornered me in the hall of TC and offered to explain, my stupid pride reared its ugly head and I'd refused to hear him out. Old insecurities were hard to shove away. Matt was not the first guy to cancel on me. He wasn't even the second. It was my experience that good-looking men had options, and when someone better came along, they took advantage of what was being offered. And besides, Matt had made it crystal clear he wanted nothing to do with me outside of the bedroom. Instead of that being a turnoff I appreciated his candor. My life was hectic. I didn't have time for games and bullshit, and after I ended things with Todd, I decided I didn't have time for relationships seeing as they were mostly games and bullshit. Yet, I was still a woman with a healthy sex drive. Matt's offer of a few nights of sex with no entanglements was perfect. Then it wasn't. I promised him I was not a clinger so I wouldn't turn into one now.

I grabbed my duffle bag and my dress I'd carefully laid across the back seat and slammed the door. I didn't bother beeping the locks. If someone broke into my old truck in a church parking lot, they needed the loose change in my ashtray and the cassette player more than I did.

By the time I entered the sanctuary, I was no less frazzled. I hated being late, which was ironic since I always was. I hated how my thoughts kept going to Matt even though I tried not to think about him. I doubly hated how good he was in bed. How sweetly he could kiss. How softly he'd trailed his hands over my back only to glide his fingers into my hair and roughly yank it until my scalp tingled. Hard and soft. Rough and sweet. Matt had sex down to a science. He knew exactly what to do to make my body catch fire. And the man didn't shy away from oral sex. Not the giving or receiving. His tongue should be bronzed and memorialized.

I caught sight of the huge stained-glass windows behind the pulpit and my face flamed.

Shit.

I should not be thinking about crazy, earth-shattering, premarital sex with Matt while in a church.

I was going to hell—straight to hell on the express train.

At least the sex had been well worth spending eternity in the bad place.

I found the hallway I needed to take me to the function room that had been transformed into a bridal suite and did my best to clear my mind of Matt.

It was Adalynn and Trey's special day.

All of my thoughts should be on the bride and groom and their wedding.

I heard laughter and music before I made it to the door and I smiled. Addy was lucky. She had a big, happy family *and* a huge extended family. Lots of aunts, uncles, and cousins. When I first met her, I was insanely jealous. But the more I got to know her, my jealousy slipped away. Adalynn Walker was as sweet as they came; she didn't take her blessings for granted. Instead, she shared them and quickly—somewhat zealously—brought me into the fold. I wasn't sure we were good enough friends for me to be a bridesmaid in her wedding, and I had a suspicion she'd asked me because Matt needed someone to walk down the aisle with. Which brought me to my new freak-out.

Yup. I was walking down the aisle with Matt.

Without knocking, I opened the door and took in the scene. Not a single woman in the jam-packed room turned toward the door. Their attention was on Addy.

"Holy crap," I whispered and closed the door behind me.

Adalynn's long black hair that was normally pulled up into a ponytail was flowing down her back in messy, loose curls. A chunky three-strand braid went diagonal from the top left of her head, stopping just behind her right ear. But what made the style unique was the waterfall braid just under the other braid. The stylist had joined the two braids together with a beautiful barrette adorned with crystals.

"Right? My sister's gorgeous," Hadley said without looking away from Addy.

Hadley and Addy's sister, Quinn, snorted a laugh and muttered, "You know, calling your identical twin gorgeous is the same as calling yourself gorgeous, right?"

Hadley looked at her sister and smirked.

"You're just in time," Delaney, the eldest Walker sister, said. "Your turn in the hot seat."

Hot seat?

"What?"

Delaney didn't explain when she bossed, "Drop your bag and hang up your dress."

I didn't argue, mainly because I was late and still needed to do my hair and makeup and asking a bunch of questions would delay both. But also because Delaney had used her I'm-a-high-school-teacher voice on me. Which was half mom-voice, half I'm-the-boss-of-the-classroom-don't-argue-with-me voice.

Not that I actually knew what a mom-voice was from

hearing my mother give directives. I'd only recently, after meeting Emily Walker, heard how a real mother spoke to her children. Then there was Reagan Clark, Blake McCoy, and Lily Lenox, who all shared Emily's soft but firm tone to convey something important.

It was a strange thing, reaching my thirties before learning how a mother behaved, but there you have it; I didn't grow up with a mom who cared much about anything, including me. It was also a strange thing not knowing if that was just the way she was or if the years she'd been with my father had drained her of her will to live. I'd only spent eighteen years with the man, and God knows he sucked me dry. He, and my brothers who were just like him, unfortunately. Overbearing, high-handed, and all-around assholes.

"Hello?" Delaney called. "Earth to Chelsea."

"Sorry. Where do you want me?" I asked as I hung my dress on the rolling garment rack.

"Over here." Meadow Clark motioned for me to sit in the chair in front of her.

I noted the makeshift workstation with eyeliner pencils, mascara tubes, and a bunch of other makeup scattered around.

It was then I understood.

Meadow was married to Addy's cousin Nick. She was a stunning redhead who looked like she could be a runway model. Speaking of models, I looked around the room for Meadow's sister-in-law Tuesday who at one time was an actual model but I didn't see her. She must've been running late as well. Of course, she had a better excuse than I did. Emily had made some last-minute changes to the reception, which meant Tuesday was responsible for implementing them seeing as the whole reception was a surprise for Addy and Trey.

I scooted by Hadley, who was curling Liberty's hair, and made my way to Meadow. But before I got there, I stopped in front of Addy.

"Your hair looks amazing."

Careful not to move her head, she only lifted her sparkling green eyes to look at me.

"Are you sure? I was a little worried there was too much bling."

"Is there such a thing as too much bling?" I asked.

Addy gave me a stunning smile and shooed me away.

"Go let Meadow make you even more beautiful than you already are."

That was sweet, but not true. I was not beautiful. I couldn't hold a candle to the Walker girls, but then ninety percent of the population couldn't compete with their dark hair, green eyes—or blue in Delaney's case—and fabulous bone structure.

That was what happened when two beautiful people spawned children.

Superior genes for the win.

My ass had barely hit the chair cushion before Shiloh blurted, "What the hell is going on with you and Matt?"

My gaze sliced to her and I gave her my best "shut the hell up" look. Unfortunately, Shiloh was too badass for my nonverbal dagger to work.

"Don't give me that look," she said. "You'd have to be clueless *and* stupid *and* maybe even blind." Shiloh stopped and shook her head. "Nope, not blind. The tension was so thick you could feel it. Spill, sister, what the hell is going on?"

So, perhaps there was a little tension between Matt and

me last night. It wasn't uncomfortable, but we definitely had been dancing around each other.

"Nothing's going on."

Which was the God's honest truth. Nothing was going on, and whatever was going to go on was no longer happening, so I wasn't lying.

"Liar," Liberty Hayes said. She was another cousin who used to be a McCoy but recently got married to Drake.

"I'm not lying. There is absolutely nothing going on."

"Well, that's disappointing," Quinn mumbled.

"But you want something to be going on, don't you?" Hadley asked.

I felt my face heat up and I cursed my inability not to hide my blush.

"There's nothing—"

"You've said that," Lauren interrupted. "For months, we've watched you watching him. And we've watched him watching you. There's some serious sexual tension going on, so don't deny it. I thought for sure after the other night at Balls Deep, the two of you finally figured it out. The two of you were in the backroom for a long time."

"Are you sure you're not talking about you and Logan slipping into the bathroom, thinking the rest of us wouldn't notice?" Quinn laughed. "The two of you were in there for a *very* long time."

"We were talking," Lauren obviously lied.

"Yeah, sure, talking about the best way to christen the newly remodeled bathroom, maybe," Delaney mumbled.

"We're not here to discuss my sex life. We're here to talk about Chelsea's," Lauren returned.

"Actually, we're *not* here to talk about my sex life. We're here for Addy."

"So, you admit there's a sex life to talk about," Addy joined the conversation.

"Traitor," I hissed.

Thankfully there was a knock on the door before it opened, and Carson Rose entered, followed by her mom, Honor.

"Oh, good, your hair's done," Honor said and lifted her camera.

Honor was a photographer. She mostly did nature and still-life photography, but somehow Addy had talked her into shooting her wedding.

"I've already finished with candids of the guys," she continued.

"How are they doing?" Addy asked. "Is everyone there?"

"Yes. And your mom's over there, so they're on schedule. But just a heads up, Carter's bringing Ford over. He said he's hungry."

"I pumped and gave him a bottle," Delaney said and weirdly lifted her hand to feel her breast.

"Um, why are you feeling yourself up?" I asked.

"Sorry, habit."

It was unclear why Delaney was in the habit of grabbing her boob. However, I was thrilled beyond measure the topic had been changed. I would happily discuss Delaney's strange practice of feeling herself up in public—she did seem partial to her right breast—again, strange but welcomed.

"How is baby Ford?" I asked.

And just like any new beaming mom, Delaney smiled and said, "He's perfect."

Ford's actual name was Ethan Ford Lenox, named after Carter's brother. It seemed the Lenox family liked recycling names seeing as Carter and Ethan's father was Carter. And

Ethan named his son after his father and brother. Thankfully, Carter Hudson also went by his middle name.

Three Carters plus two Ethans equals too confusing.

"How's Emma getting on with him?"

"She loves being a big sister."

"Stop grabbing yourself so I can get some shots of you before Carter gets here," Honor demanded.

Carson looked up from her phone and laughed.

"Mom gets bossy when she's working."

"Mom also pays the sassy teenager's cell phone bill."

Carson's smile widened and she smartly retracted her statement. "What I meant was, Mom's good at directing when she's working."

"That she is, Squirt," Ethan said, coming into the room. "Special delivery. I have a hungry nephew."

Ethan cradled Ford against his chest and the sight damn near made my ovaries explode.

What was it about a hot guy holding a tiny baby?

"Your nephew's always hungry," Delaney mumbled and took her son from Ethan.

"I'd explain to you why that is, but you're married to a Lenox, so it's likely you know we grow—"

"Ethan," Honor warned.

"I was going to say, into big, strapping, handsome men."

"No, you weren't."

"Gross!" Carson complained.

"Come help me with your brother," Ethan started. "He's tearing apart the room."

"He's always tearing apart something," Carson mumbled.

"True story, darlin'."

Ethan caught his daughter around the shoulders and

pulled her to his side. Carson melted into her dad and rested her head on his chest.

I felt my nose start to sting, and I couldn't stop myself from wondering what it would've been like to have a dad like Ethan.

"Hey," Meadow called. "Are you alright?"

"Yeah. I'm great."

She gave me a sad smile and picked up a foundation brush. "Let's get started."

Conversation flowed around me. Laughter filled the room. Champagne was consumed, though Hadley had sparkling water seeing as she was pregnant. The vibe was happy and mellow, but for some reason, I couldn't shake my sadness.

The bridesmaids were all dressed. We were putting on our jewelry and Hadley was finishing buttoning the back of Addy's wedding dress when it happened.

There were two raps on the door before it opened. As if they could feel it, all four Walker sisters looked at the door and watched their father walk into the room. Though Jasper didn't walk far; his step faltered and he stood stunned, staring at Adalynn.

"Jesus."

I felt his tortured whisper stab me in the heart.

His gaze skidded around the room, pausing just for a second when his eyes landed on one of his daughters before they returned to Addy.

"My sweet Adalynn. I didn't think it was possible for you to be more than your usual beautiful, but, darlin', you look..." He stopped to clear his throat. "*Beautiful.*"

"Thank you, Daddy."

Daddy.

God, I wished I had that. I wished that just once in my

life, I'd be so overcome with emotion I'd call my father "daddy." Just one time, I wanted to know what it felt like to be stunned by my father's love.

Before I turned into a blubbering mess, I needed to leave the room. I finished putting my earrings in and did my best to ignore the way Jasper was staring at his daughter.

Someone's phone chimed, then Liberty announced, "Everyone's ready."

"No one forget your flowers," Delaney started. "Hadley, you're in charge of Addy's bouquet."

Adalynn had decided not to have a maid of honor—or maybe it would've been a matron of honor since all of her sisters were married. Instead, she had a huge wedding party, and we were all included equally. Though Hadley would be standing closest to Addy when she and Trey exchanged vows.

Pandemonium ensued as everyone made their way to the door. I hung back until the others had their flowers, and when it was just Delaney, Quinn, and Hadley left, I took that as my cue to give the Walker girls a moment alone with their father and sister before the ceremony.

I grabbed my flowers—six long steamed, pink Gerbera Daisies tied together with a simple lace ribbon. Addy's bouquet included daisies, but it was mostly blush-colored peonies—her favorite flower.

Simple but elegant—just like Adalynn.

I gently closed the door behind me and nearly ran into Sawyer's back. I didn't know her well, and if it weren't for her ever-changing hair, she might've slipped into the background without anyone noticing her.

"I haven't had the chance to tell you," I began. "I love the purple."

The top three-quarters of her hair were different shades of blonde, but the bottom faded into a deep purple.

Sawyer craned her neck to look back at me.

"Thanks. I was tired of the pink."

I didn't get a chance to tell Sawyer I loved the pink tips, too.

Instead, my breath caught and my heart rate tripled.

Matt Kessler in a tux should be outlawed. He was so freaking hot it was damn right criminal.

"Ready?"

His gruff tone hit me in places, and those places started tingling. Places that were not appropriate to quiver in a church.

God help me.

How was I going to make it down the aisle on his arm without having a spontaneous orgasm from just touching him?

Dylan walked around the corner and stopped next to Matt.

Holy smokes, he, too, looked hot in a tux.

"Ready to roll?" Dylan asked Sawyer.

"Wanna switch?" she muttered.

Yes.

My virtue was safe with Dylan. No doubt he was good-looking, but Dylan didn't do it for me the way Matt did.

Before I could answer Sawyer, Quinn came out of the bridal suite sniffling.

"Damn my dad." She wiped under her eyes before she stormed off.

I glanced back at the door as it opened again. This time Hadley was sniffling, and Delaney was smiling.

"They'll be out in a moment. Dad wanted some time alone with Addy," Delaney told us.

Without any way to get out of my impending doom, I glanced back at Matt.

"I'm ready."

Matt's gaze latched onto mine—his eyes were dull and listless. The pain of seeing that seared a blazing hole through my heart. He blinked away some of the gloom, attempted a smile that in no way communicated happiness, and jerked his chin toward the sanctuary.

"Let's go line up."

Something was very, very wrong.

6

"Everything alright?"

I tipped my eyes down and to the left to look at Chelsea.

Seeing her in that dress nearly made me forget how shitty my life had become. It had definitely stolen my breath and left me momentarily paralyzed. I'd never seen her in anything but jeans, shorts, and workout gear.

And the heels.

Christ.

Adalynn had not chosen provocative dresses for her bridal party. The fabric more than covered Chelsea's curves, but weirdly it made the dress sexier. The hem landed right above her knees, giving just a hint of leg. The unfortunate part was I knew what was under all that material. I knew what her thighs looked like when she spread them open for me. I knew what they felt like under my palms. I knew just how strong they were when they were wrapped around my waist.

It had been days, and I couldn't forget.

"Matt?"

"Yeah, everything's fine," I lied.

Everything had gone to utter shit.

Not only was my sister on the warpath, but my father had been released on bail. He, too, was now blowing up my phone along with his attorney. The only person who had yet to call me, even though I'd left a dozen messages, was my mother. I'd declined all calls from Alessandra and my father. I wasn't ready to speak to either of them and had communicated this through Roland. Though, my father disregarded my wishes and continued to call.

I wasn't ready to hear his excuses—or worse, his denial.

"If you say so," Chelsea muttered.

It would've been comical the way she held herself away from me even though her arm was bent into the crook of my elbow if it wasn't so goddamn infuriating.

I bent my neck so I could whisper, "I don't bite, Chels."

"Yes, you do."

Her quick and honest response had me belting out a laugh, garnering attention from our friends who were also paired up and waiting for their cue to start walking down the aisle.

"You're right, I do," I conceded. "Though I promise not to do it while we're in God's house."

Chelsea hummed. What she didn't do was slide closer.

"Listen—"

"They're ready," Carson chirped excitedly, interrupting Chelsea. "Ariana, hold Emma's hand. Nolan, don't let Hudson run."

Despite my shitty mood, I couldn't stop myself from smiling at Ethan's daughter. She was certainly a Lenox. They were a bossy bunch, the lot of them right down to baby Ford who'd screamed his head off until his father had given in and fed him. And when one bottle hadn't been enough,

Ethan took his nephew and promptly delivered him to his mother.

Carson shuffled the little kids off to the side to wait their turn, and the wedding coordinator, who was scarier than any instructor I had while at BUD/s, nodded to someone I couldn't see. A moment later, an instrumental version of Ed Sheeran's "Perfect" started.

And just like we'd practiced five thousand times last night, as soon as the piano joined the cello, Hadley and Brady started down the aisle. After they were a couple steps in, Quinn and Brice followed, then Delaney and Carter, Liberty and Drake, Shiloh and Luke, Lauren and Logan.

Finally, it was our turn. And since she couldn't protest in front of a hundred guests, I pulled Chelsea closer. I only had fifty-six steps to enjoy her nearness, feel her warmth, pretend that the woman at my side wanted to be there. And I took every one of those steps and invented an alternate universe where Chelsea was mine. A place where I was capable of being everything she'd ever need. The truth was, if there was ever a woman with whom I could see myself spending the rest of my life, it would be Chelsea.

We only had three steps left when I leaned over and whispered, "You are the most beautiful woman here."

I heard her swift inhale.

Then once again, I let her go.

I took my place next to Logan and watched Dylan walk Sawyer down the aisle. Right behind them were the kids. Ariana and Emma tossed handfuls of flowers into the air. Nolan was doing his best to control Hudson, who was alternating between stomping on the petals and batting them out of the air.

"I think Carson's figured out she's lost control," Dylan mumbled.

He wasn't wrong. Carson had given up and was laughing right along with her cousins.

Once the little kids made it to the front, Lily Lenox and Reagan Clark quickly ushered their grandchildren to the front pew to watch the ceremony.

I was busy watching little Emma throw one last handful of flowers at her cousin, hitting him square in the face, so I missed the doors to the sanctuary shutting, but when the music changed—which was not part of the rehearsal—my gaze shot to the mother of the bride.

It must be noted, Emily Walker had it going on. Total knockout. I would've said she was a MILF if I wasn't worried that Jasper would cut off my balls. I relaxed when I saw her staring at Trey, smiling. If something was amiss, Emily would've been all over it.

The doors were pushed open just as the first verse to the song began.

One look at you, my whole life falls in line.

Adalynn Walker stood in her beautiful wedding dress, holding her father's hand.

They did not move as the song continued.

I prayed for you before I called you mine.

Still, Addy and Jasper didn't start walking.

Addy smiled at Trey.

Jasper was the picture of fatherly despair. The man looked like he was ready to scoop his daughter up and run out of the church. I heard a few sniffles and more than a few throats being cleared. I looked from Jasper to Trey to find my friend wiping his face.

In some faraway place in the back of my mind, I wondered what it would feel like to love a woman so thoroughly, so completely that the mere sight of her makes the rest of the world fall away.

Finally, Jasper and Addy started walking.

I heard the collective inhale from all the women in the room.

They walked slowly. So slowly, I wasn't sure who was being tortured more—Trey or Jasper. Trey looked like he was nearing the end of his patience, and Jasper looked like he was being led to his execution.

Jasper stopped five feet from Trey, and the battle began. And make no mistake, the two men were at war—just not with each other. Jasper was battling his emotions, and Trey was fighting the urge to rush and take Addy.

The song came to an end, and Jasper finished leading his daughter to Trey.

The room fell silent, Trey stepped forward, and Jasper cracked a smile.

Jasper lifted Addy's hand, kissed the back of it, and reluctantly set it in Trey's. However, Jasper didn't move. He grabbed Trey's forearm and held on.

"Today, I've handed you the world. I am giving you everything you'll ever need to be happy." Jasper stopped to clear his throat then he looked over at Addy. "Your mother and I are proud of the woman you are. We're proud of all that you've accomplished. Today when you take your vows, know that you have chosen a man who will never fail you."

I felt my eyes start to sting. I hoped the church was filling with noxious gas and I hadn't somehow grown a vagina in the last ten minutes because damn if I hadn't teared up.

"I am blessed," Jasper whispered. "Embarrassingly blessed."

Jasper let go of Trey's arm, but before Jasper could move, Trey's hand shot out and grabbed Jasper's bicep.

"I will not fail," Trey vowed.

"I know you won't, or you wouldn't be standing here."

And that was the God's honest truth. Trey had proven himself to Jasper.

I spent the rest of the ceremony staring at Chelsea and only half-listening to the vows.

I watched as she wept and discreetly wiped away her tears. I watched her smile. I watched her face go soft when Addy said, "I do." I watched her suck in a breath when Trey said the same.

Throughout it all, I wondered what she'd look like on her wedding day. Would she wear cowboy boots or heels? Did she want a big church wedding, or did she want something small? But when my mind wandered to her groom an overwhelming bitterness crept in.

And during the fifteen-minute ceremony, I finally had to admit I'd been lying to myself about all the reasons I'd stayed away from Chelsea. It had not one thing to do with our friends or things getting awkward when I'd inevitably stop inviting her to my bed. It was because I knew once she was there, I'd never want her to leave.

And damn if I hadn't been right.

"It is my pleasure to introduce Mr. and Mrs. Trey and Adalynn Durum."

Deafening cheers rose from the pews, filling the church with hoots, hollers, whistles, and clapping.

I guess I missed the kiss.

Oops.

Trey and Addy started down the aisle and everyone started to file out behind them. Once I had Chelsea's arm back in mine, a sense of relief washed over me.

"That was perfect," she breathed.

Her head tipped back, a big, bright smile beamed up at me, and I did something I'd wanted to do for days. I leaned down and brushed my lips over hers. When I straightened, her eyes were wide and full of shock.

"Have I told you how beautiful you look?"

"Yes," she whispered.

"Well, I feel the need to tell you again. You're absolutely stunning."

"Move it along, Romeo." Dylan laughed.

I ignored Chelsea's disgruntled gasp and moved it along.

There'd be hell to pay for this lip touch.

But it was damn well worth it.

7

"Relationship Goals," Sawyer said and plopped herself down in the chair next to mine.

She wasn't kidding.

I'd been watching Lenox and Lily, Jasper and Emily, Levi and Blake, and Clark and Reagan sway on the makeshift dance floor under the strings of lights I'd help set up in the middle of Tuesday's beautiful orchard.

The evening was winding down and I was dead-on-my-feet tired. Thankfully, Ty had agreed to change my training from first thing in the morning to late afternoon. After all the dancing, food, and cake, I needed a good ten hours' worth of sleep before I'd be functional.

"What are you guys talking about?" Quinn sat down across from me.

"Relationship Goals," Sawyer told her and pointed to the couples dancing.

Quinn glanced at the dance floor and sighed.

"This place is magical."

Quinn wasn't wrong. The orchard looked like something out of a movie.

"Gross," Quinn grumbled.

Her gaze left the dance floor just as mine went to it to figure out why she was scowling.

Jasper's hand was on Emily's rear end, and he was kissing her.

"At least they like each other," I found myself saying.

"Your parents don't like each other?" Sawyer asked.

I shrugged and continued to stare at the couples.

"I have no idea. But I've never seen them kiss. Hell, I've never even seen them hug or hold hands."

"That's horrible," Quinn told me. "I know I complain when my dad makes out with my mom in public, but I don't really mean it. Well, I don't want to watch them do it, but I love that my mom has a man who loves her so much he can't keep his hands off of her. And I love that after all these years, my dad still chases her around like if she's not in his arms, he can't breathe."

I was happy Quinn had that. I was happy that everyone in the Walker, Lenox, Clark, and McCoy clans all had four great role models.

Again, relationship goals.

I had nothing to base a future relationship on. I didn't know what a partnership looked like. I had no idea how a man loved a woman, especially after thirty-plus years of marriage.

Actually, I had nothing at all, and watching the way these men behaved with their sons and daughters made that truth more painful. It had been a long time since I dwelled on what I didn't have growing up, but the longer I was around Addy and her family, the closer I got to them. I couldn't stop the comparisons.

They had love and closeness.

I had mild interest and detachment.

"So…" Quinn drawled. "Let's talk about that kiss."

"Which one?" I inquired, thinking about how brave Trey had been to lay a long, wet one on Addy at the church.

Then, of course, there was the one he gave her while they were in the middle of their first dance. That one could be described as damn-near pornographic, and they'd even stopped dancing in the middle of "You are the Reason" to make out. Okay, I was exaggerating a tad bit. It wasn't pornographic, but it wasn't PG-rated either. They'd slipped into NC-17.

"There's been more than one?" Sawyer laughed.

"Trey—" I started.

"No, not Trey. You and Matt," Quinn corrected.

My gaze sliced to Sawyer. "You told?"

"It wasn't me." Sawyer held her hands up and smiled.

"Everyone saw," Quinn proclaimed.

"You didn't see. You were in front of us."

Quinn waved off my statement and continued. "I thought you said nothing was going on."

Shit.

I was going to kill Matt as soon as I was done avoiding him. Which I'd decided to do for the rest of my life.

"There isn't. Weddings and funerals do weird shit to people."

"That's the lamest excuse I've ever heard."

It was pretty lame, but that was all I could come up with.

"I don't know," Sawyer started. "I *did* see it, and it was pretty damn hot." Sawyer looked at Quinn and went on. "It wasn't a real kiss. It was this sexy lip brush."

"Oh, really." Quinn drew out her words and I closed my eyes. "Tell me more."

"I didn't think Matt had it in him to be all sweet and gentle. But I saw it with my own two eyes. He just softly brushed his mouth over Chelsea's and told her she was stunning."

Sawyer wasn't lying. The lip brush was sexy. It was also confusing. And he'd told me I was beautiful as well as stunning, which was just as puzzling.

"Well, she *is* stunning," Quinn said, sounding affronted, and my eyes shot open. "It's about damn time he tells her he thinks so." Then her gaze shifted to over my shoulder and she smiled.

"Dance with me."

I wasn't breathing; therefore, I couldn't answer Matt. But even if I could have, I would've said no. There was no way I was dancing with Matt and ruining my plan to avoid him until the end of time.

"Chels?" Matt called.

The jerk didn't wait for my answer. He grabbed my hand resting on the table and pulled me out of my chair. I teetered on my heels and in one smooth, probably practiced move, Matt spun me so we were facing each other. I didn't want to think about how many women he'd plucked out of chairs. Further from that, I didn't want to think about why I cared.

I was silent as he led me to the dance floor. I said not a word when he lifted my left hand and placed it on his shoulder. I continued to do my best impression of a mute when he slid his arm around my back and started to sway.

"Are you having fun?"

Since I wasn't speaking to him, I nodded.

"Are you still not speaking to me?"

It was good he'd noticed he was on my freeze-out list though he seemed completely unaffected by my efforts. Case in point—he'd plucked me from my chair and we were dancing. Well, *he* was dancing. I was doing what I could not to step on his feet and make a fool out of myself.

"You can't avoid me forever, baby."

"Wanna bet?" I snapped.

Matt lifted a brow and smiled.

Damn.

"Sure, let's bet. Winner takes all."

"What's that mean?"

"Whatever the winner wants it to mean."

"That's not how a bet works. There need to be clear parameters."

Matt's arm around my back tightened, which meant my front was now plastered against his chest. The feel of him overwhelmed me. The smell of his earthy cologne could only be described as clean, fresh, and sensual. Though it smelled better directly on his skin when mixed with sweat.

"How's this for parameters—no rules, no limitations, no restrictions, no fear. Live a little, Chelsea."

I wanted to laugh. Matt's advice to live a little was in direct contradiction to everyone else, who had always told me to live less. Even Ty had jumped on the bandwagon and was telling me I needed to reconsider my life and give up my dream.

The tips of Matt's fingers dug into my hip and a flash of a memory made me tremble.

"I *am* living, Matt."

"Then take the bet."

Shit, what are we betting on?

Oh, right; me avoiding him forever.

Considering we shared a lot of the same friends, I'd lose the bet. I couldn't actually avoid seeing him unless I wanted to live like a hermit.

"You're a good dancer," I said. My hasty change in topic was solely to evade having to admit I couldn't take the bet.

"I started lessons at five."

"Five? Did you have aspirations to become the next Fred Astaire?"

"Actually, Elvis."

My mouth dropped open at his declaration.

"Seriously?"

"No, baby." He chuckled. "I hated dancing."

"Then why would you take dancing lessons?"

Something unhappy moved over his face before he schooled his features.

"It's what was expected of me."

Expected.

I knew all about family expectations.

"Expectations suck," I muttered.

"You got that right."

We fell silent and Matt effortlessly moved us to the music. It was then I started listening to the words of a song I'd heard a thousand times. Thomas Rhett crooned on about dying a happy man, and for the millionth time in my life, I wished I was the type of woman who could inspire a man to write a song.

Alas, I was not.

According to my daddy, I was a hardheaded idiot who never listened. According to my brothers, I was one of those stupid feminists who didn't know her place. I didn't know what my mother thought I was because, again, she'd never expressed an opinion of her own. She was simply a mouthpiece parroting what her husband thought.

I was not beautiful or stunning. I was average. I was just like the rest. There was nothing about me that stood out or was memorable.

"Hey," Matt whispered.

"You shouldn't have kissed me in the church," I blurted out. "Everyone saw, and they're talking about it."

"And that's a problem?"

Had he lost his mind?

"What happened to, 'It matters because if things go bad, it will be uncomfortable?'"

Those were his exact words the night he found me in the back hall of Balls Deep. The excuse he gave me for why he'd been avoiding me.

"And what happened to the woman who dared me to kiss her?"

Shit. I'd done that. In my frustration—and, yes, desperation—to end the months I'd watched and waited for Matt to make his move, I'd dared him to kiss me.

It was the best kiss of my life.

It was also the worst.

It was the kiss that proved there'd never be another Matthew Kessler. There'd never be another kiss as good. I'd live the rest of my life knowing there was something better out there, and I'd never have it.

I should've stuck to the shitty kissers.

Later that night in his bed, he'd shown me a whole new world. One in which I was the center of his universe, and for those few hours, his sole purpose was to worship me.

It was funny how one experience could be both your best and worst.

A dream and a nightmare.

"We didn't have an audience," I hissed.

"Right. You wanna know what I think?" He didn't give me a chance to tell him I absolutely, unequivocally, did not want to know what he thought before he continued. "I think you talk a big game. I think you're bold and straightforward until something important is on the line. I think you're brave until you have to face something that scares you. I think you're tough as hell, absolutely fearless when you climb on the back of a two-thousand-pound animal hellbent on tossing you off. But you're scared as fuck to admit that you care about why I stood you up, and you're too damn afraid to hear the reason why."

Everything Matt said hit way too close to home. My insides burned with embarrassment.

I was a total fake. The only way I could make it through the day was to pretend I didn't care about anything but my next ride. My problem was I cared too much. I cared that my family had turned their backs on me. I cared that my brothers laughed at me. I cared that my daddy was a dick and didn't believe me. I cared that my mother was spineless. And I cared that I felt bad for thinking bad thoughts about the woman who'd raised me.

"Let me go!" I demanded.

"Made that mistake once." Matt shook his head and corrected. "Actually, I made that mistake twice. Brace, baby—there's not gonna be a third."

"What?"

"First time was when you nabbed that fucking hair tie off my nightstand. I caught your play, and it wasn't until I was lying there after you left that I figured out why it bothered me so much. I was letting you go, letting you erase yourself from my room. Second time was when you wouldn't agree to dinner, and instead of explaining what happened while we were standing there, I let you walk away. I thought I was doing the right thing—both times. Letting you untangle yourself from me. I was wrong. It was a mistake, and I'm not making it a third time."

I hadn't yet digested everything Matt had said, but something had struck me as strange.

"My hair tie?"

"Women leave shit as an excuse to call or come back," he said bluntly. "But not you. Not even a rubber band that I'm fairly certain came in a pack of fifty for five bucks. You snatched that shit up quick and double-checked the floor to make sure you had everything. *You* didn't want *me* to have an excuse to call you."

"I agreed to come over again," I reminded him.

"Your terms. You were coming to me so you could up and leave when you wanted to. And don't deny it, you already told me that was the reason."

Damn.

He was correct about everything.

"Well, sorry to tell you, stud, but you don't get to *let* me do anything. When I want to leave, I leave."

"I believe that."

"What's that mean?"

"I believe that when you want to leave, you leave. I bet you're good at it, too. I bet, like me, living up to all those expectations taught you a thing or two about being your own person. Being what other people think you should be is fucking exhausting. Being used by people teaches you how to build a wall to keep the manipulators out."

When Matt stopped speaking, I was breathing hard and he was staring intently into my eyes. I didn't bother looking away. He'd already seen too much.

"But, just to point out—baby, you haven't left yet."

Every muscle in my body spasmed and my spine snapped straight.

Why hadn't I left yet?

I was about to rectify my mistake when Matt dropped

his mouth to my ear and whispered, "I fell asleep on the couch in my office."

That did it. I started to pull away. I didn't need him to lie to me.

"A few hours after you rolled out of my bed, the FBI was at my door to tell me my father had been arrested. I spent the rest of the day unraveling years of lies. I didn't mean to fall asleep, I knew you were coming over, and I was looking forward to it. But it's not every day you find out that everything you thought you knew about your father was a goddamned lie—"

"Your father was arrested?"

Holy shit.

"Racketeering and money laundering."

Racketeering? Wasn't that what gang members and mobsters get arrested for?

Matt's father was in a gang?

"That can't be right," I blurted out.

"Went through no less than two hundred pages of evidence that says it is absolutely right."

"But you're not in a gang."

That's right, I blurted that right out, too.

Matt's head tilted to the side and his eyes blazed with righteous anger.

"Hell, no, I'm not. Though my father's tied to the mob."

I hadn't noticed we'd stopped dancing and the song had changed to something upbeat until people started bumping into us.

"C'mon." I pulled out of Matt's embrace and grabbed his hand.

I didn't stop walking until I found a secluded table no one was occupying. But when I sat down, nerves got the best of me.

We're not that.

I wondered if that still applied if we weren't sleeping together.

If there was no sex, could we be friends?

Before I could give into my insecurities, I went for it.

"Are you okay?"

"Nope."

"Do you want to talk about it?"

"You sure you wanna hear this?"

"Yes."

Matt didn't hold back when he told me about his father's criminal activity. But it felt like there was more to the story than his father getting caught up with the mob. But I knew what it felt like to withhold certain details about your life, so I didn't push.

By the time Matt was done telling me about his dad, the wedding guests were all leaving. I was undecided about what to do next when Matt made the decision and walked me to my truck.

He didn't kiss me goodbye.

He didn't make any more advances.

He simply helped me into the driver's seat and told me to drive safely.

That night, I didn't sleep.

Sleep deprivation—that was my excuse for what I did next.

8

I set the bar on the rack and listened.

More knocking.

I sat up on the bench and glanced at the clock. Nine after nine.

Thank fuck it wasn't another six A.M. wake-up call. Though everyone I knew had been out late at Addy's wedding and wouldn't be knocking on my door this early.

Shit.

Not bothering to grab a shirt, I walked down the hall and through the living room. The knocking started again just as I threw the door open.

"Morning," Chelsea chirped, and my scowl deepened. Her eyes widened and she took a quick step back. "Damn, Matt, I'm sorry. I didn't think about banging on your door first thing in the morning."

I wasn't tracking why she was sorry.

"What?"

"The FBI—"

Hell, no. I wasn't talking anymore about the FBI.

"Why are you out of bed?"

Last night we hadn't left Tuesday and Jackson's house until after one in the morning. I hadn't missed her exhaustion, nor had she been able to cover her yawns.

"Wake up early every morning." She shrugged. "I brought breakfast. If you consider donuts breakfast."

Chelsea held up a big paper bag from the bakery around the corner from my house.

She mistook my silence as reluctance and blathered on, "I know what we are and what we are not. I thought about it last night. If nothing else, we can be friends."

We can be friends?

Oh, we were going to be friends all right. Good friends who shared a bed and had wild, mind-blowing sex. We were also going to be the kind of friends who ate dinner together and the occasional breakfast, too.

"And friends surprise friends with calorie-laden junk food that clogs arteries?" I asked.

"Only the best kind of friends. Boring friends bring oatmeal and fruit."

I barked out a laugh and stepped to the side.

Still chuckling, I said, "Well, then, *best* friend, please come in."

Happiness flared in her pretty eyes, making me feel ten feet tall. The woman needed to smile more.

I shut the door behind Chelsea but didn't get a chance to move away from the door when she stopped and looked back at me.

"Five Finger Death Punch." She noted the music coming from the back room I used as a home gym. "I approve."

"Didn't take you for a heavy metal kinda girl. I approve."

"I listen to it before a ride. It sounds crazy, but it centers me. The violence of the rhythm gets me ready."

"Doesn't sound crazy at all," I told her. "I'm gonna go grab a shirt. Make yourself at home."

Chelsea's gaze dropped to my chest. If she was attempting to hide her blatant interest, she'd failed miserably.

"That is, unless friends eat breakfast together shirtless," I started. "In which case, please feel free to remove yours."

Chelsea's face flamed red but she didn't miss a beat.

"Only special friends eat breakfast shirtless, Matt."

"How do we become special friends, Chels?"

Chelsea shrugged.

"I don't know, never had one."

That was interesting.

I knew she'd had at least one steady man in her life. I couldn't remember the dude's name, but she'd had a boyfriend when I'd met her. And looking back, it was funny how that was not one of my reasons for keeping my distance. That was not my style. If a woman had a man, she was off-limits—period. But I hadn't given him a second thought when I was coming up with lies to stop myself from getting too close to her.

"I've never had one either."

"Is this when I'm supposed to offer to pop your cherry?"

Christ, she was funny.

But I held back my laughter. Her pretend offer was too good to pass up.

"If you're offering, baby, I'm fully on board and up to the task. I've never been anyone's first, but I promise to be gentle."

Chelsea rolled her eyes and laughed.

"Unfortunately, I have been someone's first. It was clumsy and not fun. So I'll take a pass on the deflowering."

Unholy jealousy spiked in my gut.

"You've been someone's first?"

Shit, am I growling?

"Yep. And it's not a story worth telling and not just because it lasted approximately four minutes and two seconds."

Poor bastard.

"How old were you?"

"Nineteen."

Nineteen?

"What, were you robbing the cradle? How old was he?"

"Nineteen."

I had so many questions swirling around in my brain I didn't know where to start.

"He was my first, too," Chelsea sighed. "I didn't know he was a virgin, as well, or I probably wouldn't have done it. I know that sounds bad, but I kinda wanted my first time to be...better."

I did not want to give headspace to some guy fumbling around, not knowing what to do with a virgin Chelsea. Mostly because I was jealous as fuck about something that happened sixteen years before I knew her.

"Did he at least..." I trailed off, not knowing how to ask or if I even wanted to know the answer.

"Can we please not talk about my embarrassing first time? Unless, of course, we're going to swap stories, and you're gonna tell me about yours."

I quickly clamped my mouth shut. I was not going to tell Chelsea about my first time.

"That bad, huh?" She chuckled.

My first time was the opposite of bad. I was a junior and the girl was a senior. It was not her first time, and she'd thoroughly enjoyed showing me exactly what she liked, letting me explore what I liked, and by the time we'd gotten down to the actual sex, I'd lasted a hell of a lot longer than four minutes and two seconds.

"Sure," I mumbled noncommittedly.

"Your first time was good," she surmised.

It was time to drop the subject and move on.

"There's fresh coffee so help yourself. I'm gonna go change."

I rushed through a quick rinse off, got dressed, and turned off the music. By the time I got back to the kitchen, Chelsea had found plates and poured me a cup of coffee.

"Sorry, I don't know how you like it," she said, pointing to the mug.

"Just black."

Chelsea made a face and pointed to her cup. It didn't even resemble the color of coffee.

"I hate the taste but need the caffeine."

I glanced back at the milky-colored liquid and shook my head.

"How much milk did you add?"

"Half coffee, half milk," Chelsea said and jostled the bag of donuts. "I didn't know what kind you liked, so I bought a dozen."

I ignored the donuts and focused on Chelsea in my kitchen. Since I bought this house, not a single woman had ever been in this kitchen. And for some bizarre reason, I liked that.

"You're the first woman who's been in my kitchen," I told her.

"I'm not sure if I should feel honored or feel sorry for the women who've seen the inside of your bedroom but not the inside of your fridge."

Maybe I should've kept my trap shut.

"Do you even offer them a glass of water, or do they have

to cup their hands under the bathroom faucet to get a drink?"

Damn.

I walked straight into that.

"Depends. The quitters have to use the hose outside."

"You're gross," she grumbled.

"I'm joking. I don't invite quitters—"

A half-eaten donut hit me in the face. I watched the sugary treat hit the counter and bounce. Before it could roll off the edge, I grabbed it and took a bite.

"Maple," I said around a mouthful.

"You ate my donut," she complained.

"Baby, you threw it at my face," I said and swallowed. "Besides, you bought enough for breakfast, lunch, *and* dinner."

"Breakfast, lunch, and dinner?" Chelsea shook her head. "Sweetheart, do I look like a quitter? Those'll be polished off well before lunchtime."

I had firsthand knowledge that Chelsea was indeed not a quitter. Further, she had an ass that was meant to be worshipped, and if she got that ass from eating a box of donuts for breakfast, I was committed to the task of delivering a dozen to her every morning.

"Besides, I have a three-hour workout scheduled for this afternoon after my training with Ty. I'm sure I'll burn through the carbs."

"Who's Ty?"

I hoped my voice came across as nonchalant even though I felt anything but.

Chelsea's lips curved up into a smile that had my gut clenching.

"He used to be on the circuit. Went to the finals more times than I can remember. Took home the world championship twice and has a bunch of other wins besides. Now he trains roughstock. I moved to Georgia to be close to him."

What the hell?

"Is this the guy you broke up with?"

Chelsea's entire body started shaking before she busted out laughing.

"First," she sputtered. "His wife's not only a farrier but a blacksmith, and she wouldn't think twice about branding someone in the ass if they looked at Ty funny. Second, I adore his wife and kids. Third, contrary to popular belief, I don't do married men. And finally, he's old enough to be my father—that is, if my father had me at sixteen."

The relief I felt was short-lived.

"Contrary to popular belief?"

"To be fair, I'm not sure how many people believe I screw around with married men, but my father certainly believes I do."

Jesus.

"Your dad thinks you fuck married men?"

"Actually, just one. He heard this guy Barrett telling TJ—that's my brother—that he fucked me. Barrett was married, and he was trying to get TJ pissed off so he'd do something stupid and get disqualified. Unfortunately for Barrett, my brother not only doesn't care who I screw, he doesn't care about anything I do. Barrett's plan failed, but my father overheard and refused to believe me when I told him I'd never touched Barrett."

"That's jacked-up."

Chelsea waved her hand before she nabbed another donut.

"That's just one of the many reasons I packed up my shit at eighteen and left."

Wait. What?

"Hang on, you're telling me that you were under eighteen when some jackass was running his mouth about you, and the guy was married, and your dad didn't beat the shit out of him?"

Chelsea started laughing again, and as much as I'd been thinking earlier that I wished she'd smile more, I didn't like that she was laughing about the fucked-up relationship she had with her dad.

"I was sixteen. Barrett was at least twenty-one. And my dad accused me of screwing Barrett to distract my brother. It was an excuse because it was the second day of the rodeo, and TJ didn't have any points on the board. I was racing that weekend and was in second place. But that wasn't good enough for my dad. The golden child had yet to place, and the season was coming to an end."

Christ, what a douche.

"So, you've been doing this a long time?"

"I started barrel racing when I was five, calf roping when I was eight, and saddle bronc riding when I was fourteen. Though girls weren't sanctioned to compete in bronc riding back then."

"Damn, woman, that's some dedication. Where'd you grow up?"

"Omaha. You?"

"Greenwich."

Chelsea's torso swung back, and she looked shocked.

"Greenwich? Damn, I never would've guessed."

She took a bite of her donut and washed it down with a gulp of her milked-down coffee.

"Anyway, it's not really dedication when you're doing something you love. When I was little, the only time I felt free was on the back of a horse. I would ride way out into the pasture to get away from my dad and brothers."

Her mouth was moving, I could hear words, but I wasn't comprehending anything she was saying. I was stuck back on her comment about not guessing I was from Greenwich.

"Hello?" She waved her donut in front of my face. "Earth to Matt."

"Sorry." I shook myself from my stupor.

"What's wrong?"

For once, nothing was wrong.

"Why wouldn't you have guessed I was from Greenwich?" I asked.

Chelsea's nose scrunched and her brows pulled together when she said, "Please don't take this the wrong way, but Greenwich is a little uppity. Well, maybe that's not fair. I've only visited there once, a place called Belle Haven. There's this country club on the water where we had lunch with this bigwig who sponsored my brother Russ." She stopped to shake her head. "Seriously uppity."

My parents' estate was across the cove from Belle Haven Club. When I was a kid, I used to jump off our dock and swim over to the club. Chelsea was not wrong. It was uppity. My father lunched there at least five days a week.

She had no fucking clue who I was. Which was a douchey thing to think, but bottom line, she didn't know I came from money. Not even after I explained my father had purchased businesses for the sole purpose of helping the mob clean their dirty money.

And she hadn't put two and two together because Chelsea didn't give a single fuck about whether or not my family was wealthy. Just like she didn't care if I was.

I let that thought go and focused on what she said about a sponsor. The night I found her in the backroom of Balls Deep, she'd been upset about two things: her ex telling her she needed to move her horses and her sponsor had dropped her.

"Have you found a new sponsor?"

"Not yet. Though Ty thinks he knows someone."

That sounded like good news, so I didn't understand why she was frowning.

"Why do you look unhappy about that?"

Chelsea sighed and finished the rest of her donut. While I waited for her to finish chewing, I took in her makeup-free face. Yesterday her makeup had been heavy. She'd looked beautiful but fresh-faced she was gorgeous. Same with the dress and heels—she looked great all tricked out, but I much preferred her like this: workout gear, hair sleek and smooth, tennis shoes on her feet. This was the real Chelsea.

"The sponsor wants to promote me as a woman," she said shyly.

I didn't understand why that was a problem.

"Um, babe, you are a woman."

"That might be, but when I'm on the back of a bull, I'm just a cowboy."

"Still not trackin'."

"The bull doesn't know if I'm a woman or a man," she explained. "When I get into that chute, I'm just a rider. I've worked hard to get to where I am. I did that by riding the same bulls as the men. I've never used being a woman as an excuse or as a marketing tool, and I won't start now."

Damn, if I didn't respect the hell out of that line of thinking.

"Merit," I mumbled.

"Damn straight."

I'd already offered once and was turned down flat, but I thought I'd pitch my idea again.

"Would you consider the pool hall sponsoring you?"

"Not a chance."

"Why? I could use the tax write-off, and you need a sponsor. Seems like a win-win."

"I appreciate the offer, but I'm not riding with "Balls Deep" on my jersey or my chaps." She smirked.

Well, damn, I hadn't thought about that.

"What about if we changed it to Matt's Balls—"

"That's a hard pass, friend."

Friend.

For some strange reason, I liked that just as much as I like Chelsea in my kitchen.

Though, 'special' would be added in front of the friend as soon as I could manage.

Naked donuts with a funny, beautiful Chelsea.

Fuck yes!

"Do you know how to ride a horse?" she asked.

"Yep."

She looked at me disbelievingly.

"Do you know how to really ride a horse, or do you know how to sit on the back of one while a ranch hand leads you around?"

"Fifteen years of polo says I know how to ride a horse."

If that didn't sound uppity, I didn't know what did.

"Polo?"

She was putting two and two together.

"Why'd you wanna know if I rode?"

Chelsea cleared the curious expression from her face and answered.

"I have two mares. They need to be exercised. I was thinking if you weren't busy later, we could go out for a ride."

"What time? I have to go into the pool hall and do some work, but after that, I'm free."

"Is four too early?"

"Perfect."

The conversation turned to Trey and Addy's wedding, and for the next hour, while we polished off a dozen donuts, the banter continued. It was a novel concept—standing in my kitchen laughing with a woman. It was also the best morning I'd ever had.

9

My thighs were burning.

As luck would have it, Ty had decided today was the day he moved up to Lucky Strike. On a good day, Lucky was a tough bull; today Lucky felt like being extra ornery.

I watched Brisby, Ty's gateman, load Lucky in the chute and ignored the commotion going on around me. Ty and Daisy were mounted on their horses in the ring talking to Billy, the bullfighter who'd be the one to save my ass today if Lucky got too frisky. And Macho, the newest rider Ty had taken under his wing, was already up on the rails waiting to help me strap in.

With my rope in hand, I climbed up the rungs and took a deep breath.

"He's twisting hard to the left today," Macho warned.

"Saw that."

"The old man's got some spice in him today," Brisby added.

I swung my left leg over the rail and gently put my boot on Lucky's back—just to let him know I was climbing on. I slid my legs down between the rails around the fat beast and settled on his back. Brisby and Macho fell silent. Some riders didn't mind chatter while they were roping up.

I was not one of those riders.

This was my time with the bull. Just him and me getting a feel for each other.

I dropped the body of my rope down the right side of Lucky and looked at Brisby.

"Hook, please."

Brisby used his long metal pole to hook the knot in my rope. I was reaching down Lucky's left side to grab the rope when he decided to say hello and slammed my arm between his ribs and the gate.

"Be nice, Lucky," I mumbled under my breath.

Brisby chuckled, and once I had a hold of my rope, he backed away.

I finished tying on my rope, double-checked my hand placement, gave the tail of my rope one last hard yank then threw the extra length over my right hip. One more breath and that was it. In one smooth motion, I slid my crotch tight against my left hand, squared my shoulders, let go of the railing, and nodded my head.

Brisby opened the gate and Lucky didn't wait to clear it before his head dropped down and his back legs kicked out.

Hell, yeah, he was feeling spicy.

The thing about riding bulls was there was no time to think. Either you rode the beast, or you didn't. You went with the uncontrollable motion. There was no fighting the bull. You didn't control the twists, the kicks, the jumps. Your only job was to hold on while you were being tossed around like a ragdoll.

"Shoulder!" Ty shouted over the clanking of the bells.

Lucky dipped again and spun left, but at the last moment, he decided to go right. I set my hips, pushed my shoulder forward, and rode away from the spin. I felt my rope slip under my hand, dug my knuckles into Lucky's back, and rolled with him.

The buzzer sounded.

I opened my hand, let go of my wrap, and my hand easily slipped out of the handle. I leaned forward and started my dismount. Lucky bucked and I went flying. At the last second, I tucked my chin, landed on my left side, and rolled.

"Up! Up! Up!" Brisby shouted and stepped in front of Lucky.

I was on my feet running for the gate when I saw Matt—his boot-covered feet up on the third rail, his elbows resting on the top, his gaze steady on me.

Out of the corner of my eyes, I saw Brisby smack Lucky on his rump and the bull took off full speed through the open gate. Macho swung it closed behind the bull, and I let out a sigh of relief.

"How's the shoulder?" Ty asked and wheeled Cisco around, stopping behind me.

I rolled my shoulder and nodded. "Feels good."

"Want another go?"

I glanced over at Matt then back to Ty.

"Who's that?" Ty asked, still looking over my head.

"A friend. I asked him to come ride with me today. He must be early."

Ty glanced down at me and smirked.

"He ain't early. He's right on time."

Brisby walked over, holding out my rope with a huge smile on his face.

"And she's back!" he whooped. "Going eight!" he continued to shout.

"Macho, load up Tank!" Ty yelled. "And get Aaron out here to help. Chels needs a spotter."

My eyes narrowed and I felt a twinge of fear.

"Are you trying to embarrass me?"

Tank was just that—a tank of a bull. Young, full of energy, and he was a jumper. Whereas Lucky was old and liked to spin and buck, Tank liked to jump and twist.

"You wanna ride a ninety you need a bull that will score high. Lucky's not giving you what you need. Buck up, cowboy, or don't. Choice is yours."

There was a lot I liked about Ty. He was a great trainer with the belief that there was no one right way to ride a bull. As long as the outcome was an eight-second ride, he didn't care how you got there. His job was to teach the fundamentals and run drills. But each rider had their own style, and if it didn't look like his, he didn't fuss. The other thing I liked was that both animal and rider safety was his number one concern. But the best thing about Ty was he didn't treat me like I was anything but what I was—a bull rider. He didn't see me as a woman. He didn't put on kid gloves when he talked to me. And he'd never, not once, taken it easy on me.

"Load up Tank."

Ty jerked his chin. "Your wrap was too loose. If you need help, there's no shame in having your puller yank that shit tight. That's what he's there for. Use him."

Ty clucked his tongue and Cisco started to walk.

Now I had another choice to make—go talk to Matt or go get ready for another ride.

I chose Matt.

"Hey, am I late, or are you early?" I asked.

"I wanted to watch you do your thing."

So that meant he was early.

"And? What'd you think?"

For some dumb reason, I couldn't stop myself from holding my breath while I waited for his answer.

"I think you're insane."

I felt dread hit my belly. That wasn't the first time I'd heard that.

"I also think that you're a fuck of a lot tougher than me. You made that look easy when I know it's not. Are you going again?"

Tougher than him?

"Yeah, I have one more ride."

"Do you mind if I watch, or will it throw you off your game?"

Something deep inside me began to loosen.

"You wanna watch?"

The muscle in Matt's cheek jumped, and tiny lines around his eyes formed.

"You have no idea how special you are, do you?"

I reared back as his question slammed into my chest. The steel-lined vest I was wearing did nothing to stop the impact of his words.

"What?"

"It shocks the hell out of me that you don't get it, but here it is. There are far and few people who rise to the occasion. Who are mentally tough enough to set their fear aside and work hard to accomplish a goal. You out there on the back of that bull is no joke. That thing could kill you. Yet I watched you climb onto his back, and when you did, there was no fear. It was like when you slipped down onto him, you found your peace. It was incredible to watch you."

No one. Not my dad, not my brothers, not my mother, not my friends back in Omaha had ever got it. None of them cared enough to watch me ride. They all thought I was a joke.

Matt saw it.

He understood.

"Thanks," I whispered.

"Not sure why you're thanking me, baby. It's your hard work."

I shook my head and looked up at him.

"Thanks for seeing me and not a stupid girl with a stupid dream."

Matt's eyes went hard and his jaw clenched tight.

I couldn't process what that look meant. I had a bull to ride.

"Don't get your hopes up on another eight-second ride. Tank's a mean sonofabitch."

"Then be meaner."

"Right. I'll be meaner." I smiled. "Gotta go get ready."

"Ride ninety, baby."

Matt winked and I belted out a laugh.

"Have you been watching YouTube videos polishin' up on your rodeo lingo?"

"Maybe."

I laughed again and waved.

I took my time brushing down my rope and added more rosin, using the mundane, familiar activity to clear Matt from my mind.

This time while I climbed into the chute, Aaron was there to keep Tank steady while I settled and got myself ready. Brisby was still doing double duty as my puller and gateman.

I was stroking the tail of my rope, heating up the rosin, when Tank bucked hard and crushed my knee on the rails.

"Freaking hell," I hissed. "Pull up, would you, Brisby?"

He did as I asked and I wiggled my fingers.

"More. Yank the bitch up."

I heard Brisby grunt and that did it. I wrapped the rope tightly around the back of my hand, back over my handle, tossed the tail over my right leg, and went for it. It was easier out of the gate if my body was in motion when the bull took off. I was up on the handle, already riding my hips when I let go of the rail and nodded my head.

Brisby opened the gate, and Tank took off like a bat out of hell.

Muscle memory took over and I held the fuck on for dear life. Tank didn't let you do anything but. He didn't let you breathe. He didn't let you think.

It was a miraculous, scary, wondrous thing when a gigantic animal jumped into the air—all four hoofs off the ground while its body twisted. It felt like you were flying; for just a moment, you were weightless until the animal landed with a thud and your brain rattled.

"Ride! Ride! Ride!" Daisy chanted.

Tank reared when I thought he'd buck, and I felt my hips slip back.

Fuck!

That was all she wrote. Tank's hoofs hit the dirt, his rear spun around, and I let go.

I heard the buzzer sound as I was flying through the air.

No points.

I was in the dirt on my hands and knees, catching my bearings, when I felt Brisby's boot step on my back as a platform to launch himself at Tank.

"Move!"

I shot to my feet and glanced over my shoulder. Brisby had his arms around Tank's thick neck and he was getting tossed around. I stopped watching and started running.

I hit the gates, climbed up, and when I looked back, Tank was running through the gate.

Ty rode up and stopped.

"Anticipation killed the bull rider." Ty chuckled. "Other than that, great ride."

"Sometimes it's annoying as hell you don't miss anything."

"You pay me the big bucks not to miss when you're thinking too hard out there."

"I thought he was gonna kick," I admitted.

"And you would've stayed on if he had. The only thing you should be thinking about out there is where your hips are at." Ty glanced over to where I knew Matt was waiting, then looked back to me. "You need to ice down before you take your friend on a ride."

Damn, I hadn't thought about that.

Ty's expression turned serious. "No exception. You want that shoulder to continue to heal. You'll respect your body and continue to rehab."

I wanted my shoulder to heal.

"I'll ice it."

"Good riding today. Tomorrow you're on the barrel and your turn to man the chute while Macho rides. He's been slackin' off. It was good for him to watch you today. You lit a fire under his ass."

Macho was younger than me by about ten years. But then, I was old by rodeo standards. He was also skinny, and I was fairly certain I could whoop his ass in a fistfight. But he was a good rider.

"How's he slackin' off?"

I wasn't gossiping. I sincerely wanted to know for two reasons. The first was so I could help Macho get his head right, and the second was to make sure I wasn't making the same mistakes.

"Heart."

That was all Ty said, but that said it all.

If your heart wasn't in your ride, you'd already lost before you got into the chute.

"Does your man know how to ride?" Ty asked, and my heart skipped a beat.

"He's not my man. He's—"

"Sure looks like he is the way he was watching you."

I fought the urge to glance over at Matt and kept my eyes on Ty when I shook my head.

"I don't think he's ever watched bull riding in person. He used to play polo."

Ty's head tipped back and he belted out a long, loud laugh.

"Go on and show him how a real cowboy rides."

"Thanks, Ty."

He was trotting away when he shouted, "If he gets hurt and sues me, you're picking up the bill!"

"Sure thing!" I yelled back.

I couldn't imagine Matt getting hurt by something as minor as falling off a horse.

I was a few feet away from where Matt was when he said, "That was incredible."

"Didn't make it eight seconds."

Matt shook his head and smiled. "Baby, that fucker jumped four feet off the ground."

Only four feet? It felt like we were soaring at least ten feet off the dirt.

"Tank's young. He's still got plenty of piss and vinegar in him. Plus, I think Aaron made his flank strap extra tight."

Matt's eyes rounded and he coughed twice.

"I'd be pissed, too, if my testicles were cinched."

"Oh my God." I laughed. "That's a total myth. The strap doesn't go anywhere near the testicles. And I was joking about Aaron tightening the rope too tight. The part that goes around the flank is covered in wool. The underside of the belly is sensitive, and when the wool rubs, it tickles, and the bull bucks and jumps."

"No shit?"

"No shit."

"Well, fuck me sideways. I always thought the balls were being twisted."

"Nope."

Matt's chin was dipped down so he could look at me. There was a big, wide smile on his handsome face, and something strange started fluttering in my stomach. It felt a lot like the feeling I got right before I climbed into the chute.

Adrenaline mixed with excitement. The feeling was intoxicating and addicting.

A deadly combination when it came to Matthew Kessler.

I had a feeling there was a lot I didn't know about the man. And if I was smart, I'd stop getting to know him and go right on not knowing. The problem was the more he told me, the more I wanted to know.

"Ready to saddle up?" Matt asked.

"Do you mind waiting ten minutes? I need to ice my shoulder."

Matt's gaze dropped to my right arm, but to his credit, he didn't ask me if I should be riding while I was recovering from an injury.

Which was more respect than anyone else gave me.

10

"Why Gypsy?" I asked when we slowed to a trot.

"I didn't name her," Chelsea said. "I bought her at an auction. She's a retired jumper."

"Have you ever given her head and tried her out?"

Chelsea slowed Rebel to a walk, and with no correction on my part, Gypsy followed.

"Yeah, when I first got her. But she's getting old. When I got Rebel, her name was Breeze, but after the first week of her fighting me, I renamed her. There's nothing breezy about her. I've never had a horse bite me as many times as Rebel has."

I couldn't stop myself from smiling at the way Chelsea talked about her horses. These animals weren't her pets. They were her babies.

"You have a good seat," Chelsea commented.

"I've been given plenty of compliments before, but that one's a first."

As intended, Chelsea smiled. The more I saw her smile, the more I wanted to make her do it again—and again, and again.

I was completely and totally screwed. Now was not the right time for me to catch feelings for a woman. But it was too late. I couldn't stop thinking about Chelsea. It was something I'd emphatically avoided for years—I kept everything in my life casual and fun. But now, I wanted more.

"How was everything at the pool hall?"

A freaking mess.

"I need to fire my manager, but before I do that, I need to find a replacement."

"Why do you need to fire him?"

"I went in today and he fucked up the liquor order again. The schedule's a fucking mess. I had messages from two waitresses that they'd specifically given dates they couldn't work, and Pete has them scheduled, and he only has one bartender on for Saturday night. And that's only the bar. He's screwed up the tables, too."

"One bartender on a Saturday night? I'd kill my manager if he forgot to schedule a second bartender on a Saturday. I can mix drinks and pop tops off bottles pretty damn fast, but I couldn't handle the bar alone when it was packed."

Holy hell.

I forgot that Chelsea was a bartender at Whiskey Pete's. I'd only been there once. It was a cool place. Chill. Mellow. A place you went to sip a cocktail and have a conversation. There was no music, no pool balls smashing in pockets, there weren't people up walking around having a good time. But the place was always busy.

"Do you make good money at Whiskey Pete's?" I asked. Then I winced at how rude my question was. "I'm asking because I'm wondering how much I'd have to up what you make to come run Balls Deep."

Chelsea was quiet for a long time and I was kicking my own ass for putting her on the spot.

"Can I ask you something?"

"Sure."

Please, fuck, don't bring up my father, his arrest, or his money.

"Why'd you buy the pool hall when you already have a full-time job?"

Shit. Her asking about my dad's legal trouble would've been easier to talk about.

"The truth?"

"Why do people ask that? I wonder if anyone has ever answered with, no lie to me?"

My lips twitched, but I held back my smile.

"In this case, me coming up with a lie will make me sound less like a douche. For instance, I could tell you that buying it was a sound business investment. Or I was helping the previous owner out of a jam. Both would be the truth but not the real reason I bought Balls."

"What was the real reason?"

There wasn't much I'd done in my life I was embarrassed about. I made a decision, and good or bad, I owned it. And there'd never been a time in my life when I cared what someone thought about me. I was who I was. I couldn't be any other way. And for the most part, I was a good person. But right then, I was embarrassed. And I was embarrassed because I cared what Chelsea thought of me.

"I bought Balls so I could rename it Balls Deep. I bought it as a joke."

"You bought a business as a joke?"

Chelsea's frown said it all. She rightly thought I was a tool.

"It started that way, yes. But when I approached James,

the old owner, he was in financial trouble—not the business, him personally. His eldest is in college, and he was racking up more debt than he could afford the monthly payments on. And since he owned a business, his daughter didn't qualify for scholarships. I looked over the business's financials, liked what I saw, so I had my accountant look them over. We negotiated a fair price, and I bought Balls."

Chelsea remained silent, and the longer it stretched, the more worried I got about what she was thinking.

Finally, she said, "I'll make you a deal."

"What kind of deal?"

"The kind that's like a bet."

I thought back to last night's bet and smiled. She'd totally lost but being the good sport I was, I wouldn't rub it in.

"I like bets," I told her. "Whatcha got?"

"I'll race you back to the stables. If I win, you up my salary by ten thousand a year. If you win, you up it by eight."

"What's your salary now?"

Not that it mattered to me either way, but a man's gotta know what he's dealing with.

"What happened to, no rules, no limitations, no restrictions, no fear? Live a little, Matt."

Well, since she brought it up...

"Speaking of, you're not gonna welch on me, are you?"

"I don't know, are you gonna up my salary by ten K a year when I whoop your ass?"

I didn't feel now was the best time to explain to her that there would never be a time when she whooped my ass.

"Sure."

"I could make a lot of money," she taunted.

"You could."

Chelsea pulled back on Rebel's reins, and the horse

stopped. I quickly pulled back on Gypsy and looked over my shoulder.

"You don't care, do you?"

How do I explain without sounding like a spoiled prick?

"Money's money. You make it, you spend it. What you don't do is take it with you after you die. I need a manager. I'm willing to pay whatever I need to pay to have someone I trust in there running my business. Protecting my investment."

"That's what people with money say," she grumbled.

She had no idea.

"Does it bother you?"

As much as I'd liked to say her answer didn't matter, it did. I had no idea what was going to happen with Kessler Management. I hadn't decided what I was going to do with my shares in the company or what I was going to do with the money I'd made off my dividends, but the bottom line, even without that, I was still wealthy.

And there was another first. Normally I was trying to scrape off the gold diggers. Now it seemed the first woman I was interested in exploring a relationship with I was going to have to convince to take a chance on me and my money.

"Does what bother me?"

"That I have money?"

"Why would I care how much money you have or don't have? It's none of my business."

Jesus, was she for real?

"Oh, and something else," she continued. "No micromanaging. You're my boss, I answer to you, but the day-to-day operation and the employees answer to me. You either trust me to run your business, or you don't. But the employees will never respect me if you're in there undermining my authority."

"Done. Anything else?"

"During the season, I'll need to take some time off. I'll take care of my responsibility at the bar first, and I'll have everything in place so when I'm gone, everything will run smoothly."

"Okay."

"Agreed?"

"Agreed."

"Go!"

Before I understood what the hell was going on, Chelsea had dug her heels into Rebel, and the horse was off like the hounds of hell were on her rump.

What the fuck?

"Cheater!" I shouted and wheeled Gypsy in the direction of the barn.

"You ain't trying hard enough..." That was all I heard over pounding hoofs and wind rushing by.

Something Chelsea hadn't taken into consideration—Gypsy was a jumper, and just because the old mare had been retired from the sport didn't mean it wasn't in the old girl's blood. Chelsea had to take Rebel through the clearing. With Gypsy, I could cut straight through the wooded area.

The first downed log came into sight, and I lifted off the saddle and leaned forward.

"Take it, girl."

Gypsy cleared the log with ease.

"Atta, girl." I patted her neck and gave her head. "Take us home, Gypsy."

By the time the barn came into view, I'd forgotten about everything—my dad, Chelsea, Balls Deep, Triple Canopy, everything. It was me and Gypsy and fresh air blowing in my face. It was the steady rocking of the horse under me. I'd been transported back to a time when everything was simple, when life was stress-free and full of fun.

When was the last time I had fun?

That was a weird question to ask yourself, but I couldn't remember.

Out of the corner of my eye, I caught Rebel coming around the corner in an all-out canter, Chelsea's hair blowing behind her, looking more beautiful than ever.

"Go, Gypsy."

I dug my heels in, and like the rockstar she was, Gypsy picked up speed.

"C'mon, Rebel, go!"

She wasn't gonna make it. I had her by at least a head. Both horses shot through the open gate to the paddock, and I pulled back on the rein.

"Ho, girl."

Gypsy eased to a fast trot, then slower still until she was leisurely trotting around the ring following Rebel.

"What was that about cheating?" I yelled.

Chelsea cocked her head over her shoulder and was absolutely beaming.

"How'd she do? I saw her take the first jump but lost you when the woods got thick."

And there it was again, she didn't care she lost, she wanted to know about how her baby did.

I held Chelsea's gaze and said, "She's perfect."

And she was—the woman, not the horse.

"Any more bets you wanna make?" I asked.

"Goddamn," Chelsea's trainer called. "I didn't know that old biddy had it in her."

"Don't call my girl old. She's sensitive."

"Right, about as sensitive as a calloused palm."

"Damn, boss, I don't wanna hear about why your palms are calloused," one of the ranch hands joked.

"Manners, son."

The younger guy shook his head and smiled at Chelsea like she was a goddess.

"Next time you wanna go for a ride, give me a call, Chels."

Ty took off his hat and smacked the kid in the back of the head.

"Damn, Macho, you got any brains in there at all? See that man over there? He'll snap you in two."

Ty was not wrong. I could snap him in two and not break a sweat.

"I was offering to exercise—"

"I'd stop now," Ty suggested.

The kid's face turned red and I chuckled.

Another first; I didn't give two fucks Ty was insinuating I was Chelsea's man.

11

In my experience, there were two different kinds of bosses. The ones who were awesome and cared about their employees, and the assholes. I was lucky, and my boss at Whiskey Pete's was awesome. When I gave my notice and explained I was going to be the manager at Balls Deep, Samantha was excited for me. She even offered her help if, in the future, I had questions. And she didn't need me to work out my notice, or rather she was so happy for me that I was moving into management—even if it was at another business—that she told me not to waste two weeks and to go get started now.

I was excited but nervous.

A steady income not dependent on tips plus a raise meant I wouldn't be as stressed when rent came around. The only downside was Matt was now my boss and I wasn't sure if that was good or not. I'd tossed and turned all night last night, wondering if I'd made the right decision. I had been impulsive and off the cuff. I hadn't thought about the ramifications of managing his pool hall.

Did that mean we couldn't be friends?

Sleeping together again was completely off the table—not that it was going to happen again anyway. But now that the door was completely closed, I didn't like the finality of it. And if I was being honest with myself, knowing that Matt and I would never...never what? Be together? That was never an option in the first place. We'd never be special friends who ate donuts together naked. That hadn't been a real option either. Fuck buddies? Maybe we could've been that as long as I didn't allow myself to get lost in him. Which, there was a slight chance I already was, so keeping our relationship professional was the smart thing to do.

Professional.

I could totally do that.

It was just after seven and I was sitting on my couch debating the merits of doing a load of laundry versus going to my new place of business and sitting at the bar to get a feel for the place before I started working there when my phone rang.

I glanced down and saw Matt's name on the screen.

Nope, my heart didn't just jump in my chest. Nope. No way.

"Hey," I greeted.

"Hey, *best friend*," he returned. "Are you hungry?"

Best friend?

"Depends on what's on the menu."

That was a lie. I was starving, and part of me going to the pool hall was so I could eat and not have to cook.

"Greasy takeout, of course. A *friend* would buy a friend a healthy meal at the all-you-can-eat salad bar. A best friend offers to supply calories and carbs."

"Now you're getting it," I muttered. "And for the record, you ever try to take me to a salad place we're breaking up."

I heard Matt chuckle. I let my eyes drift closed, then I took it one step further and let myself memorize the sound.

"You have a great laugh."

Holy hell, I said that out loud.

Matt fell silent, and my stomach twisted into a knot.

"So, anyway, greasy—"

"Chelsea?"

"Yeah?"

"You have a great laugh, too."

Is this being professional?

"Maybe this isn't a good idea," I told him.

"What's not?"

"This. Us being friends like this."

"Best friends," he corrected. "Yesterday morning, you didn't have a problem with us being friends."

"Yesterday morning, you weren't my boss. Today you are. By the way, I gave my notice today, and my boss was cool about it and told me I didn't have to work out my two weeks. So I'm all yours." *Shit, goddamn.* "I mean, I can start whenever you want me to."

"I'm not your boss," he argued. "You're the boss. I just own the joint."

"Matt—"

"I'm serious, Chelsea. You're the boss."

"You are the owner."

"Okay, how about this? As the owner, I have no problems being friends with the people who work at the bar."

A thought came to me, and as hard as I tried to shove it aside now that it was swirling around in my brain, I couldn't stop wondering how many *friends* Matt had at Balls Deep. He and the rest of the guys had frequented the bar before Matt bought it, and since Matt had bought the bar, there hadn't been any turnover with the staff. Was I going to be working with a bunch of women that Matt had slept with?

The thought made me sick to my stomach.

"Chels?"

"Yeah?"

"Text me your address so I can bring over dinner. I worked through lunch, and I'm fuckin' starving."

No way was he coming to my homely, little apartment. Yesterday when he'd weirdly asked me if I had issues with him having money, I told him the truth. I didn't give a rat's rear end what he had. It was none of my business, and honestly, I hadn't realized he had money until he told me he'd bought Balls Deep as a joke. And actually, I still didn't know if he had money because people didn't buy businesses with money they had in the bank. They got loans. So for all I knew he was broke and in debt.

However, none of that mattered because I didn't invite *anyone* to my place.

"If you're starving then—"

"Chelsea. Address."

"I'll meet you at Balls Deep. I was getting ready to go there to check out how the place ran on a slow night."

"There are no slow nights at Balls Deep. It's packed every night."

"Seriously?"

"Yes. Two nights a week, the tables are reserved for league play. But even with the tables all taken, the bar's still packed."

I had no idea Balls Deep was a hot spot. I worked in a bar, I didn't have any desire to visit one on my nights off.

"Address," he repeated.

"I'll meet you at your house."

There was a beat of silence, then he asked, "Is there a reason you don't want me at your place?"

Yes.

"Of course not."

"Then give me your address and I'll pick up something on the way."

"I'll come to—"

"Fuck it," he snapped. "I'll find it myself."

"I'm a single woman, living alone. I'm not dumb enough to be listed. I've spent hours taking myself off those stupid 'find people' internet sites."

"Babe."

That was all he said, like that one word said it all.

"Matt—"

"See you soon."

The line disconnected, and realization set in. He had ways to find me. I'd heard the girls talking about how good Dylan was at finding what the guys at TC needed. They didn't jabber jaw a whole lot about it, but I knew beyond the training Triple Canopy did with police and what the guys called weekend warriors, they also did investigations.

Matt was going to find my address, then he was going to show up and probably be appalled at how I lived. He wouldn't understand that I lived in a studio apartment because I spent all my money on taking care of my horses. And Ty wasn't cheap but he was worth every penny I spent training with him.

I didn't need much. I never had. If given the choice of buying a saddle or clothes, I always picked the saddle. All of my gear was the best money could buy, but my couch came from Goodwill, as did the rest of my furniture.

I looked around my sad little apartment and sighed.

So what if there was no artwork on the wall? So what if there were no pictures of friends or family displayed? So what if my furniture was secondhand and crappy? I had a roof over my head, but more importantly, my girls were well taken care of, and I'd already paid Ty for the next month's training, and I had enough money set aside to get me to Athens. If I could score there, I'd win a little money, and that would get me through to the next rodeo. With no sponsor, this season was going to be tight. When I traveled far I'd be sleeping in my truck instead of a hotel room, and I'd be eating truck stop food, but I'd done it before and survived.

If Matt thought poorly about me because of where I lived, then so be it. I'd know he was an asshole, and maybe I'd get over this stupid crush I had.

The more I thought about it, the more I liked the idea of him coming over.

It might be just what I needed to stop obsessing over what would never be.

"Okay. So, I got you a bacon cheeseburger," Matt said as he dropped the bags on my coffee table. "I had them put the lettuce, tomato, and onion on the side. I wasn't sure if you considered that salad, and I didn't want to risk a breakup. In case you're not in the mood for that, I also got you a spicy chicken sandwich. A large fry and an order of onion rings. We can share those. Oh, and four of those apple pie desserts."

I stared down at the fast-food bags and I knew my mouth was hanging open like an idiot, but there were three bags full of food for two people.

"What'd you get yourself? A quarter cow?"

"Two cheeseburgers and a chicken sandwich. If you don't eat both of yours, I'll eat what you don't."

I lifted my gaze to Matt, and yes, my mouth was still hanging open. There was no way he could eat all that food and look the way he did. With his clothes on, you couldn't miss he was in shape. His shirtsleeves pulled tight around his biceps and not because he was one of those guys who bought a size too small to show off—he was ripped. But I'd had the pleasure of seeing him undressed, and I knew, because I'd paid special attention to the ridges on his stomach, he also had a six-pack. From top to toe, Matt was the perfect male specimen.

Totally lickable.

And lucky for me, I'd had the pleasure of doing just that. Not only had I explored every inch of him with my tongue, but my hands had gotten in on the action, too.

"Babe?"

"Mm?"

Matt's laugh filled the small space and my eyes shot to his.

Bad idea.

He was looking at me like he had when he was tearing at my clothes not even two seconds after we'd stepped through his front door. I'd never been divested of my clothing so quickly. Not that I was complaining, but Matt was well-practiced in the art of clothing removal.

That ugly ball in my tummy twisted tighter.

Of course he's well-practiced. The man is hot.

"What just happened?" Matt asked.

"What do you mean?"

"You went from looking at me like you were contemplating whether you wanted to eat me or the burger to looking at me like you wanted to punch me in the jellybeans."

"Did you just refer to your balls as jellybeans?"

"Yep."

"What self-respecting man calls his junk jellybeans?"

"No, no, no," Matt chided. "No self-respecting man calls

his package junk. Balls, nuts, testicles, jellybeans, nads, family jewels are all acceptable. Junk? No way."

"Nads?"

Matt shrugged.

"That's going old-school. Gonads, brass clankers, bangers."

"You'll call your balls bangers, but not junk?" I inquired.

"Now, Chels, not to be crass, but you've—"

"Stop!" I held up my hand. "I get it."

"Great. Now that we got that out of the way, you wanna explain why you're giving me the stink eye?"

No, I sure did not want to explain that I was jealous of nameless, faceless women who'd taught Matt how to strip a woman in three seconds flat and not damage a single article of clothing. Hell, I didn't even want to admit to myself that I was resentful of the multitude of skills he'd acquired due to the volume of women he'd practiced on.

Why am I thinking about this?

"I wasn't giving you the stink eye. I was just wondering why you were trying to give yourself high cholesterol from all the red meat you're getting ready to consume."

Matt held my eyes. I didn't miss the flash of disappointment that raced across his face.

"That's how you're gonna play it?"

Yes!

"Play what?"

"For someone who's brave as fuck you certainly hide behind that wall of yours a lot."

Matt didn't wait for me to offer him a drink. He simply walked into my kitchenette and made himself at home, leaving me to stare at the bags full of food while contemplating what he said.

It wasn't lost on me that he'd once again called me out

on being emotionally closed off and living behind a wall. Yet, from everything I knew about him, he did the same thing.

"You're one to talk," I belatedly returned.

"One to talk about what?"

"Hiding behind a wall."

Matt set the glass he'd found in one of my cupboards down on the counter, laid both palms flat on the scarred Formica, and said, "Open your eyes, Chelsea."

They were open. Wide-open. They had been all my life. They had to be so I could dodge the insults my brothers had hurled my way. I'd never had the luxury of bouncing through life with my head in the clouds. For as far back as I could remember, I had to watch my back. I learned early on no one would watch it for me.

"They're open, Matt."

"No, baby, they're not. If you were paying attention, you would've seen the moment I stepped out from behind that wall."

"We're not that," I whispered.

"We weren't, but we damn sure are now."

I shook my head in denial.

We couldn't be anything. We shouldn't even be friends. It would get complicated and awkward.

"Admit it, Chels. You know what's changed, and you know how it's changed."

"No."

"No what?" he scoffed. "No, you're not going to admit it? Or no, you're going to lie and pretend you don't feel about me exactly how I feel about you?"

"You don't feel—"

"The night we kissed in the back room of Balls Deep, you were right. I'd been avoiding you for months. I admitted it then, but I still didn't tell you the truth. I avoid relationships—period. I do that to protect myself, and I knew there was something about you that I didn't want to protect myself from and that scared the shit out of me. So I did everything I could to never be alone with you so I wouldn't be tempted. Then we kissed, and the first thing I thought was that you tasted like a dream I never wanted to wake up from. And from there, the night only got better. You weren't a dream—you were real, and you were in my bed, and I didn't want you to leave. I wasn't ready to ask you to stay, but I did ask you for another night because that was the only way I knew how to communicate I wanted more time with you. It was bullshit. I didn't want another night of you in my bed."

Matt paused and took a breath. I did not. I was out of breath and couldn't catch it. I couldn't calm my racing heart, and I felt like I might pass out at any moment. "Okay, I wanted another night of you in my bed. But more than that, I wanted to feel it again. It had been so long since I'd felt *it* I didn't understand that first night. I laid in bed all night trying to figure out why I was so pissed at you for walking out on me. It wasn't until days later, even after you walked out on me without hearing me out, that I got it. The feeling was a connection. I like you, Chelsea. You. The person you are. I like how tough and brave you are. I like how you are with your friends. I like how you are with my friends. I like how you take life by the balls, and you go for it. It's refreshing. It's beautiful. When I'm with you, you make me remember what a rush life can be. I don't know why you've built your wall, though I can guess it has a lot to do with your father. Who, no offense, baby, sounds like a monumental asshole."

Matt stopped again, and I wasn't sure if he was waiting for me to validate his assumption that my father was an asshole or if he wanted confirmation that I lived behind a wall. I wasn't sure of anything because I couldn't get my lungs to cooperate and draw in a breath. I was stuck on the part where Matt said he liked me. I was reeling from him telling me I tasted like a dream. My mind was spinning a million miles an hour.

I did the only thing I could and nodded.

"I built my wall when I learned that women will use me. It started when I was a teenager. I wasn't Matt, I was a Kessler. Girls didn't like me because of me. They liked my last name. After I moved away from Greenwich—*from Belle Haven*—women no longer knew who a Kessler was, but they sure as hell didn't miss that I'm rich as fuck. They liked what I could buy them, and they asked me to buy plenty, but they didn't care about me. It only got worse when I made the Teams. Now I had women chasin' me because I was a SEAL, wanting nothing more than bragging rights that they banged a Team Guy. They didn't give the first fuck about me. So that wall got higher and higher until no woman could scale it."

He lived in Belle Haven. The neighborhood I'd called uppity.

"You're rich?" I whispered.

"As fuck," he returned.

Matt was rich as fuck.

"I don't know what to say about that."

"As I said, refreshing. I tell you I've got money, and instead of your eyes lighting up like you've hit the jackpot, you look disgusted."

"I'm not disgusted you have money. I'm disgusted that women would ask you to buy them things. I'm disgusted that a woman would bang you just to brag about it. That's disgusting. How much money you have is completely irrelevant."

"Refreshing," Matt muttered.

I felt myself getting pissed on Matt's behalf. What kind of bitch used a man for money?

"What those women did is gross. I don't understand it. But I think you're wrong. Those women did like you for you. I'm not saying that some of them didn't have shady intentions, but to say none of them liked or cared about you is crazy. Saying that means you don't see what a great guy you are. It's impossible to spend more than five minutes with you and not like you. I understand the need to protect yourself. But I'm betting there were women in your past who genuinely liked you for you."

Matt pushed off the counter but made no move to come closer. Not that we were very far apart. My whole apartment was less than five hundred square feet, but he remained distant when he said, "Your turn."

"My turn?"

"Why'd you build your wall?" he clarified.

Matt had opened himself up to me. He'd been honest and freely given me something I didn't think he gave very many people. My issues with my family weren't a secret. Anyone who was part of the circuit knew all about my father's disapproval. Everyone knew what my brothers thought about me. Or at least, they knew my father's side. No one knew mine.

"I didn't leave home at eighteen. I was kicked out," I started. "It just sounds better if I tell people I moved away. And, honestly, I've repeated the lie so many times I've started to believe it myself. But that's not what happened. The day of my eighteenth birthday, my dad told me to pack my shit and get out of his house. I was an adult, and he no longer had a legal responsibility to take care of me."

If I wasn't careful, the memory of that day would pull me under. The fear I'd felt had been devastating.

"Chelsea."

I ignored Matt's gentle tone and sucked in a breath. It was now or never. I'd started, so I had to get it all out or I never would.

"I dropped out of high school," I admitted. "I don't have a diploma. It's a good thing you didn't make me fill out an application, or I would've lied on it just like I have for the past sixteen years. I had nowhere to go. No money. No car. A backpack full of clothes but nothing else. I left that day not knowing where I was going to sleep that night."

I felt wet hit my eyes.

So damn weak.

I closed my eyes as tightly as I could to stop the tears from falling. It had been sixteen years, and the memory still hurt so freaking bad I couldn't stop myself from crying.

I felt Matt's arms around me, then my feet were no longer on the floor. By the time I had the courage to open my eyes, Matt was sitting on the couch and my butt was in his lap. But that was not the alarming part; he was rocking me like I was a child.

I tried to free myself, but Matt's arms around me got tighter.

"Don't move."

"I'm not a child that needs to be rocked."

"No, you're a woman who I care a great deal about. And I just found out her father's a motherfucking piece of shit. So cut me some slack, baby, and stay where you are."

He cared about me a great deal?

"It was a long time ago," I reminded him.

"Yeah? Then why did I feel your fear fill the room and watch your legs shake when you told me you didn't know where you were going to sleep? That shit might've happened sixteen years ago, but, Chelsea, terror is tattooed on your soul."

He wasn't wrong.

The feeling of being abandoned never completely went away.

"That's why I built my wall. It wasn't because my dad and brothers were dicks to me my whole life. It wasn't because he called me names. It wasn't because my brothers lied to my dad all the time to get me in trouble. I built the wall because my mom sat on the couch and watched her daughter walk out the door with no place to stay. She didn't argue with my dad. She didn't offer me help. She didn't chase after me or leave him. I walked for miles alone with nothing. And with each step, I added another brick. I'm not tough or strong or brave. I'm scared and weak and stay in the safety of my own company so no one can ever abandon me again. I've never loved a single boyfriend I've had. I've never loved another living thing except my girls."

"They'll never leave you," he whispered.

"They'll never leave me," I confirmed.

Matt's hand slid over my hip until he found mine. He threaded our fingers together and squeezed.

"You're wrong. You're the toughest person I know."

I wasn't, but I didn't have it in me to argue.

"Aren't you glad you decided to be best friends with a high school dropout with mommy issues?"

Matt leaned forward and kissed the top of my head. The sweet gesture made my back stiffen. If Matt noticed, he didn't let on. And when he started to speak, he did so with his lips at my temple.

"I know plenty of stupid people who have great educations. And some of the biggest assholes I know have Ivy League degrees displayed on their walls and more money than they'll spend in their lifetimes. Intelligence doesn't come from a piece of paper. What I'm getting at is, I don't give a single fuck if you have or don't have a high school diploma. I do care your mom sat on the couch and watched you leave. I do care your dad and brothers abused you. But none of that changes the fact that me deciding you're my best friend is the best decision I've ever made—in my life."

I didn't see how being my friend could possibly be his best decision, but again, I didn't argue.

I sat there wishing it was the truth.

I'd never been anyone's best anything.

12

"It's been two weeks. I can't believe you haven't gone to Connecticut yet."

Dylan pointed to my ringing phone sitting on top of my desk.

It hadn't been quite two weeks since my father had been arrested, but I wasn't going to quibble over a few days one way or the other.

"I was going to go up there a few days ago, but Chelsea took over managing the bar, and I wanted to be around in case she needed me."

"Right, because you know so much about ordering kegs."

I didn't know shit about running a bar or liquor orders, but I did own the place. Therefore, I was making an effort to learn. It was a fact I'd bought it as a joke, but I didn't want it to fail. And now that Chelsea was running it, I had all the more reason not to look like a total douche and take care of my investment.

"Dylan, brother, that's not the help he was offering," Logan put in.

Dylan jerked back in his chair and shook his head.

"No shit?"

"Are you blind? You're the one that saw him kiss her. And I know you saw them dancing at the reception."

"Yeah, but we're talking about Matt."

Christ. I actually felt the bile churning in my gut.

It wasn't that my reputation wasn't earned but hearing a close friend's disbelief that I was interested in a woman beyond a night was not a good feeling.

"Chelsea's different."

My declaration was met with wide, skeptical eyes.

"Different how?" Dylan pushed.

"Different in that we're not talking about her."

"That's not different. You never talk about any—"

"Different in a way that if you compare her to a random hookup, I'm gonna be pissed as fuck," I retorted.

"You like her?" Dylan asked incredulously.

"Damn, Dylan, a little slow on the uptake." Logan laughed. "Are you running low on Red Bull or something?"

"I must be. Either that or hell has frozen over. Never thought I'd see the day Matt Kessler turned domesticated. Then again, I never thought I'd see Logan in love. So, yeah, hell has turned frosty."

Domesticated?

Shouldn't the mere insinuation about me being house-trained piss me off?

Actually, the more important question was, why didn't it?

I'd spent every day since Addy's wedding with Chelsea. Sure, most of the time we spent together was in the evenings at Balls Deep, but twice I'd surprised her with breakfast at her apartment before I had to be to work, and she had to go train. She was just as uncomfortable about me being in her small apartment as she was the first time I'd been there. But yesterday, when I showed up, she just opened the door and told me to make myself at home while she finished getting dressed. I think she finally understood I didn't give a shit where she lived, and I certainly wasn't going to make a comment about it. Though with that said, I hated with every fiber of my being that she lived in a small, lifeless apartment. But that was me caring about Chelsea, not me giving a shit it was the size of a shoebox. I cared that she didn't have anything special in her space because she'd never *had* anything special. No keepsakes. No happy memories to display.

My phone stopped ringing only to start again.

Alessandra was like a dog with a bone. She kept digging and digging.

I stabbed the reject icon and looked at Logan.

"You think since my dad's all wrapped up with Zanetti, he'd cut me a deal on a hit?"

Logan laughed before he asked, "What's that, the third call this morning?"

"Those were four and five. Back-to-back calls—she's getting desperate."

"Hasn't she been desperate?" Dylan asked.

"Yep. Part of the reason I'm dragging my feet going up there. It's driving her crazy I'm not coming to heel. That and my head might explode when I see my dad."

"We offered to come up with you," Logan reminded me.

All the guys individually and collectively had offered to fly to Connecticut with me. I appreciated the offer, but I didn't need them there to witness my humiliation. Thankfully, my dad had stopped calling, but his attorney had resorted to emailing me every day with updates. Though they were laced liberally with instructions not to speak to the feds and outlined the damage I'd already done by admitting my family had a close and familiar relationship with the Mancinis.

Every email got the same four-word response: I will not lie.

That was about all I had to say to my family at the moment.

I knew I had to face them.

But it would be on my terms, not theirs.

"If we're done writing up the schedule, I got shit to do," I said.

"Schedule? I thought we were picking apart your love life," Dylan joked.

"Tell me something, brother. Did you lose your dick somewhere?" I asked.

"Yeah, last night in a nice—"

"Please, for the love of all things holy, don't finish that," Logan griped.

Dylan pushed back from the table and crossed his arms over his chest.

"You know the best part of being the last man standing? No competition."

I looked at Logan and shook my head.

"He's straight-up lying," I told Logan. "He thinks he's smooth, but I didn't miss him chatting Sawyer up."

"Sawyer?" Dylan scoffed. "Have you lost your mind?"

"Nope. But you have if you think I missed you picking her hair off her shoulder and giving it a tug. Which, brother, was a third-grade move but I'm gonna give it to you because she smiled at you like you'd lit her world."

Dylan scowled and stood. What he didn't do was deny he was flirting with the pretty Sawyer.

"She's hot." Dylan shrugged.

"She's sweet and quiet unless she's around Hadley. But

that's par for the course. Hadley brings out the wild in most people."

"You're not lying," Logan agreed. "Last week, I caught Hadley and Lauren pulling into the parking lot coming back from lunch. Hadley was bumping 2 Live Crew. Two white girls throwing hands and rapping. The girl is a menace. Jasper deserves a medal just for getting her to adulthood."

Jasper Walker was a man with infinite love for his children. I was pretty positive Quinn and Hadley had put his patience to the test while they were growing up. Delaney and Adalynn were the quietest out of the bunch. And then there was Jason; the man was protective of his sisters and was all about family. A trait he'd learned from his dad.

A trait I thought I'd learned from my father as well.

"You've got a class in ten minutes," Dylan reminded me, suddenly eager to leave now that I'd brought up Sawyer.

Logan gathered the schedules we'd filled out and stood.

"I'll take these to Quinn before I head out."

Quinn still handled the scheduling, but now that Hadley had left her job at the library to come work for Triple Canopy, she'd soon take over the scheduling, leaving Quinn to the all-important job of taking care of TC's accounting.

The only two family members who didn't work for TC were Ethan Lenox and Jackson Clark. Jackson was a firefighter. He was living his childhood dream, and I highly doubted he'd be leaving his job any time soon. Ethan was a detective, and like Jackson, he loved the work he did.

"Where are you off to?" I asked Logan.

"Dylan got the goods on the fraud case I'm working on. I'm taking a drive to check out the dude's house. If I can set up cameras today, I will. If not, I'll go back tomorrow morning."

"You found him?"

"Wasn't hard," Dylan returned. "Assholes always slip up. You just have to know where to look."

Dylan was being humble. The Hecker family had hired Triple Canopy to find the man who scammed their grandmother Jena out of twenty thousand dollars. They'd gone to the police and after a year of them not being able to find the man, they'd hired a PI firm out of Savannah, and after six months of getting nowhere, they came to us. The case hit Dylan's desk a week ago. It was an eighteen-month-old case, and he'd solved it in seven days.

"Let me know if you need a hand with those cameras. Luke and I will be done with the class by lunch."

"Will do."

I followed Dylan and Logan out of the conference room. They went left, and I went right toward the armory.

I unlocked the door and made my way to one of the four safes on the back wall. I opened the one that secured the long-range rifles and smiled when I saw the Barrett MRAD was missing. Luke had already been in and selected a .308 for today's class. *Nice.* I took in all the beauties before me, and I grabbed my personal Accuracy International AXMC configured in .300 Win Mag. A modified version of what I used when I was still in the Navy.

As always, the moment I had my rifle in my hand, a sense of peace washed over me. It was not the damage of the bullet or the violence of the weapon. For me, it has always been about precision. The skill and patience it took to lay in wait. The minutes, sometimes hours, of silence. Being a sniper meant being the best among the highest caliber of men. It meant pushing myself mentally. I had one shot to get it right. One chance to hit my target. There was no room for error. No excuses. No bullshit. Timing was everything.

I closed the safe, gave the handle a pull to make sure it was locked, then I went to find Luke.

"You don't have to stay," Chelsea said through a yawn.

It was just after midnight. The bar was closed, and she was finishing the nightly deposit.

"Don't ever take the deposit to the bank on your way home."

Chelsea looked up from the stack of money on the desk in front of her and scowled.

"I don't have a death wish walking around with cash in the middle of the night," she retorted.

Well, that was debatable. Every time she climbed on the back of a bull, there was the possibility of death.

I settled back on the small couch next to her desk and stretched my legs out in front of me.

"Why bulls?" I asked.

"Why not bulls?"

Her answer made me smile, or maybe it was her sass. No, she wasn't sassy. She was spirited, vivacious, brazen. She could also be playful and funny when she wanted to be. There were many sides to the woman sitting next to me—all of them I liked. All of them I wanted to get to know better.

"Point taken," I returned.

"I would think someone like you would get it."

"Get what?"

"Why I do it."

I thought I was beginning to understand, but still, I wanted to hear it from her.

"The rush?" I prompted.

"That's part of it," she admitted. "The first time I got on a bull, I was so scared I thought I was going to throw up. The first time I was bucked off one, I thought he was going to trample me to death. But as the fear started to fade, the adrenaline kicked in."

"Adrenaline's addictive," I noted.

"It is," Chelsea agreed. "I'm sure you know all about the rush of extreme emotions. The moment anxiety and panic disappear and you become hyper-alert. Everything snaps into focus. Everything slows down, and euphoria takes over."

"I know that feeling well."

Chelsea smiled and whispered, "I know you do."

"So, is that what drives you to continue? Are you chasing the high of danger?"

"For the first few years, yes." Chelsea exhaled, and her shoulders squared. Something I noticed she did a lot when she felt like she had to defend herself or her motives. "There's still something inside of me that has to prove my dad wrong. It's probably not healthy, but it's a need that I can't squelch. For so many years, all I heard was how stupid I was. How I didn't know my place. How I was making a fool out of myself and my family. How no one would accept me on the circuit, and they'd all laugh at me. So I admit, I'm pushing myself hard to get to Omaha."

"What's in Omaha, besides that's where you grew up?"

"River City. My dad and brothers never miss that event."

Suddenly more than anything, I wanted Chelsea to make it to River City.

"Have they ever seen you ride?"

"Barrel racing, calf roping, and saddle bronc, yes. But my dad's never seen me on a bull. TJ has. He caught me out at old man Coleman's ranch and ran home to tattle. My dad was red-hot pissed. He beat my ass bloody and—"

Anger surged, and I growled, "Come again? He beat you bloody?"

"Hell, yeah. He took a leather strap to my ass and told me he'd beat the stubborn out of me. All he did was make me want to do it more. I couldn't ride for a month, not even on Penny, an old pony we had. But when I healed, I went right back to Coleman's ranch and got back on."

Jesus Christ.

Fucking hell.

"Baby—"

"Don't, Matt. It was a long time ago. That wasn't the first or the last. But it was the beating that I remember the most because with every slash of that strap, I vowed he'd never break me. And he didn't. He could never beat the stubborn out, and he tried."

"You're not stubborn," I grunted, unable to get my anger in check. "You're fucking tough and determined. You're strong-minded and formidable. I'd guess you're everything he's not. And I bet your brothers don't have half the talent you have."

"I don't think I'm—"

"You are, Chelsea. And you're right. He didn't break you."

Chelsea held my gaze, and the longer she did, the farther I fell for her.

As the silence stretched, the more I came to realize that timing wasn't everything. Not when hearts and happiness were on the line.

"Can I ask you something personal?" Chelsea inquired softly.

If any other woman, including my best friends' women, asked me that, I'd shut them down in a heartbeat. I'd spent the majority of my adult life keeping my personal life personal. I didn't answer any questions. I didn't let anyone in. I gave what I gave, and that was just enough to be friendly. But no one got the real Matt Kessler.

But I wanted Chelsea to have all of me.

"Sure."

"Why haven't you gone to see your family?"

Of course, Chelsea would cut straight to the point.

"Because I'm not ready to hear my father's excuses. I'm not ready to face the lies. I grew up thinking I had a great dad, a good family. All of that is now gone. I'm afraid of what I'll find when I go up there. I'm afraid my mother knew my dad had gotten involved with organized crime. I already know my sister knew. And if my dad asks me straight out to lie for him, I'll lose what love I still have for him."

"Your sister knew?"

"My sister's a mooch. And that's me being generous. She's never lived off the estate. She's never had a real job. Her position at Kessler Management is a sham. She takes clients to dinner and basically sucks up to them. She lives the high life and blows through money like its water. She got the same inheritance I got from our grandfather. I'm not gonna lie, it was a sizable chunk of money. But the way she lives, I don't know how she hasn't blown through hers yet. My only guess would be my parents give her money beyond her salary from Kessler. She's a minority shareholder..." I trailed off.

Besides my father, I'm the majority shareholder.

If the board ousted my dad, Alessandra would likely be next. She'd lose her salary. And if all of my father's assets were seized, she'd have nothing. The bitch thought if I took over for our father, I'd save her ass.

Always conniving.

She wasn't worried about our dad. She was worried

about keeping herself dripping in diamonds and fancy dinners.

"What's that mean?"

I blinked and took in Chelsea's office. When I'd remodeled Balls Deep that included the back of the house. New paint, new flooring, new furniture, and a top-of-the-line computer system. The space looked nice. The whole remodel turned out far better than I'd imagined. But the office was about a fourth of the size of Alessandra's office at Kessler, and my sister might spend an hour a week at the office.

"Do you like working here?" I asked.

Chelsea scowled at my abrupt change of topics.

"Um...yeah."

"Is the office okay? Would you like anything changed?"

Chelsea glanced around the space then focused back on me.

"The office is fine, Matt. I don't get it."

No, she wouldn't get it. Chelsea didn't care that her apartment was tiny; to her, it was a place to sleep. She didn't care that her office was a windowless room in the back of a pool hall.

Chelsea cared about the important stuff. She'd rather have mud on her cowboy boots while riding her horse than wear a five-thousand-dollar pair of heels while eating at an expensive restaurant. I doubted she knew that five-thousand-dollar high heels existed.

"Refreshing," I mumbled.

"You keep saying that, but I don't understand. The office is an office. I'm in it a total of two hours a night. The rest of the time, I'm behind the bar or helping with the tables. If you want to change anything, the servers could use another station. When we're busy, the two we have get backed up, and the servers have to wait to put orders in. But other than that, the place runs great. You did a great job revamping the place. The vibe is awesome."

"When's your next day off from training?" I asked.

Once again, Chelsea blinked at my change of conversation.

"Thursday."

In two days.

Before I could think better of it, I blurted out, "Fly to Connecticut with me on Wednesday night. I'll have you back by training on Friday."

"You want me to go home with you?"

"Nothing says best friend like throwing you right under the bus," I joked.

"Are you sure? I don't really fit in with—"

"Thank fuck for that. I'll get us a room so we don't have to stay at the estate."

"Just one room?"

Her smile took the sting out of her not wanting to share a room with me.

"I'll sport for two rooms."

"I was teasing. Two rooms would be a waste of money. I'm sure the hotels around Greenwich are fancy. The couch will be nice and comfy when you sleep on it."

A waste of money—not reserve the penthouse suite.

"I'm sensing best friends don't share a bed?" I quipped.

"Nope." Chelsea shook her head and gave me a megawatt smile. "Only special friends share a bed."

Well, fuck me, what did I have to do to upgrade to special friend?

13

My first thought was: I'd lost my mind. My second was: this was how the other half lived. The other half being people with money.

I was sitting in first-class, and even the seats were bigger, more comfortable, and had way more legroom. First-class was the bomb. Forget the champagne the flight attendant had offered. I was all about the warm blanket.

"If you wrap that any tighter, I'm afraid you'll suffocate yourself," Matt teased.

"If I ever win the lottery, the first thing I'm buying after I buy a piece of property big enough to have my girls with me is a towel warmer."

"A towel warmer?"

"Yep. You know, so when you get out of the shower, your towel's toasty warm. Of course, I've never actually used a toasty warm towel, but it sounds divine. Do you think there's a blanket warmer on the plane? Is that how they get the blankets so hot?"

Matt was staring at me like I was crazy. And that was precisely how I knew I'd lost my mind. I didn't belong in

Matt's world. I didn't fly first-class. I'd never been to a house that was called an estate. Hell, I didn't even have anything in my closet that was appropriate to wear on the plane, forget meeting his parents and sister.

I'd had to dig through my drawers to find a pair of Levi's that weren't stained and worn. And it was sheer luck I'd found a dress I'd worn to a rodeo dinner five years earlier that still fit. I'd even had to polish my boots—which were scuffed, but they looked halfway decent.

Going to Connecticut with him was a bad idea.

"I have no idea if there's a blanket warmer on the plane," Matt said. "But I have used a towel warmer, and you're correct, a toasty towel is divine."

I couldn't stop my chuckle from escaping.

"What's funny?"

"You saying, divine."

"Why's that funny, baby?" he asked and leaned closer to me.

I shrugged, not knowing how to explain that hearing the big, rough, former SEAL Matt Kessler say 'divine' sounded silly.

Matt kissed my temple and straightened back in his seat.

"Are you sure you don't want something to drink before we take off? Gin, Jack, vodka? Alcohol will make it easier to digest my family."

I hated that he thought alcohol was needed to deal with his family. Further, I hated how he used the word digest.

"Did you always feel that way? That dealing with your family was a chore?"

Next to me, Matt exhaled. And when he turned his head to look at me, all I could see was pain.

"No. I used to love going home. And for the first day of my visit, I could even tolerate my sister. My parents still live in the house I grew up in. I have a lot of good memories there. Despite what I've learned about my dad, I had a great childhood. And that's what pisses me off; now every memory is tainted."

I wondered what was worse, having shitty parents and a shitty childhood or having a great one only to learn later it wasn't as great as you thought. At least I knew my father was a dick. He'd never pretended to be otherwise.

"Why are the memories tainted?"

Over the last week, asking Matt questions had gotten easier. And answering his questions about my life no longer gave me anxiety. I didn't even care when he showed up at my apartment unannounced. I'd been worried about nothing. Matt was not like any rich person I'd ever met. He truly didn't care where I lived or how I dressed—he'd never looked down on me because I didn't have his wealth.

"I feel the need to preface this by reminding you I'm not a douche."

"Why would you need to remind me? I know you're not."

I'd learned a lot about Matt, and it was safe to say I loved everything I'd learned.

"It might be that what I have to say is going to sound so damn pretentious I might gag a little as I say it."

"Just say it, tough guy. I'll hold the barf bag for you."

I startled when Matt barked out a loud laugh.

"I love that about you."

Chills raced up my spine and goose bumps erupted on my arms.

Matt loved something about me?

Then why the hell was he driving me bananas with his temple kisses and hand-holding? Why had I caught him staring at me like he wanted to make a move, yet he never did? Why did he flirt then back off? Why did he admit he wanted me in his bed, yet he hadn't actually invited me back? Why did he make a bet with me at Quinn's wedding, win that bet, and not attempt to collect? Not that I was completely sure what he'd won, but he hadn't done anything to make me believe he wanted anything beyond friendship.

Did *I* want something beyond friendship?

Hell, yes.

Was I insane for wanting it?

Hell, yes.

But the more time I spent with Matt, the more I realized I didn't have a crush on him; I was falling in love with him. Which would make it especially painful if I was going to be stuck in the friend zone for the rest of my life.

"What do you love?" I choked out.

"That you'd hold a barf bag for me."

"I was joking."

"No, you weren't."

Wow, that had gone from teasing to serious in a nanosecond.

The flight attendant came over the loudspeaker to tell us the cabin door had been closed, effectively ending our conversation.

I wasn't sure if I was grateful for the reprieve or if I was sad the moment had been broken.

I was staring out the window, starting to doze off, when I felt the blanket covering me jostle, then Matt's hand landed on my thigh.

"Every memory is now tainted with the knowledge my childhood was financed by dirty money. Every polo lesson, my swim meets, my sailing, the clothes I wore, the house I lived in, the cars I was given, the vacations we took. The dinners I sat through honoring my parents for their generous donations to various charities. Playing tennis at the club. All the luxuries I grew up with. I thought my father's hard work and integrity had afforded us that privilege. Now I know it's all a lie."

I let go of the blanket and covered Matt's hand with mine. When he spread his fingers so mine could slip between his, I pressed down harder.

"Not all of it, sweetheart. You told me your grandfather started Kessler Management. Obviously, the company was thriving before your father took it over. Not all the money is tainted. And even if it was, honey, those memories aren't. They're yours, and they're about happy times. Don't let your father take them from you."

The pads of Matt's fingers dug into my thigh.

He'd heard me.

But I knew he didn't believe.

I was showered and dressed for bed when I came out of the bathroom. The hotel was beautiful, much nicer than any place I'd ever stayed but not over-the-top fancy, which I appreciated because I already felt out of sorts.

I stopped dead when I saw Matt shake out a blanket before he draped it over the couch.

"What are you doing?" I asked.

"There are two more blankets on the bed, woman, and three pillows. Please tell me best friends at least get a pillow."

Smartass.

He was taking this best friend stuff too far.

"I was joking about you sleeping on the couch."

"Thank fuck. This thing is lumpy."

I wouldn't know if the couch was lumpy or not, and I doubt Matt had even sat on it.

"Warning," I rapped out. "If you snore, you're sleeping in the bathtub."

"I don't snore."

"How do you know you don't? Did one of the many women who spend the night in your bed confirm you're a quiet sleeper? If that's the case, I want names and references."

That was an absolute lie. I did not want the names of the women who'd slept in Matt's bed, and I didn't need references to know that he was a perfect ten in every category.

Matt crossed his arms over his broad chest and stared at me.

After a few moments of silence, he said, "I haven't slept next to a woman in over ten years."

How was that possible?

"You don't believe me?"

He sounded hurt that I'd question his integrity—even in my mind. But seriously, I wasn't stupid. Matt was a good-looking man in his thirties. The hours I'd spent in his bed were off-the-charts good. So good I knew he wasn't born with the level of skill he possessed, which meant he'd learned it the old-fashioned way—with practice.

And besides, it wasn't my business.

"It doesn't matter what I think."

"It matters to me, and I damn well want it to matter to you."

"Why?"

Matt let out an exasperated sigh and dipped his chin down. Without looking at me, he shook his head.

"I see you're annoyed with me," I said. "But I don't understand why telling you it's not my business who you've had sex with or slept next to would upset you."

"Maybe because I want you to be just as jealous as I am." He told the floor. "Maybe I want you to feel something when I tell you that I haven't slept next to a woman in ten years. Even if that something is you telling me I'm an asshole for not staying the night with a woman I've had sex with."

I felt my stomach clench. I didn't want to think about anyone who'd come before me.

Matt's head came up. His eyes found mine and they were no longer angry, but they were troubled.

"All these firsts mean something to me," he mumbled. "First woman in my kitchen. First woman I've shared breakfast with in a decade. First woman I've opened up to. First woman I've seen every day for weeks but still can't get enough of. The first woman I've wanted more with. The first woman who's made me want to buy her a castle—"

"I don't want a castle," I whispered.

"Jesus, Chelsea. I know you don't!" he exploded. "I know one hundred percent I'm all you need. Just me. Not my money. Not my name. Just fucking me. Never has anyone besides my brothers given me that. But you do. I'm good enough for you."

By the time Matt was done, my heart felt like it was going to pound out of my chest.

"But am *I* good enough for *you*?"

My question slipped out, and once it was out there, no matter how badly I wanted to pull it back, I couldn't.

"You even asking me that pisses me the fuck off," Matt snarled. "Your father should be hung, your brothers right alongside him. And while I'd never harm a woman, your mother might be the exception. You cannot see your worth through all the shit that they left you—but mark this, Chelsea, you will. I will not stop telling you, showing you, badgering you until you come to understand how magnificent you are. How beautiful. How smart. How strong, capable, resourceful, brave, tough. You have a backbone made of steel. So please, baby, don't ever ask me again if you're good enough for me. When it is me who will never measure up to you."

The weight of his words settled over me, and dread wrapped around my heart.

When Matt left me, I'd crumble. The pain would be unbearable. It would be worse than being kicked out and homeless.

"I won't ever recover from you," I said.

"What do you mean, recover?"

"When you walk away," I explained. "I won't recover from that. If I let myself have you, and you leave."

"Baby—"

"It's like I have multiple personalities," I said through gritted teeth. "One minute, I'm asking myself why you're torturing me with your flirting and sweet kisses to my temple and why you're not making a move for more—"

"More?" Matt interrupted me.

"Yes, more. You said you wanted me back in your bed. You said you wanted more. Have you changed your mind?" I demanded to know.

"Make no mistake, you'll be back in my bed," he growled and took a step closer. "But the more I want is not just your sweet, naked body under me. The more I want is donuts after you've spent the night. The more I want is making you a ridiculous mug of milk-coffee in the mornings. The more I want is you knowing that I'm willing to wait for you. I see it, baby. Sometimes you look at me like you're ready to strip me down and fuck the hell out of me. But other times, you look at me like if you get too close to me, I'll shove a knife in your back."

"Why am I crazy?"

"You're not crazy."

I sure felt like I was.

"Then why are there times when I want nothing more than to be with you—really be with you? And other times, the thought of it scares me so badly I can hardly stand?"

"Because sometimes you can push what those assholes did to you into the back of your mind, and sometimes you can't. The times you can't are the times when I'm being honest with you. When I flirt and tease you, there's no fear of emotion. When I tell you I'm falling in love with you, it sends you into a panic."

I felt myself sway, and my arm shot out to find purchase on the dresser before my legs collapsed.

"Falling in love with me?" I breathed.

"Chels, I'd tell you to open your eyes, but I've already said that once so now I'm asking you to pay attention."

"I'm falling in love with you," I admitted.

"I know you are. *I'm* paying attention."

Of course, he was paying attention. I didn't think there was much Matt missed.

Which was annoying.

"You didn't let me win," I told him.

"What?"

"When we raced. You didn't let me win. That's when I knew you understood me. You could've pulled back on Gypsy, but instead, you pushed her harder."

Matt's mouth curved up into a slow, sexy smile that did

insanely wicked things to my girly parts. I stood rooted to the floor as he prowled across the room. I didn't move a muscle when he stopped in front of me and lifted his hands. I stayed stock-still when feather-soft, his palms glided over my cheeks until his fingers tangled in my hair.

"Baby, please, pay attention to this. I understand you. I understand your fears. I understand what drives you. I understand the rush you get when you're doing something you love. I understand the need to prove yourself. I understand your passion. And, Chels, I understand that you would kick me in the jellybeans if I let you win. Proving you're the woman who was made for me because even if you wouldn't severely damage the jewels, I would never let you win. That's not me. Like you, if I'm committed to a task, I'm giving it everything I have."

Matt tipped my head back just a smidge and leaned closer. "Here's the important part. I'm committed to the task of making this work. I want you comfortable about where we're going. I want you to believe me when I promise you I'm ready for this. I'm not pushing to get back into my bed because the next time you're there, you won't be leaving it, and I need to know you're ready for that. You think you won't recover? I'm gone for you. Totally and completely gone. You rolling off me and rolling out of my bed like you did the first time will kill me. You think you're scared? I'm downright fucking terrified of losing you."

Every single word he said broke my heart even as they healed my soul. No one in my life had ever understood me, but I supposed there were a lot of people in the world who were misunderstood. That wasn't what made my heart hurt. It was that no one had ever loved me. No one had ever been patient or kind. No one had ever trusted me to lay themselves bare and give themselves to me. It was humbling. No, it was beautiful. Matt's honesty healed and hurt and made me hate my dad even more. Was it too much to ask a father to show a little gentleness to his daughter?

"I want to see myself like you see me. Please don't give up on me."

"I won't," he promised.

"You won't lose me. You were right." I rolled up onto my toes, slid my arms around him, and brushed my mouth against his. Then against his lips, I whispered, "You're all I need. Just you. Just this."

I felt his groan vibrate on my lips. One of his hands left my hair. Seconds later, it was cupping my ass.

"You're not gonna leave my bed."

It wasn't a question, yet I felt it vital I answer.

"I'm not gonna leave your bed."

"Are you ready for us?"

How could I not be ready after everything Matt had shown me over the last week? He'd made it a point to see me at least once a day, sometimes twice. I'd learned he wasn't big on talking on the phone, and he didn't text, but he'd shown up. I couldn't remember a single person showing up for me. Beyond that, he'd opened himself up to me, and he promised to be patient with me as I learned to do the same.

I was scared as all get-out, but I wasn't stupid.

I had a once-in-a-lifetime chance at something good.

"I'm ready."

Matt's mouth came down hard on mine. I opened for him and his tongue spiked in. I'd missed the taste of him, the feel of him, the way my body responded to him. The kiss wasn't gentle. It was demanding, deep, greedy. Matt took more and more. And in return, I gave him everything. All of me. Everything I could give, I gave. By the time he broke the kiss, I was wet and ready and growling in protest when he pulled away.

"Have I told you today how beautiful you are?"

"Huh?"

"You're so damn beautiful, Chels."

I wanted to tell him he was beautiful, too. That he was perfect in every way. I wanted to tell him I wanted to keep him for the rest of my life.

But I settled on, "You're the first man I've ever loved."

14

Chelsea was pouting.

It was cute as hell.

"Matt," she whined and bucked her hips.

I lifted my head and took her in. The swells of her bare breasts, her tight puckered nipples, the blush covering her chest, her rosy cheeks, her messy hair fanned over the pillow.

"Yeah, baby?"

"I'm dying."

A moment ago, she told me I was torturing her.

It was safe to say, Chelsea had no patience. Luckily for her, I had enough for both of us. And I was determined to take my time.

I lowered my head and continued kissing my way down her stomach. My hands slid under her bare ass and scooted farther down the bed freeing her legs, and they immediately opened.

"Wider, Chels."

The moment my tongue circled her clit, her hips jerked and I heard her sigh. I gave her another flick of my tongue, slid my right hand from under her, and used the tip of my finger to tease her opening.

"You want my tongue or fingers, baby?"

"Both."

I slid two fingers inside her and sucked her clit into my mouth. Wetness flooded my fingers, her moans filled the room, and my cock ached, which meant I didn't go slow. I didn't go gently and build her orgasm. I wanted it too fucking bad. So I took it hard and fast, fucking her with my fingers until her back arched off the bed. I pulled my mouth off her clit, dragged my fingers out of her pussy, and replaced them with my tongue. Chelsea's hands came off the bed and fisted my hair, holding me where she wanted me. She took over and fucked herself against my face.

Christ, perfect.

When Chelsea wanted something, she took it. And I was more than happy to give her whatever she wanted.

I listened to her moans and waited until they turned into cries. She was close and reaching for it, so close her pussy was spasming around my tongue, her excitement dripped down my chin, and I was done. My thumb circled her clit and she cried out. I pressed down and she started to gasp. I rubbed harder and she rocked her hips. I rolled her clit between two fingers and she exploded.

Magnificent.

Before her orgasm waned, I hooked her around the back of the knee, pulled it up and around my hip, and came up over her as I fisted my cock and guided the tip to her slick pussy. Without pausing, I drove deep.

"Ohmigod," she breathed.

With her pussy still convulsing, I kept driving in hard. The need I felt overwhelmed me. The hunger—all-consuming. This...her...was what I'd been missing all my life. I thought it was the connection, and it was, but it was bigger than that. She'd awakened something inside of me. It was so huge I couldn't put a name to it. It felt like I'd been electrocuted, like my nerves were raw.

"Matthew," she groaned and wrapped her other leg around me.

"I want another one, Chels."

"Yes."

Her hips lifted in time with my thrusts, her nails dug into my ass, our breaths mingled together, and peace settled over me.

"Everything about you feels beautiful, baby."

"Everything about you is perfect, sweetheart."

Fuck, that felt good.

My eyes closed and my pace slowed.

Her hands left my ass and traveled up my back—not slow, but not fast, just taking her time exploring. That felt good, too. Her hands on me, her legs wrapped around me tightly, holding on like she wasn't going to let go.

When I opened my eyes, she was staring at me, and I saw it.

Fucking amazing.

"You falling in love with me?"

"No," she whispered.

"No?"

"I've already fallen."

Jesus.

Fuck.

My head dropped into the crook of her neck, and her arms circled my shoulders.

I shifted up to my knees, Chelsea's thighs tightened around my middle, and I pounded harder.

"Don't stop."

I heard the hitch in her voice. It was building in her again.

"Harder, Matt."

Her pussy spasmed around my cock and I clenched my jaw.

"Christ, Chels. Come, baby."

Her limbs tightened, pulling me closer, and with a throaty moan, her climax hit. And with hers, mine broke.

Pleasure coursed through my veins, it pounded through my muscles, it pulsed through every cell in my body.

I was suspended in a place where it was just Chelsea and me. No other thoughts invaded. No words were needed.

"Matt?" she whispered, and I pulled my face out of her neck.

"Yeah, baby?"

"Are you okay?"

Fuck. I rolled to my elbow, taking some of my weight off of her, and she smiled up at me.

My breath caught in my throat, and there was another first: Chelsea was the first woman to ever render me speechless.

I nodded and brushed her hair off her face.

"Are you sure?"

"Yeah, Chels. Everything's perfect."

Her hand went to my face and traced my jaw with her fingertip.

"You're beautiful, too. Every time I look at you, I'm amazed at how hot you are."

My lips twitched, but I bit back a smile—just barely.

"Glad you think so."

"One day you'll have to share your secret with me."

"What secret?"

"How you can eat three bacon cheeseburgers and a large

order of onion rings and still have a body that should be on the cover of Muscles Weekly."

"Is this a magazine you have a subscription to?" I teased.

"No, but if you were on the cover, I'd buy a copy."

I couldn't stop my body from shaking with laughter, which was an unfortunate thing—though it was another first. I'd never in my life laughed while my dick was still buried in a woman. However, the movement meant I slipped out, and when I did, I felt our combined orgasms drip down my thigh.

"I took you without a condom," I told her.

"I'm on the pill."

Right, birth control. Why wasn't I relieved she had us protected?

"I've never had sex without a condom."

"A first." She smiled. "For both of us."

Damn, but I liked that.

"Let me clean you up, then we'll get some sleep."

Chelsea's legs locked around my hips, and she shook her head.

"No."

"No?"

"Neither one of us is rolling out of this bed."

Jesus.

I laid there staring down into the eyes of the woman I'd fallen in love with. I let that feeling seep deep, I memorized the look, and I locked it down into my soul.

I shifted off Chelsea, rolled to my back, and she rolled into me.

Once she was settled with her head on my shoulder, her arm resting on my chest, and her knee on my thigh, I curled my arm around her back.

After a few beats of silence, I felt her body start to shake.

"What's funny?"

"Am I leaking on your thigh?"

"Yep."

"Is it gross?"

I thought about it for a second, and what I came up with wasn't gross. For some reason, it was sexy as hell that my come was leaking out of her.

"Nope."

"Then I don't feel bad since I'm lying in the wet spot."

"Another first?"

Her laughter became audible, and her body shook harder.

"Yeah. I can confirm I've never laid in the wet spot before."

For some reason, jealousy didn't surface. She was mine, and her past no longer mattered. None of the men she'd been with before were smart enough to see what they had. I, on the other hand, was not stupid. I understood full well the treasure I held in the curve of my arm.

"Night, baby."

"Night, sweetheart."

Chelsea cuddled closer.

It didn't take long for her to fall asleep.

It took me hours.

Shockingly, it had nothing to do with the nine A.M. meeting I had with my father and Roland Huston and everything to do with not wanting to miss a second of the first time I had Chelsea sleeping next to me.

15

"No!" my father shouted. "Matthew is not involved. Not in any way."

"Vernon," Roland sighed. "Please listen to me. The family has to put on a united front."

My father's gaze slid from his attorney to me, then to my sister. Pain flashed across his face as he shook his head.

"Father, Mr. Huston is right," Alessandra cooed. "I was able to postpone the board meeting, but we need to present a strong family unit. They have to see that you are still in charge and that we *all* support you."

I didn't miss my sister's snarky emphasis, but I was too busy reeling from my father's outburst to pay her any mind.

"Alessandra, my love, we are not united in anything," my father returned. "You, your brother, and your mother must distance yourselves from me."

"Vernon, that is not wise," Roland mused. "Not wise at all. The board has motioned to have you removed. You'll be going to trial and—"

"Stop," my father interjected. "I need a moment alone with my son."

I did not want a moment alone with my father. I wanted to get this over with so I could go find Chelsea and we could leave. Since the moment we'd pulled up to the front gate of my parents' house, I regretted asking her to come. Her discomfort seeped out of her pores as she shifted in her seat. Her hands had tugged at the hem of her dress, and no amount of reassurance would take the uneasiness out of her eyes. I should've known she'd be uncomfortable—not only meeting my family for the first time under the extreme conditions, but also their extravagance was so in-your-face it was almost sickening.

I'd left her in the library with a kiss and a promise to be quick. She'd given me a smile that didn't reach her eyes, then she lied and told me she'd be fine.

Now I was standing in my father's office with guilt eating at my gut. Conflicting emotions at seeing my father warred inside of me. Distrust and skepticism were winning out but anger and fury were coming in a close second.

Then there was Alessandra. Every word that came out of her conniving mouth pissed me off. There was no doubt she was angling to make a move. The problem was I couldn't figure out her game. Did she want to be the next CEO of Kessler? Did she want my mother to step up and take over? Surely she knew our father was going to prison; barring the federal building that housed evidence against my father burning to the ground, he was fucked.

Speaking of my mother, I'd yet to see her. She was not in the foyer with my father, Alessandra, and Roland to greet Chelsea and me. She had yet to return any of my calls.

"Where's Mother?" I asked.

My father's pain-filled eyes focused on me, and damn if he didn't look sorry.

"She's gone to stay with your Aunt Rosie in Boston."

It wasn't just my father's side of the family who was wealthy. My mother had come from money as well. They had homes in Bar Harbor, Boston, and Nantucket. Homes that belonged to my mother and her two sisters.

"And she's not answering my calls because?" I pushed.

"Likely because she's furious with me and didn't believe me when I told her that you had no involvement in my—"

"Vernon," Roland clipped.

My father's spine stiffened and his eyes narrowed. Gone was the sadness I'd seen moments ago; in its place was the astute, shrewd businessman I'd always known him to be.

"Roland, I'm aware you're doing your best to protect my interests. However, I can assure you if you ever interrupt me again while I am speaking to my son, I will find your replacement. Now, I'd like a word with Matthew alone. Alessandra, please take Roland into the conservatory and offer him a drink."

I heard my sister's heels clicking on the marble floor of my father's office. I didn't have to look at her to know she was pissed. My father had not only ordered her out but also ordered her to get Roland a drink—something she would feel was beneath her. Yet, in reality, that was her job. She was an overpaid hostess for Kessler Management.

I vaguely wondered if my sister had ever had any aspirations, any dreams. Was there something that she'd wanted to do or try, or had she always been a lazy sloth?

The door closed behind Roland and my father wasted no time.

"Thank you for coming."

Is he serious?

"Why?"

"Will you sit?"

My father pointed to the set of leather wingback chairs

that sat in the corner of the room. Chairs that we'd sat in dozens of times. When I was a kid, I'd sit there and draw or read while my father worked. Later, when I was a teenager, I sat there and listened to my father fumble through an uncomfortable conversation about girls and the importance of using protection. As an adult, I'd sat with my father in this room many times. Sometimes it was enjoying an after-dinner drink discussing nothing of importance, simply spending time together. Other times it was because I'd sought him out for fatherly wisdom, which he'd always had time to impart.

Now, however, I was in this room staring at the man who'd been nothing but a great father and wanting to spit on his Italian leather loafers.

Talk about a mind fuck.

"I think I'll stand."

"I need to explain," he stated the obvious. "I never meant for everything to get this far."

"And what exactly is *this*?" I asked.

"My involvement with Zanetti."

When he stopped and it was apparent he wasn't going to go on, I prompted, "Involvement?"

"It started with the restaurant. Arnie was a good friend. I knew he wasn't on the up and up, but he was still a good man, a good friend, and Sophia and your mother were close. With your mother not having her family in Connecticut, Sophia was like a sister to her."

"Please, fuck, tell me you're not blaming this mess on Mom."

"Of course I'm not," he spat. "I did this. It's all my doing. Your mother had no idea. She might've had her suspicions about Arnie, but we never discussed them. I just want you to understand that I didn't go looking for...trouble."

My dad's hands came up, and in an uncharacteristic turn of events, he shoved his fingers into his graying hair.

A Kessler never showed vulnerability.

And Vernon Kessler never showed weakness.

Not as a man, not as a father, and never in business.

Therefore, I'd never in my life ever seen him rake his fingers through his hair.

"Arnie came to me and asked if I would invest some money for him. He was honest from the start. He never hid where the money came from."

"And where'd it come from?"

"Gambling. He ran poker tables. He split the house's take with Zanetti."

That was shockingly upfront, and something inside of me started to loosen.

"I took the money and invested it for him. A few years later, Arnie came to me again and asked if I wanted to buy a building in White Plains. It wasn't in the greatest of neighborhoods, and I didn't see the value. But Arnie guaranteed he could get me ten thousand a month in rent which was double the mortgage, and I'd get monthly bonuses. I knew then if I bought the building, I'd be opening a door I shouldn't."

"So why the hell did you?"

My father dropped his hands and leveled me with an icy stare.

"Greed."

I felt all the oxygen in my lungs whoosh from my chest. After that, I felt nothing. I was completely numb. *Greed.* That was why my father destroyed my family.

"I bought the building, and the poker games moved to White Plains. I was still investing Arnie's take through Kessler. Then Zanetti approached me and asked me to take over some of his accounts—legitimate accounts from rental properties. About a year later, Zanetti made another approach and asked me to buy a check-cashing business. I bought it. The year after that, I bought a pawn shop. It wasn't until many years later that together we bought a few apartment buildings and a business park. Those were on the up and up. Clean money coming in for Zanetti."

I knew all of this already. I also knew about the dry cleaners and three warehouses he owned with Zanetti.

"How did Mom not know? Hell, how didn't I know?" I shook my head and put my hand up. "No, the real question is, did Alessandra know?"

"Not in the beginning. But a few years ago, she saw me having dinner with Zanetti."

I wasn't tracking how seeing my father and Zanetti having dinner would clue my sister in on my dad's illegal dealings.

"I don't get it."

My father's head tilted slightly to the side as he intently studied me. An emotion I didn't like came over me, a feeling that I'd missed something big.

"You see what your sister wants you to see. What she wants everyone to see. Alessandra likes nothing more than to be underestimated. But make no mistake, your sister is far smarter than she lets on. She never misses an opportunity to sink her teeth into her prey."

He sounded proud.

"Jesus, Dad, you're talking about your daughter."

"Indeed," he agreed. "I know who she is because she's the woman I made her into. The woman I needed her to be."

I recoiled in disgust, and once again, the anger crept in.

How in the hell was this the same man who'd raised me?

He wanted my sister to grow up to be a nasty bitch who

sank her teeth into her prey. And who in the actual fuck was her prey?

"I don't get it. Why would you need her to be a manipulative, scheming bitch?"

"Your sister is resourceful and cunning," he contradicted. "She's my eyes and ears."

"So, she saw you having dinner with a mob boss, and she figured it all out? Then what? She was thrilled there was more money to be made and happily jumped on board?"

"We never spoke of it. I knew she knew. And the reverse was true for her. Alessandra understood the need for discretion and went about her duties at Kessler."

I was so dumbfounded from the shit I was listening to I was actually at a loss. A total loss. I had nothing to say. I felt nothing. I didn't want to hear any more of this bullshit. I wasn't angry, I wasn't sad, I wasn't even surprised.

The only thing I was, was done.

Totally and completely done.

My life hadn't been a lie.

His life had been a lie.

My father was a fucking fraud.

"I'm selling my shares in Kessler."

"I understand," my father softly said.

"I won't be meeting with the board, and I will not lie to the FBI if they show up again."

"Understood, son."

It was the gentle way that he said "son" that had me seeing red. A simple word I used to cherish now felt like a dagger through my heart.

"That's it?" I roared. "You fuck up our family, and all you have to say is 'understood?'"

My father's face twisted into an angry mask of fury. He

balled his fist and slammed it down onto his desk while yelling, "A man does not make excuses!"

"But he says something to his son after he's destroyed everything."

"The only thing left I can give you is your freedom. I will not allow you to be dragged into this. I made the decisions. I made the deals. It was my greed. It was my behavior. And now I will take responsibility. I will not make a plea. I will not proclaim innocence. I'm guilty, goddammit. I might be a criminal, but I'm not a liar. I'm a goddamn *Kessler,* and we do not make excuses for our shortcomings." My father ended his tirade and looked at the floor. "I failed this family. Saying I'm sorry will not fix what I have done. Sell your shares and disassociate yourself from Kessler. Your investments are secure; I've made sure of that. Your accounts are healthy and won't be subject to seizure. All of your assets are safe, Matthew, I swear it. I can't give you anything more than my promise that I will not drag this family through a trial."

"I can't believe I'm having to say this to the man who carried me into the house bleeding when I was ten and fell out of the tree. I can't believe I'm looking at that man, who was covered in my blood, rushing to get me to the hospital so I could get stitches, the whole time telling me I was going to be okay when you were so scared for me you had tears in your eyes." I couldn't stop the anger from consuming me until I shook with it. "I don't give a fuck about the goddamn money, Dad. Fucking hell! I would've rather have been dirt poor and you clean, not facing twenty years in prison."

"That's what rich people say, Matthew."

The motherfucking nerve.

"No, Dad, that's what a son who loves his father says."

"Matt—"

"No. We're done." I turned to walk out but stopped

when I got to the door. I looked over my shoulder, and crushing pain filled my chest. "I wish I could leave here telling you I didn't care that you'll never see me get married or have kids. I wish I could say that it doesn't kill me knowing that my children will never jump off the dock like I did, or they'll never get to sit in this office and watch their grandfather work behind his big desk. They'll never read the books in the library or run around on the lawn. They'll never know you, or the you I thought you were. But that Kessler honesty's a real sonofabitch, and I can't lie."

I turned back to the door and left.

I took a deep breath, then two, then three. When I had my heart rate under control, I went in search of Chelsea.

I found her where I'd left her, though she wasn't alone, and all that deep breathing was for naught when I heard my sister's vile mouth running.

"Tell me what it'll take."

"Are you crazy?" Chelsea's tone was full of indignation. "I don't want your money."

"Please," Alessandra huffed. "A girl like you? You need my money. Besides, it'll be easy. All you have to do is whisper in my little brother's ear that he should come home, and fifty thousand dollars will appear in your bank account."

"Damn, Ally, fifty thousand, that's it? Who knew on top of being a royal bitch you were a cheap bitch?"

Both women turned toward the doorway and I smiled.

It was either smile or rip my goddamn sister's head off.

"You need to come home and take care of the family."

"From what Dad just told me, he's trained you well. I think you'll be able to handle everything just fine. I told Dad, and now I'm telling you, I'm selling out. I want nothing to do with Kessler. And I'm never coming back up here again."

"You can't do that!" Alessandra screeched.

And it was sheer curiosity that had me asking, "Why can't I do that?"

"Kessler will…"

My sister trailed off, and I had enough for one day. And so had Chelsea. She was standing off the side of the room near the built-in bookcase with her arms wrapped around her middle.

"You ready, baby?"

"Absolutely."

Chelsea skirted the large antique reading desk giving Alessandra a wide berth. I couldn't blame her. I didn't even want to be in the same room as the bitch.

"You were always weak," Alessandra spat. "So weak that Dad needed me to help him run the company because you were too spineless to do it."

Chelsea rocked to a halt, her head snapped in the direction of my sister, and her eyes narrowed.

"Do you have any idea who your brother is?"

"Yeah, sweetheart, I know my brother a hell of a lot better than you do."

"Then you're either brave or stupid, *sweetheart*." Chelsea matched my sister's sarcasm. "There's not a damn thing weak about your brother. A weak man would've wrung your neck. Oh, and just so we're clear, you can take your fifty thousand dollars and shove it up your ass."

"God, nothing's changed. You still like the uneducated twits with foul mouths."

"Careful, Alessandra, I feel my control slipping," I warned. "Keep your insults directed at me."

"Or what?"

"Or *what*?"

"Yes, Matthew. Or what?"

"It's like I've entered the Twilight Zone and slipped through time to second grade," I mumbled.

"Weak."

"You know, that might be an effective slur if there was one goddamn thing I respected about you. But here we are, and I've yet to find a thing even remotely salvageable about you."

Without missing a beat, my sister seethed, "I hate you."

Christ.

"Yeah, you hate me because while you've treated me like a dog my whole life, I've yet to allow you to walk me like one."

I turned and looked at Chelsea, held out my hand, and waited for her to take it.

We walked to the door, but before we could escape, Alessandra had to have the last word.

"You're making a mistake."

I kept walking.

"You're going to regret this, Matthew."

That made me stop. I turned, and with me, Chelsea did, too.

"I'm gonna give you one warning. One solid piece of advice I hope you heed. Do not fuck with me, Alessandra. Do not push me into a corner. You think you know me, but you have no idea what I'm capable of. Don't make me do something *you'll* regret. I will shred you until there's nothing left."

Chelsea squeezed my hand and I took that as my cue it was time to leave.

I walked out the front door of my childhood home with

the knowledge I would never be back. Even if my mother got to keep the house, I'd never step foot it in again.

I'd never ask Chelsea to come back.

It was a shame she'd never know the beauty. But the real tragedy was our children would never see where their father grew up.

16

Uncomfortable didn't begin to touch the vibe in the rental as Matt drove away from the house—and calling it a house was a gross understatement. It was a mausoleum. Bigger than a mansion. Decorated with furnishings that cost more than I could begin to imagine. Every room Matt had shown me was cold and emotionless. Which was a weird way to describe a room, but it was the truth. The library was the only place that I saw that remotely had any warmth. It was hard to visualize Matt growing up in that place. To be fair I'd only seen about a quarter of one wing. So maybe there were family living spaces tucked in there somewhere.

I watched the manicured gardens fly by as Matt sped down the long driveway, and I struggled to find something to say.

"Hungry?" Matt asked when he stopped to let the huge gold gate open.

I absentmindedly wondered if the gate was solid gold—which wouldn't surprise me—or if it was just painted gold.

"Chels?'

"Is the gate solid gold?"

"Hell, if I know. Maybe?"

I pinched my lips to stop the hysterical laughter that was bubbling up.

Out of the corner of my eye, I saw Matt rest his head back and scrub his hands roughly over his face. I reached over and grabbed his right forearm and gave it a squeeze.

"What can I do to help?"

"Forget you saw any of that."

"Matt, seriously, what can I do?"

Matt dropped his hands from his face and captured one of mine. He placed it on his thigh, then left his covering mine.

"I'm being serious. What would help me is if you could forget you ever saw this place because I promise you, we're never coming back. Forget all that shit you heard my sister spewing. And please do not hold that shitshow against me. I'm so fuckin' sorry I didn't think about how uncomfortable you'd be. It was selfish wanting—"

"Quiet," I interrupted him. "It wasn't selfish. You asking me to come with you made me feel special."

"Like a special friend?" Matt attempted to joke, but in his current mood, it fell flat.

"Yeah, like a special friend, without the donuts and bacon cheeseburgers."

Matt's mouth started to curve up, but his lips never made it into a full smile.

"Fuck," he whispered.

"Do you want to talk about it now or later?" I asked.

"Later."

"Okay," I agreed. "Where are we going now?"

"Would you think I was a total douchey prick if I flew us down to Manhattan for lunch before we flew home to Georgia?"

I blinked, then I blinked again as I tried to digest his question.

"Fly to Manhattan?"

"Have you ever been on a helicopter?"

"No."

"Do you wanna fly in one?"

"Sure, Matt, let's find an airport that rents helicopters and dash to New York for lunch at Times Square," I blathered sarcastically.

Matt said no more as he pulled through the now-open gate. The neighborhood of Belle Haven wasn't very big. It only took a couple minutes to get to the interstate. But instead of getting on 95, which would take us back to the hotel, he drove under the overpass and continued to drive through another residential neighborhood.

I was beginning to get scared Matt was being serious about flying to Manhattan.

"Where are we going?"

"You'll see."

More and more houses flew by until a few minutes later, there was a small industrial area in front of us.

"Matt?"

"Almost there."

I was afraid of where "there" was.

A sleek glass building came into view with a black glossy sign that read "Velocity."

Matt pulled into the lot and parked in the space nearest the front door.

"Matt?"

He ignored me and got out. I watched him round the hood, then he opened my door and offered me his hand.

"Why do I get the feeling that this is going to be douchey?" I muttered and took his outstretched hand.

He pulled me from the rental and didn't stop until I was flush against his front.

"Because this is going to be as douchey as it gets. But I promise you're gonna love it."

"I'm not sure," I started and shook my head.

"Trust me, Chels."

What was I supposed to do? I was in Matt's arms, and he was asking me to trust him. So what if he was going to rent a helicopter so we could fly to Manhattan instead of driving there?

"I trust you."

Matt's smile melted my heart, which made this environmentally unfriendly trip worth it.

"Thank you."

He dropped his mouth to mine and gave me a hard, closed-mouthed kiss. When he pulled away, I told him, "You owe me big time for this. I expect at least three orgasms for—"

Matt's head tipped back and he belted out a laugh. And after the morning he'd had, on a day when his sister had said mean, despicable things to him, including telling him she hated him, watching him laugh was the best gift I'd ever received.

"You're beautiful when you laugh."

Matt sobered, his eyes came to mine, and they were still dancing with humor when he said, "You're always beautiful."

Matt and I walked to the door. He held it open and motioned me through. My breath caught as soon as we entered. More opulence. I didn't want to seem ungrateful, but damn, I'd be happy when we were back to our normal lives.

"Mr. Kessler," a well-dressed man greeted. "A pleasure to

see you."

"Likewise, George. And, please, it's Matt."

George dipped his chin but didn't agree on the usage of Matt's first name.

"What can I do for you?"

"I was hoping you had something available to take us to Pier 6. There and back. We'll only need a few hours in the city."

"Of course," George purred.

And, of course he purred because that was what men in three-piece suits did when a *rich as fuck* man asked to rent a helicopter for a jaunt to the city.

And yes, I thought that in my head in my best hoity-toity Mr. Belvedere impersonation.

"I have a Eurocopter AS350 if that will suit your needs."

"That'll be perfect, George, thank you."

"Have a seat." George swept his arm in the direction of a fancy-schmancy seating area. "Would you like me to send Sarah out with something to drink?"

"Chels?"

"Um. No, thank you."

"Nothing for me, either."

George bustled away and I wanted to kick Matt.

"Why'd you ask me? You could've answered for both of us."

"I was being polite." The rat-bastard chuckled.

"Well, from here on out, don't be polite, and please answer for me. Pretend I'm mute. No, pretend I don't speak English."

"Okay, what language shall I pretend you speak?"

"Gah! Don't say "shall" now you sound like them."

Matt's big body started to vibrate, and I was afraid he was going to laugh in the luxurious...shit, I didn't know what to call the space we were in. It looked like a reception area of an office building, only way fancier.

"Don't laugh in here," I snapped.

Now the vibrating had turned to quaking.

"Why can't I laugh?"

"It's rude," I told him and gave him my best 'duh' face.

Oh, no. He lost the battle and busted out a long, very loud laugh that echoed off the walls.

"What the hell has gotten into you?" he asked through his chuckling.

I glanced around the room, hoping George couldn't hear him.

"Nothing, *Mr. Kessler*."

"Baby."

One word, yet it was full of understanding.

"Remember when I told you about my wall?"

I bit my lip and nodded.

"It wasn't just to keep the women who wanted to use me away. It was to keep everyone out. George is a nice enough guy, but you wanna know why he knows my name?"

"Because he knows you?"

"This might be the third time I've met him. He knows my name because he's paid to know my name. He's paid to know every rich family's name in a hundred-mile radius. I bet if I asked him to stock the helicopter, he'd have my favorite beer, vodka, and gin. He'd also know I'm not fond of whiskey. That's his job. He's paid to make me feel special."

None of that sounded pleasant. Actually, it sounded bad.

"Are there a lot of people who kiss your ass to make you feel special?"

"Now you're getting it. In my old life, before I left Greenwich, ninety-nine percent of people I came into contact with kissed my ass. Now, no one does. Unless I'm up here in Connecticut."

I hated that for Matt.

"Well, you did come in here all hoity-toity asking to rent a helicopter so you and your girlfriend can go eat lunch in New York," I defended George.

"Is that what you are, Chels, my girlfriend?"

Oh, crap.

Was it too soon?

Was he not my boyfriend?

I mean, he hadn't asked.

Oh, shit!

"I was, um, just kidding with you." I tried to backpedal.

"I know you were teasing me about flying us to New York," he said and captured my chin when I tried to look away from him. "Tell me, Chels. Are you my girlfriend?"

"I thought so. I mean last night..."

I ran out of words when he lowered his forehead to mine.

"Yeah, last night," he whispered. "You told me you were in love with me and I told you I felt the same."

"Right. So why are you acting weird because I said I was your girlfriend?"

"Because you don't feel like my girlfriend." My heart slid into my throat, and my panic swirled in my stomach.

"I...I don't?"

"No, you feel like my future. You feel like the mother of my children even though we don't have any. You feel like my wife even though we haven't gotten married. You feel like more, like everything, like a dream come to life."

At that moment, if it were possible, I would've roped myself bodily to Matt just to make sure he never left me. But since I couldn't do that, I let his words wash through me until they touched my soul. Once they were there, I felt the sweetness settle deep.

"I'm keeping you forever," I croaked out, my throat clogged with so much emotion I knew I sounded funny but didn't care. "I won't let you leave me, Matt. If you try, I'll fight you. I'll find a way to make you stay."

"You won't have to fight me," he whispered. "I'm not going anywhere."

"But I will. I'll fight for you."

"I know you will."

"I wish we weren't in a hotsy-totsy helicopter rental place because I really want to kiss—"

Matt's mouth came down over mine and he kissed me. It wasn't a PDA-acceptable kiss—it was a full-blown make-out—deep and wet and delicious. Highly unacceptable but I didn't give the first flip. I was kissing the man who thought I was his future—which meant he was mine.

A throat cleared and Matt broke the kiss but didn't let me go.

"Excuse me, Mr. Kessler, your helicopter is ready."

Matt rolled his eyes.

"Thank you. We'll be there in a moment." Then still holding my gaze he muttered, "*Presto amore mio, così posso darti il primo orgasmo su un elicottero.*"

"What does that mean?"

Matt winked, grabbed my hand, and started to walk.

I guess I was taking my first ever helicopter ride.

17

"This is delicious," Chelsea said after she swallowed the last of her hot dog.

"Told you."

We were sitting in some hole-in-the-wall burger joint near the Staten Island Ferry terminal, which was, thankfully, only a short walk from the Heliport. I was fairly certain after the helicopter ride, Chelsea's head would've popped off and spun in circles if I'd ordered us a town car. I didn't take public transportation while in New York City—ever—and I was already over my douchey quota for the day.

The waitress skidded to a stop at our table and smiled at Chelsea. "What'd you think?"

"I wasn't sure what Pushcart sauce was, but you were right. It was great."

The waitress beamed and nodded to Chelsea's empty plate. "Would you like another one?"

"No thanks. I'm stuffed."

"How 'bout you?"

"No. Just the check, but we're in no hurry."

"That's a first for around here," the woman muttered and jogged off.

Yes, jogged. We were in New York, after all.

"Thanks for bringing me here." Chelsea glanced around the busy restaurant. "This place is awesome."

It still amazed me how totally and utterly different Chelsea was from any other woman I'd ever met. I knew she enjoyed the helicopter ride because she'd nudged me every few minutes to point something out. She held my hand and squeezed during takeoff and landing. She'd smiled and happily bounced in the plush leather seats. But she was not impressed. No, not Chelsea; what she thought was awesome was a hot dog smothered in sautéed onions, ketchup, and hot sauce.

"When I was a kid, I'd fly down here with my dad. He'd go to meetings and have fancy lunches. I'd walk around and look for the dirtiest diners I could find and eat there."

"Dirty diners?"

"Cut me some slack. I was like ten or eleven. I needed to do something to entertain myself. It was dirty diners or stuffy lunches. And I hated wearing ties."

"You walked around New York City alone when you were ten?" she gasped.

"Thinking back it was a little crazy my dad let me loose while he worked. But when I was a kid, I didn't think anything of it."

It was more than a little crazy, it was downright dangerous, but there was no use thinking about something that happened twenty-plus years ago. Though I couldn't help but wonder if my dad let me wander the streets so I wouldn't have to sit through lunch with his good ole pal Zanetti.

"And for the record, this was not one of the places I

found when I was a kid. I'm sure the health department has long since shut them all down."

Chelsea's smile died and she started fidgeting with her napkin. She was cute when she was building the courage to ask me something personal. Over the last week, the shyness had mostly gone away, but I noticed she still wrung her hands together when she wanted to ask me something she thought would offend me.

"Do you like being rich?" she rushed out.

"I don't know how to answer that," I told her honestly. "Do I like knowing I have the means to take care of my wife and the family we create? Yes. Do I like that I can fall asleep at night and not have to worry about how I'm going to pay my mortgage? Yes. Do I like being able to give to Women, Inc.—which is a dumb name, and someone should've talked Liberty out of calling it that—but I digress. Do I like being able to write a check to help fund a worthy cause? Yes. But do expensive dinners excite me? No. You've seen my house, the truck I drive, the clothes I wear. I live in a nice house in a quiet neighborhood, I drive a decent truck, and the clothes I wear are at least ten years old. So, again, I'm not sure how to answer your question."

"The helicopter," she mumbled.

"The helicopter was the means to an end. I needed to get the fuck out of Greenwich and away from my sister before I strangled her. So, if you're asking if I frequently charter helicopters, the answer is no. I've never chartered a jet or a yacht. And I only fly first-class because the legroom in coach sucks."

Chelsea nodded, obviously finding my answer acceptable, and I couldn't stop my smile.

"Baby, you do know that you're the first woman I've ever had to defend my money to."

She jerked back. Her eyes went round, and she shook her head.

"You don't have to defend your money. I was just curious."

"I know you were curious, and I don't care that you asked. I *like* it when you ask me questions. And I like that me flying us to the city doesn't impress you because it sure as fuck doesn't impress me. Today my father told me straight-out he got involved in what he did because of greed. He didn't deny it or sugar-coat it. Straight up greed. That's what money does to people. When they get it, they want more. Some people work harder, and that kind of ambition is impressive—admirable even. Then there are some who let it rule their lives. You have every right to wonder what kind of man you're with. If I'm full of greed or if I'm comfortable living off the money I make at Triple Canopy. Which, by the way, is the money I use to live on."

"You impress me."

"Chels—"

"You impress me," she repeated, leaning deeper in. "Everything about you impresses me, not just how you handle your wealth. Which, that alone is damn impressive. Most people with the kind of money I saw today would be happy to sit back and live off their trust funds and interest. But instead, you left. You followed your dream. You went out and became your own man. You joined the Navy—which is impressive, too." She paused, weighing her next words. "I know the story."

"What story?"

"About why you left the Navy. Liberty told me what happened with her and Drake. I know Trey and Luke got hurt. You didn't. You could've stayed in, but you left with your team. Your loyalty and love for your friends impresses me. I know you're great at your job because Shiloh brags about you all the time. She says you're the best marksman out of anyone at TC. She values your help and says she's better at what she does because of you. And I know you said you bought Balls Deep as a joke. But really, you bought it because the old owner needed the money from the sale to put his daughter through college. You're smart, so I know it was a sound business investment, but you still would've bought it even if it wasn't just so a man you didn't know would be able to sleep at night knowing he wasn't in debt to his eyeballs and his girl got the education he wanted her to have. That's the kind of man you are. That's Matt Kessler."

Throughout Chelsea's words, I felt my throat clog with emotion.

"But more than all of that," she continued. "You're open and honest. You say what's on your mind. You're giving, and by giving, I don't mean the over-the-top helicopter ride you gave me. I mean, you give your time, your thoughts, your feelings. You give me *you*. You think it's refreshing I don't want your money. Well, I think it's refreshing that you're the type of man who knows his mind and isn't afraid to voice how he feels. It impresses me that after the morning you've had, you still had patience with me and my insecurities. You still have it in you to smile and laugh and sit across from me and still be open when most people would've closed down. I know I don't have to tell you this, but there's not one weak bone in your body, Matt. You're the strongest man I know. And for the record, never, and I mean never, did I think that you were motivated by greed. I wouldn't question your integrity."

Since my throat was clogged and I could say nothing, I stretched my hand across the table and rested it palm up.

When Chelsea placed hers over mine, I curled my fingers and held on tight.

"Whenever you're ready to talk about what happened, I'm here to listen," she told me. "And if you don't want to tell me, no hard feelings. I get how difficult it is. I understand the mixed emotions. Even after everything my parents did to me, there's still a part of me that wants their approval. My dad threw me out, not caring that his daughter was going to sleep on the street. Yet, just once, I want to hear him tell me he's proud of me. It's fucked up. I shouldn't want that from him. But the way we feel about our parents isn't always logical. It's okay to still love your dad. He made a mistake." Chelsea paused and gave me a small, sad smile. "A big mistake. But he's still the father you remember him to be. That wasn't a lie. How he made some of his money was illegal. That was a lie. But your childhood wasn't. The love he gave you is real. And I hope in time, when the wound heals, all those good memories you have will bring you comfort instead of pain."

Goddamn.

I dropped my head forward and stared at the scarred plastic table.

"I hope you're right, baby, because right now, I feel like thirty-six years have been erased, and it hurts so fuckin' bad. It feels wrong to love him. But it feels worse turning my back on him. He was flat-out wrong. He's guilty, he admits it, and he takes full responsibility for everything he's done. But taking responsibility for it doesn't change anything."

I glanced up from the table, took in Chelsea's beautiful face, and something new came over me. It wasn't peace, though when I was near her, I certainly felt at ease. It was an awareness, a recognition, that I was looking at the woman I didn't know I'd been waiting for. A woman who had been through hell but hadn't let her dad's abuse break her. A woman whose determination matched mine. A woman who was strong. A woman who would not run away at the first hurdle we faced. A woman who would stand by my side.

I'd danced around the words. I'd told her I'd fallen in love with her. But I hadn't given them straight out. And right then, I needed her to know.

"I love you, Chelsea."

I heard the hitch in her breath, felt her hand tighten in mine, saw the wetness hit her eyes.

"No one's ever said that to me before."

Her admission was barely a whisper, but I felt those words like they'd been shouted in my face and shoved down my throat.

"I love you, Chelsea," I repeated. "And I'm gonna remind you every day."

As I watched the tears roll down Chelsea's cheeks, I hoped that one day I'd get to meet her father and brothers. I hoped that one day our paths would cross, and they'd see the beautiful, resilient woman she'd become. And right after Chelsea got her pound of flesh—and I knew my woman, she'd get hers—I was going to strap her father's ass the way he'd done to his baby girl until it was his tears rolling down his cheeks.

"I love you, Matthew."

Sweet Jesus, that felt good.

Better than any rush of adrenaline.

The only thing that came close to feeling as good as hearing Chelsea tell me she loved me was feeling her sleeping in my arms.

18

"Gin and Tonic. Botanist if you have it," the man said.

I finished making change for a Bud draft and looked up at the new patron at the bar. Then I looked down at Tony's end of the bar and noted he was just as slammed as I was.

"Sure thing," I told the G and T man as I set the bills down in front of my last customer.

"That's for you, darlin'." The draft man pushed a five back and added a wink.

A five-dollar tip on a three-fifty beer was ridiculous, but I had feed to buy for my girls, so I wasn't going to quibble.

"Thanks, bud."

I pocketed the tip, gave him no room for further conversation, and turned to grab the gin off the back wall. I was pouring the drink when Matt came up behind me.

"You need anything?"

"Do you know how to change out a keg?" I asked.

"Yep."

I wasn't sure why that surprised me, but it did.

"You do?"

I finished the drink, reached around Matt, and grabbed a lime out of the tray.

"I told you I worked at the club when I was a teenager. Might not have been legal letting a fifteen-year-old change out kegs, but I did it all the same. And before I took over Balls, I got a refresher course. So, yeah, I know how to change out a keg. Which one needs to be replaced?"

"Blue Moon."

"On it."

"Hey, boss, Blue Moon's sudsy!" Tony yelled over the noise of the crowd.

"Matt's changing it!" I yelled back and set the drink down.

"Six dollars," I told the man.

"Is that Matt Kessler?" the man asked, looking in the direction of the door Matt had just walked through.

The hair on the back of my neck stood on end. It was a Saturday night. The bar was packed, all the tables were full, and there were wall-to-wall people. I didn't have time to ask why this man was asking after Matt, and I didn't like the way he was staring at the door.

"Six dollars, please."

"That's not Matt?" The man asked the same question, just a different way, and I didn't like that either.

He wasn't catching the hint that I wasn't going to share.

"Sorry, but I can't give out the names of the people who work here."

That was a total lie, and the man knew it.

"I'm a friend of Matt's," he tried again.

"Two Millers!" a new customer shouted. "Bottles."

"Well, if you're a friend, then why are you asking me his name?" I didn't let the guy answer before I went on. "Six dollars now, please."

The guy tossed seven bucks on the bar, grabbed his drink, and left.

I grabbed the money and went back to serving drinks.

It was nearing on ten, and some of the pool tables were now empty, but all of the tables surrounding the pool area were still full. I'd scheduled three waitresses but I was thinking I needed four on the floor, or I needed to hire a busser to help clear the tables. I knew what it was like to have to serve and clear, and when you were slammed, someone picking up empties was a big help. I made a mental note to ask the girls what they preferred. Tips were gold, and I didn't want to take money out of their pockets, but I didn't want them stressed and for the service to suck.

"Tony? You good here? I'm gonna do a quick walk-through."

"Got it. On your way back, can you grab another bottle of Jack?"

"Will do."

I grabbed a plastic bus tub and hurried out to the floor, picking up empties as I went. Donna, a tall redhead, passed me with her tray full of drinks.

"You good, Donna?"

"Yep. But Karen needs to pick up the pace," Donna complained. "She's got drinks sitting on the bar getting watered down."

Then why don't you grab them and serve them?

I didn't say that. Correcting staff on the floor wasn't my style. It was rude and disrespectful. But damn if Donna didn't need to learn the meaning of being a team player.

Not that Donna waited for me to reply before she rushed to a four-top and smiled at the men. The smile was flirty; it said, 'I'm open to going home with you', and from what I heard, she actually did go home with a lot of men from the bar. Matt didn't have any rules in place about staff fraternizing with customers, so it wasn't my business. And I wouldn't make it mine unless it became an issue.

I spotted Karen. She looked more than a little frazzled.

"Hey, girl, what do you need?"

"Those two guys thrown out," she mumbled.

I glanced at the table and my neck got tight. One of the occupants was the man who'd asked after Matt.

Shit, where is *Matt?*

I'd been so busy I'd lost track of him. Not that I was keeping tabs or anything, but he was damn pretty to stare at. The last time I saw him, he'd finished changing out the keg and was helping Skylar at the pool desk. Monday through Thursday, the bartenders handed out the pool balls. But Friday through Sunday, Skylar worked and handled the pool tables. She'd gotten overwhelmed with the check-ins, so Matt had gone over to help.

Another thing that impressed me about Matt, he jumped in wherever he was needed. Over the last week, since we'd been home from Connecticut, I'd seen him clean tables, wash dishes, help deliver food. He'd delivered drinks, and tonight he'd changed kegs and restocked bottles.

The last week had been the best week of my life. Better than the week before. And that week had been awesome, too.

Karen said something, and I realized I'd drifted.

"What was that?"

"It's nothing. Forget I said anything."

"Hey, wait," I told her before she could walk away. "Are they bothering you?"

"They're just assholes. I can handle it."

"Uh-uh. No way. You never put up with bullshit. Tell me what's going on."

Karen blew out a breath. I didn't miss the relief that washed over her face.

"The bald one won't stop asking me for my number," she started. "And the one in the baseball hat has grabbed my ass three times. He—"

"He touched you?" I snapped.

"Yep."

She squared her shoulders, and I wasn't sure if it was because she was pissed or thought she was going to get into trouble.

I quickly disabused her of the notion she'd ever be in trouble for some dick putting his hands on her.

"No one ever puts their hands on you, Karen. Not fucking ever. And certainly, they don't ever do it in my bar. Do they have a tab, or are they paying as they go?"

"Paying as they go."

"Perfect. You've got a choice; go behind the bar with Tony or come with me. But if you come with me, I want you to know I'm kicking their asses out. Whatever you prefer to do is fine."

Karen glanced at the table and took a moment to think. When her gaze came back to me, it was full of fire but also fear.

"They're really big," she noted.

They were. And the one in the baseball hat who'd asked about Matt looked like he was a wall of muscle. I also didn't give a shit.

"Maybe Tony—"

"Karen, I'm the manager. It's my job. But I'm also smart enough to know my limitations. I'm asking them to leave. If they give me trouble, I'll ask Tony, or I'll find Matt."

"I'll go with you. But you talk."

I gave Karen a smile. She was young, just twenty-two;

she was also a tiny thing only coming up to my chin, and I'd guess she weighed all of a hundred pounds fully clothed and soaking wet. I understood her trepidation. But I was also proud she wanted to come.

I weaved through the crowd and made my way to the table. When I stopped next to the men, the bald one looked up and smiled.

"Look what we have here," Baldy drawled. "Smalls brought us a friend."

Smalls?

What a dick.

The guy in the baseball hat turned his attention to me and I felt my skin crawl as he eyed me up and down.

"You'll do," the guy sneered.

"I'll do?"

I already knew whatever came out of the jackass's mouth was going to piss me off, so I should've let his comment go and simply asked him to leave. I didn't know why I bothered asking—morbid curiosity, maybe? Or maybe I didn't like that some jerk thought he had the right to make a lewd comment.

"Yeah, darlin', you'll do," he semi-repeated. "Not the prettiest but not the ugliest."

"I think it's time for you two to leave," I shared.

"Oh, c'mon. Denny was just kidding," the bald guy said. "You're totally hot."

"Time to leave."

"Christ, bitches. So sensitive. Can't a guy pay a compliment anymore without your panties twisting?"

That was when I lost my cool.

My hands slammed down on the table and I leaned across until I was face-to-face with the asshole, close enough to smell the gin on his breath.

"Your compliments suck," I spat. "But I'm kicking your ass out because you seem to have a problem keeping your hands to yourself. Learn some goddamn manners, asshole, or don't come back."

"Fuck you. She didn't have a problem—"

I saw red. That was my only excuse for what I did next.

My hand shot forward and my aim was true. I closed my fingers and pinched his nipple through his shirt as hard as I could.

"Bitch!" the hat guy shouted and swatted my hand away.

"Yeah, did she like it like *you* liked it? Huh? Did she really want your fucking hands on her?"

I stopped twisting his nipple and backed away.

Before I could stand to my full height, my back hit a wall of muscle, and two steel bands wrapped around me.

"Baby, what the fuck?"

I took a moment to enjoy Matt's arms around me. The bad news was, it was short-lived. More bad news—the guy in the baseball hat jumped to his feet and lunged at me.

One second, I was standing in front of Matt. The next, I was behind him, and Mr. Baseball Hat was flat on his back, surrounded by tipped-over chairs.

What the hell just happened?

The bald guy stood but stepped back when Matt held up his hand.

"What the fuck do you think you're doing, Denny?" Matt growled.

So he did know Baseball Hat Guy.

With very little grace, Denny rolled to his side, then up to his hip.

"I'm gonna—"

"Careful, Denny," Matt started.

"Fuck you, Matt," Denny said and scrambled to his feet.

"You good?"

My head snapped to the side, and I saw Dylan standing next to Matt with his arms crossed over his chest.

"All good," Matt returned.

There seemed to be some sort of silent battle playing out between Matt and Denny. I wasn't sure if they were using the time to calm down or if they were plotting murder. I figured Matt was waiting for Denny to make his move. And the red-faced Denny looked dumb enough to make it.

"I was telling Denny and his friend it was time for them to leave."

No one said anything.

"So, I think it's time you did that now, Denny. You and your friend need to leave."

Still, no one said anything.

Denny just kept scowling at Matt.

Matt just stood there with a bored look.

I stepped out from behind Matt and his arm came up, halting my movement.

Denny smiled; it was one of those smiles that felt icky. The kind that came before a dickhead opened his mouth and said something you weren't going to like.

"You've trained her well."

Yep. There it was.

Asshole.

Matt didn't take the bait. Dylan didn't move. But Karen did. She flew forward, and in a flash, she smacked Denny across the face. Dylan yanked her back before Denny could do something stupid, like hit her back.

"That's for grabbing my ass!" Karen shouted. "When a woman asks you not to touch her, you don't touch her."

You go, girl!

"Wait," Matt grunted, his voice vibrating with anger.

"You touched one of my employees?"

Oh, no.

Dylan gave Karen a gentle shove in my direction, and I quickly grabbed her hand and pulled her close.

"It fucks me I gotta tell you this with you being a cop *and* married," Matt snarled. "No means no, motherfucker."

"She didn't tell me no."

Hold on.

Back up.

Denny was a *cop*, and he was *married*?

"She said she asked you not to touch her," Matt reminded Denny. "But she doesn't actually have to say *no*. She has to say *yes*. And since she slapped the fuck out of you, I'm guessing she didn't say *yes* before you grabbed her ass. Now you got a choice—walk your ass out of my bar and never come back, or I call your wife and ask her to come pick your ass up while Karen files a police report."

"I bet your punk ass would love to call my wife."

"No, my *punk ass* would like you to walk outta my bar without me having to call Nadine. Heard she's ready to pack up your kids and leave your *cheating ass.* Bet her knowing you're sexually assaulting my employee would tip her off the fence."

Jeez, this guy was a monumental asshole.

"C'mon, Denny," Baldy waded in.

There were a few more moments of Denny trying his best to look like he was a tough guy, but once again, he had to prove he was the asshole the whole bar had heard him be.

"Watch your back, Kessler."

I heard Dylan chuckle, and a second later, Matt followed suit.

"I'll do that, Denny."

"I'm fucking serious, asshole."

Matt kept right on chuckling when he said, "I bet you are."

"Denny!" Baldy snapped.

Karen and I stood behind Matt and watched Denny and his buddy leave.

They didn't dally, and when they were out the door, the bar erupted in cheers.

Matt spun around, his hands went to my hips, he yanked me forward, our bodies collided, and he shoved his face in my neck.

What in the world?

"Are you okay?"

His big body was trembling. No, it was quaking—shaking so violently I was moving with him.

"You gave that motherfucker a titty twister," he roared with hilarity. "Goddamn funniest thing I've seen in my life."

"Well, he deserved it."

"Yeah, Chels, he did. I'm shocked you didn't tear the thing off. He was howling in pain."

"He was?"

"Yeah, baby, he was. But you just kept on twisting. Fucking hilarious!"

Okay, so it was funny I'd given a grown man a titty twister, but it wasn't good that I'd been so mad I kind of blacked out for a moment.

"We were so busy, I forgot to tell you that guy Denny was at the bar earlier—before you changed out the Blue Moon keg. He saw you and asked if you were Matt Kessler."

"What'd you tell him?"

"That I couldn't give out employees' names. He said he was your friend."

"That asshole is not my friend. He's been to TC once for hand-to-hand combat training. He was such a dick Jason called his captain and told him Denny was not welcome back."

Why did that not surprise me?

"Sorry I forgot."

"No worries." Matt turned to look at Karen and asked, "Are you okay?"

"I'm great," she chirped.

"If you want to press charges, we'll go in the office and—"

"Nope. Chels giving him an epic titty twister and me getting a slap in was good enough for me. Besides, I hit him and I don't want to get into trouble."

"I didn't see you hit anyone," I chimed in. "Dylan, did you see Karen hit Denny?"

"I didn't see a thing," Dylan played along.

"If you're good, then I'll get this mess cleaned up," Matt said.

"Oh, shit. Tony needed a bottle of Jack. I have to run."

I got one step away before Matt tagged my hand.

"As funny as that was, Chels. Next time there's a problem, you get me, or Tony."

"She's the manager." Karen came to my defense. "She had everything under control. But we were going to get Tony if it got out of hand."

"Seems it got out of hand," Matt pointed out.

"No. Chelsea had him in hand." Karen winked.

"Yeah, his nipple," Matt huffed.

I really needed to get back to the bar, so I did the only thing I could do and leaned forward and kissed Matt.

Then I ran away before he made me lie to him by agreeing to get him or Tony should I need to throw another patron out of the bar—because that was not going to happen.

19

"What in the sam fuck is that?" I grouched and kicked Matt to wake him up.

I felt Matt's hand leave my belly, then his heat left my back, but the pounding continued.

The bed dipped, I heard clothes rustling, but I kept my eyes closed.

The doorbell rang and I heard Matt growl.

"I swear to God someone better be dead," he yelled.

I reached behind me, grabbed Matt's pillow, and shoved it over my head to drown out all the banging, ringing, and yelling.

I had no idea what time it was, but it felt like I'd only slept for ten minutes.

"Jesus, Hadley..."

That was all I heard before the door slammed shut and I sat up in bed, holding the covers up to my naked chest.

A few moments later, I was still sitting in bed when Matt stepped through the door, scowling.

"Hadley's here," he announced.

"What?"

"And Quinn, and Liberty, and Shiloh."

"What?"

Matt didn't repeat himself. He stripped his sweats off, put his knee on the bed, and crawled back in.

"Have fun."

His head hit the pillow and his eyes closed.

What the hell was happening?

I glanced at the clock and saw it was after ten. I attempted to do mental math, which wasn't working out very well because I was tired as hell. The last time I'd looked at the clock last night it was four A.M. Giving up on calculating the hours I'd slept, knowing in my bones whatever the number, it wasn't enough, I scurried out of bed.

Thankfully, Matt had the foresight to shut the bedroom door because I was butt-assed naked, and none of those women in the living room knew there was such a word as privacy. I rummaged through the clothes on the floor and found a pair of jeans I'd worn a few days ago and shoved my legs into them. I glanced around, looking for a bra and shirt. Commando was one thing. Braless was a no-go. I rushed as fast as I could to finish getting dressed before one of them came knocking. I didn't bother brushing my teeth or my hair before I quietly exited the bedroom.

I was at the mouth of the hallway when I was greeted by my four friends, all standing in Matt's living room with their hands on their hips.

"Nothing's going on with Matt?" Hadley started.

"Well..."

"Hey, Chels, what's going on with you and Matt?" Quinn mocked. "Oh, nothing."

My gaze went to Shiloh and she just shrugged. Then I looked at Liberty and she was smiling.

"I'm just here for the coffee," Liberty said. "Drake's out

this morning with Luke playing basketball, so I had nothing better to do."

"I'm in love with Matt," I blurted out.

"I knew it," Quinn whooped and turned to Hadley. "You owe me ten dollars."

My mouth dropped open. Once my momentary shock wore off, I scowled at Hadley.

"You bet I didn't love Matt?"

"No. Quinn said within the first five minutes, you'd spill the beans," Hadley explained. "I said it would take a half-hour."

"Whatever," I grumbled. "Did someone bring me coffee?"

The women shared a look and all of them shook their heads.

"Evil bitches," I said under my breath. "We didn't go to sleep until four."

"Four? Doesn't the bar close at two?" Liberty laughed.

I ignored Liberty's comment and made my way to the kitchen.

I had the coffee set to brew when Shiloh remarked, "You sure do know your way around Matt's kitchen."

"I've never been here before," Quinn said, looking around the house.

My brain wasn't functioning on all cylinders. Hell, I wasn't sure it was functioning on one. At least that was my excuse for offering up more information than I should've.

"I can't remember the last time I slept at my place."

Before Connecticut.

My clothes were all over Matt's bedroom floor. He was tidy. He picked up his first thing in the morning. I just kept kicking mine into the corner.

Shit. Why hadn't I gone home?

"Oh, hell, she's gearing up for a meltdown," Hadley muttered.

"This is serious," I hissed.

"It looks serious," Hadley agreed.

"What if he doesn't want me spending the night?"

Matt hadn't said anything. But that was the thing, he hadn't said *anything*. He'd been at the bar every night since we'd been home from Connecticut. After I finished closing the bar and counting the money, Matt walked me to my car, gave me a kiss, and said, *see you at home*.

I figured he meant his home since my apartment wasn't really home.

That was an invitation, right?

But the last two nights, he hadn't said, 'I'll see you at home.' He'd just kissed me and said, 'I'll follow you.' Did that mean he didn't want me to go to his house?

"For the love of all things holy, someone please pour her a cup of coffee," Quinn pleaded.

"It's not done brewing," Shiloh said. "It'll ruin the pot if you pour a cup."

Shiloh was absolutely right. All of the water needed to percolate through the grounds or it tasted funny.

"He didn't ask me to come here last night," I whispered. "He just said, I'll follow you. Did that mean, he'd follow me back to my place? Is he sick of me being here?"

"Girl." Quinn chuckled. "The bar closes at two. That means you left there at two-thirty at the latest. At that time of night, it takes ten minutes tops to get here, and you didn't go to bed until four. That means there was some hanky-panky going on. At least an hour and twenty minutes of it. That doesn't say he's sick of you being here. That says he's got stamina. So quit your freak-out and spill."

I didn't quit my freak-out, but I did spill. I told them

about my trip to Connecticut. I left out all the ugly parts because it was not my place to tell Matt's business. They all knew I'd taken over as manager at Balls Deep, so I skipped all of that. But I did tell them about the helicopter ride.

"Seriously? A helicopter?" Shiloh laughed. Her gaze went to his living room then back to me. "If I hadn't heard the guys joke with him about being rich, I'd never guess."

That was the thing about Matt; if you didn't know, you didn't know. He didn't flaunt his wealth. He didn't talk about it. He didn't live like he grew up in a Belle Haven estate on the water.

He was just Matt.

"Best hot dogs I ever had," I told the girls. "And did I mention in first class you get heated blankets? *Heated*. It was amazing."

"The man took you to meet his family," Quinn started. "No. Actually, he took you because he couldn't face his family without you with him. And you're having a mini-breakdown because you're worried you've overstayed your welcome? You're crazy. He didn't *ask* you to come back to his place with him because it's a given where you're gonna sleep. Settle in, Chels. You're home."

Home?

And she called me crazy. Was Quinn insane?

"Are you insane? He hasn't asked me to move in."

"Uh, yeah, he has. You just missed him asking."

I will admit, I'd missed a lot of signs in the beginning. Matt had asked me to open my eyes to what was happening. Then he had to tell me to pay attention. But I hadn't missed him asking me to move in. That was something I'd never forget. I would've savored the question before I danced around. I would've memorized the moment before I shouted yes.

"She's only had one cup of coffee, cousin," Liberty said. "She's not ready to hear that Matt is moving her in one day at a time without her noticing. I have to hand it to him; it's a smooth move."

"He's moving me in?"

"Just drink your coffee and forget we said anything," Hadley suggested. "Addy will be home next week from the outrageous honeymoon Matt gave her and Trey as a wedding gift. Will you have time to squeeze in a Women, Inc. meeting?"

Wait. Matt paid for Addy's honeymoon?

"Matt sent Addy and Trey to the Galapagos?"

"Galapagos, Peru, and Ecuador. Twelve days. Pululahua Crater, Dragon Hill, Santa Cruz Island, Floreana Island, Lima, Sacred Valley, Machu Picchu, and Cuzco." Quinn highlighted Addy's honeymoon.

"Damn, girl, you got all that memorized?" Hadley laughed.

"It's Addy's dream vacation. How do you *not* have it memorized? She's only been talking about it since she was ten."

Matt paid for Addy's dream vacation.

He hadn't told the whole truth when I asked him if he liked being rich. He forgot to add he liked giving his friends their dream vacations.

"I'll pay one of you fifty dollars to run to the bakery around the corner and pick up a dozen donuts," I blurted out.

"Damn, girl, how many calories did you burn last night?" Shiloh asked.

"Fifty bucks? I'll go." Hadley pushed away from the counter.

Shit. I was a horrible hostess. We'd been standing in the kitchen huddled around the coffee maker that whole time.

"Should we go to the living room and sit?" I asked.

"Too late now," Liberty returned. "I have a feeling as soon as Hadley gets back, we're being kicked out. Refill your coffees now, ladies."

Shiloh was the first to move to the coffee pot, and as she walked by me, she bumped my shoulder with hers.

"Happy for you, Chels."

I had the best friends in the world. A devastating injury that I'd thought was going to end my career brought me to Addy. Through her, I'd met the rest of the women. A boon that the universe had given me—my first ever. A blessing that had led me to Matt. A windfall that had changed my life, given me a place to belong, a family.

My bank account would say otherwise, but I was rich beyond measure.

I had everything in life that was worth anything.

As soon as the girls left, I stripped off my clothes, left them in a pile on the living room floor, and grabbed the bag of donuts.

I opened the bedroom door and was happy to see Matt on his back asleep.

I climbed on top of him, and before I was settled, his hands were on my hips and he was smiling. But his eyes were still closed.

"They gone?" he asked.

His sexy morning voice did crazy things to me. It was rougher, deeper, scratchier.

"Yep."

I reached into the bag, pulled out a donut, and took a huge bite. Crumbs hit his bare chest and he cracked an eye open.

"Time for naked donuts," I told him.

Both of his eyes opened. His smile turned wicked. His hands moved from my hips up my ribs and finally stopped when he cupped my breasts.

I arched into his touch, losing interest in the doughy goodness I was attempting to swallow.

"You're getting crumbs in the bed."

"Are you gonna kick me out?"

"Fuck, no!"

"Then quit complaining and start eating."

I held the bag up in offering. Matt snatched it out of my hand, dropped it on the bed, and bucked me off his lap.

When he rolled on top of me, he paused to say, "It's a good thing you ride bulls, baby."

"Are you saying I ride bulls better than your cock, or are you saying I'm easy to get off? Because I'm all for testing—"

Matt's mouth lowered to my breast, his tongue circled my nipple, and I stopped speaking. When his mouth closed around the sensitive peak, my mind blanked. When his hand went between my legs, I groaned.

"You want my mouth or cock?" he asked.

Hm. That was a hard question. And in my current state, I couldn't think about which one I wanted more. Though there wasn't a wrong answer. I knew he'd made the decision for me when I felt the head of his cock tease my opening.

"Let's see how easy I can get you off."

Yes. Please.

Matt drove his hips forward, filling me with one long, hard stroke, and my breath caught.

I was home.

Here, my apartment, a hotel room in Connecticut. As long as I was with Matt, I was exactly where I needed to be.

My legs went around Matt's hips, my hands went to his ass, and my mouth went to his throat.

It took me a moment to catch my breath, but when I did, I told him, "I love the way you feel."

Matt groaned. His thrusts turned punishing and I held on.

"Love the way you feel, sweetheart."

"Fuck," he snarled.

He shifted his weight to his left elbow. His right hand went to the back of my thigh and he hitched my leg higher. When he had me where he wanted me, his hand stayed on my thigh. His pace turned brutal. I arched until my back was mostly off the bed, and I was as close to him as I could get.

Matt rolled, taking me with him. Our quick change of position meant I had to let go of his ass. This was unfortunate. He had a great ass. There was something erotic about holding onto it while he took me. The feel of the muscles tightening under my palms with each drive. But being on top gave me a better view. Not only of his chest and abs but his handsome face. I got to watch as he experienced pleasure. I didn't miss when his orgasm took him under.

My hands went to his chest and slid up to his broad shoulders. I took my time enjoying the feel of his warm skin under my palms.

"Ride me, Chels."

I slowly started to ride. Took my time with that, too, relishing the feel of him. Savoring every inch of his shaft as I slid up and down.

"Harder," he demanded.

His strong fingers dug into my hips and I rode him harder.

"Matt," I breathed.

"Lean back," he demanded. "Hands on my thighs."

I arched back and found his legs.

"Tip your head down and watch."

A shiver rolled through me, and excitement flooded my body. I loved when Matt got lost in his pleasure, and his demands got dirtier and dirtier. When his control snapped and he took me however he wanted, as rough and hard as he could. I loved knowing it was me, it was us coming together that pushed him beyond his constraint.

My head fell forward and I watched myself slide up Matt's cock then slam back down.

"Can you see how wet you are?"

"Yes," I groaned.

My belly warmed and my pussy contracted.

One of his hands left my hip. I braced for his touch, but it never came.

"I love you, baby," he said. My gaze sliced to his, and my breath arrested. "I love everything about you."

Before I could return the sentiment, his thumb circled my clit and my hips jerked.

"I love how you respond to my touch." Matt continued to circle, sending shards of pleasure through me. "I love how you wrap yourself around me." He added pressure to his circling. "I love how tight you get right before you come." Matt pressed harder and flexed his hips as I slammed down. "I love the way you look at me. I love the way you touch me. I love the way you kiss me. I love the way you taste. I love how much you love me. I love every fucking thing about you, Chelsea."

I'd vaguely heard the last of what Matt had said. In a

distant place in the back of my mind, I'd heard the words but couldn't comprehend their meaning. I was too far lost in Matt. Lost in him. Not what he was saying. Not what he was doing to my body. Just him. I was lost in a way that would never end. So lost that there was no way to find my way out. He'd consumed all of me. He'd made me believe I was strong and beautiful and capable. He'd proved it by loving me the way he did. Wholly and completely.

I heard Matt groan. I felt his cock twitch inside of me. I felt weightless and euphoric. I felt like I was floating, and the only thing anchoring me to earth was Matt.

"Jesus, baby," he growled.

Matt jackknifed up, wrapped his arms around me, and slammed his mouth on mine.

I kissed him through the rest of my orgasm. I tasted his on his tongue and groaned mine into his mouth.

When we came down, he was still kissing me. Slow and gentle, easing me back to reality. He broke the kiss, unwrapped his arms, and grabbed my face.

"You okay?"

I blinked at the insanity of his question. I'd just experienced the best orgasm of my life—an out-of-body event that had left me hollowed out, and he was asking me if I was alright.

"Yeah," I croaked. "Why?"

My throat felt scratchy and raw.

Matt's thumbs glided over my cheeks. His eyes stayed glued to mine, but they were full of concern.

"Baby, you're crying."

"Crying?"

I batted his hands away and felt my wet cheeks.

"Did I hurt you?"

"No," I rushed out.

Matt twisted and lowered us to the bed. The white donut bag momentarily caught my attention before Matt's hand went back to my face and he recaptured my attention.

"You sure?"

"Positive. You didn't hurt me. I didn't even know I was crying."

He was still staring at me with concern, and in an effort to put his mind at ease, I told him the truth.

"I was thinking about how much I love you. How overwhelming it is to know that you love me. How beautiful I feel when I'm with you. How powerful and strong. I was thinking how much I love the way you look at me when we make love. How much I love when you snap and get growly and say filthy things to me. I was lost in the moment and didn't know I was crying. It was like I blacked out for a moment—all I could do was feel."

"You believe me."

Matt wasn't asking. He knew I believed. I could tell by the gruffness in his tone. Yet, I still answered.

"I believe you."

He graced me with one of his megawatt smiles that lit his eyes.

Damn, I loved that smile.

"You blacked out, huh?"

"Don't be arrogant."

"Oh, baby, I'm not being arrogant. I'm being smug *as fuck*," he corrected. "And there's no way for me not to be. You fucked me so hard I couldn't breathe. And when your eyes glazed over—"

I put my hand over his mouth, effectively shutting him up, yet I still verbalized my demand.

"Shut it."

I felt him smile under my palm.

When I removed my hand, he asked, "Ready for naked donuts, special friend?"

"I'm afraid the donuts are toast."

Matt twisted and glanced over his shoulder. I didn't bother looking; I already knew the donuts had spilled out of the bag.

When Matt twisted back, he was laughing.

"There's strawberry filling on the sheets."

"Yep."

"If I would've known you'd planned on making such a mess, I would've kicked you out of bed."

"Liar."

"I might be serious. You seem allergic to laundry, and since I don't have a spare set of sheets, that means I have to wash them. I hate washing sheets and making beds."

Uh-oh. In a roundabout way, he'd mentioned my dirty clothes on the floor. But right then, addressing his aversion to making beds took precedence.

"You don't like making the bed?"

"I had years of room inspections. I can strip a bed and remake it with perfect, crisp corners in less than two minutes."

That was impossible.

"No, you can't."

"Bet."

"What's the wager?"

Without hesitation, he said, "If I win, you do your laundry, hang up your clothes in my closet, and move in with me. If I lose, you do your laundry, hang up your clothes in my closet, and we continue to play this game where I pretend I'm not slowly making you bring your clothes over with the intention of having you move in with me."

My heart was thumping so hard in my chest I was afraid

I was going to break a rib. Quinn was right. Matt had been slowly moving me in. I wanted to get out of bed and happy dance. I wanted to jump on top of him and kiss his handsome face. I wanted to get dressed, go buy more donuts, and bring them back so we could eat donuts naked to celebrate.

I didn't do any of those things.

There was a bet to be made.

So I made it.

"I accept your—"

I didn't finish my agreement. Matt rolled on top of *me* and kissed *my* face. Then he kissed other parts of me that he'd neglected during round one. I got his mouth on all the places I loved. And by the time my third orgasm of the morning was blistering through me, I had strawberry filling in my hair, and I was pretty certain the sheets were ruined.

20

"Yo." Logan poked his head in my office. "You busy?"

I looked up from my computer and took in my friend's wide smile.

There were days his happiness still took me by surprise. It wasn't that he'd been unhappy before, but there was something different about Logan since he'd asked Lauren to marry him.

"Nope, just finished the ammo order. What's up? And why are you smiling like that?"

"Got a phone call from my mom this morning. Ian asked her to marry him. She said yes."

I was wrong; there wasn't something different about Logan. *Everything* was different about him. It wasn't that long ago Logan's mom, sisters, and Ian Webster had come to Georgia for a visit. The trip had started with Logan having a shit hemorrhage his mother was dating again, and Logan had made his unhappiness known in a variety of ways. One of those ways was to straight-out tell Ian he wasn't pleased he was dating his mother. But somehow, Lauren had talked Logan around, and by the end of the trip

—which had been extended due to someone attempting to kill Logan and Lauren—Logan had accepted Ian. Logan had even given Ian his blessing to ask his mother to marry him.

I was actually surprised it had taken this long for Ian to ask.

"That's good news."

"The better news is, they're moving away from Bad Axe next year after he retires. They're thinking about Florida."

Indeed, that was better news. Logan hated Bad Axe. Hated that his mother and sisters still lived there after the horrors they'd gone through when Logan was a child. His disdain for the town had prevented him from visiting his mother and sisters with any sort of frequency.

"What about Jill and Jackie?"

Logan had three sisters. Unlike my sister, his were sweethearts; he was close to all of them.

"Jackie's still talking about moving to Georgia." Logan paused when he caught my smile. "Don't."

"Don't what?" I feigned innocence.

"Don't bring up her and Echo."

"I wouldn't dream of talking to you about your sister and Echo," I lied.

Shiloh's brother Echo was a standup guy. Much like Logan had done with his sisters after his father died, Echo had stepped up and raised his siblings after his father had gone to prison. The two men were very similar, and Jackie had taken a liking to Echo. Something had gone on between the two while Jackie was visiting, but neither of them had said what exactly that something was.

"She could do worse than Echo," I told him.

"That's you talking about it," he pointed out.

"Fine, I won't remind you that Echo's a good guy and

your sister deserves to be happy." I held up my hands in surrender.

When Logan didn't say anything, I asked, "Did you come in here to gossip, or did you need my help?"

"I was going to ask if you wanted to come with me to pick up the cameras I installed now that the Hecker case is closed and grab some lunch. But I'm reconsidering."

I glanced at my computer to make sure the order I'd sent had gone through. When I saw the confirmation screen, I logged out and pushed back from my desk.

"Where are you taking me for lunch?" I asked and nabbed my phone off my desk.

"The Thai place. But warning you—talk about the possibility that Echo nailed my sister and I'm punching you in the face."

The thought of Jackie and Echo doing the deed made me queasy.

"Brother, I've known Jackie a long time. She's like the little sister I wish I had. *I* don't wanna think about the possibility that Echo nailed her."

"So," Logan drawled. "Chelsea's moving in."

There was the real reason Logan had asked me to help him remove the cameras around Jayden Pickett's house. He hadn't needed my help. Logan had them disconnected and down in minutes without me doing a damn thing but standing there watching.

Now we were at the restaurant waiting for our lunch to be served and he'd finally asked what he'd wanted to know since he'd poked his head in my office an hour ago.

"Shocked it took you so long to ask," I said.

"Shocked I had to ask," he returned.

Damn, he actually looked hurt I hadn't told him.

I sat back in the chair and attempted to gather my thoughts. I wasn't sure how to explain why I hadn't said anything without sounding like a total idiot.

"You ever get the feeling something's too good to be true?"

"Every damn day when I wake up next to Lauren."

Jesus.

"I can't tell you how fuckin' pleased I am that you feel that."

"Not as pleased as I am."

Logan fell silent and waited for me to continue. Over the years, I'd closed myself off to everyone but my brothers. I'd never hidden who I was from them. Yet it was still uncomfortable voicing how I was feeling.

"She hasn't moved in yet," I started. "I didn't want to say anything until she moved in completely."

"Because you're afraid she'll back out?"

"No. Yes. I don't fucking know."

Logan eyed me skeptically, and asked, "What's really going on? Are you having second thoughts about her—"

"Hell, no," I interrupted him. "I want her to move in. I want to spend every minute I can with her. I'm exhausted working at TC all day then goin' to Balls Deep and staying there until close. But I can't stand the thought of her at the bar all night without me being there." I paused and shook my head. "And that makes me sound like I'm a pansy-ass."

"Six months ago, I would've agreed with that assessment. But now I get it, wanting to spend as much time with your woman as you can. I don't wanna piss you off, but shit's extreme for you right now. You're moving fast. And not with just asking her to move in."

I felt my temper start to simmer and had to remind myself that Logan was a good friend—the best. We'd been through all kinds of hell together. Had each other's backs when it mattered—life and death situations where you had to trust the other person to keep you alive.

But still, I warned, "You're pissing me off."

"Yeah, and I get why even though it's not my intention. I like Chelsea. So, I hope you get me asking you if you're sure you're ready for this is as much for me as it is for you."

I clenched my jaw and felt the muscles in my neck tighten.

"Pot, have you met kettle?" I ground out.

"Yeah, brother, I've met me, and I've also met you. Before Lauren, you and I were the same for different reasons. The difference is, when I met Lauren my life wasn't jacked-up."

"*Your* life wasn't jacked-up? Really?" I asked. It was a fucked-up question, and I knew it, but I was pissed as fuck. I didn't give him a chance to answer before I went on. "Yes, shit's extreme right now with my family. My dad's a fucking idiot and my sister's true colors are shining bright. I always thought she was a leech. Now I'm learning she's not only that but also a master manipulator. And it fucks me to admit this, but I underestimated her. She's more involved in Kessler than I thought. She's smarter than I gave her credit for. My mother's still not taking my calls, she's left my dad, and likely divorcing him. I don't know where she stands with Alessandra because she won't fuckin' talk to me. I don't know how the news that the CEO of one of the largest investment firms on the East Coast has been arrested hasn't hit the twenty-four-hour news cycle, but thankfully it hasn't. The feds have visited my home and questioned me. I've got a bad feeling in my gut about Mancini and Zanetti. I find it hard to believe they're just sitting back without a care after my dad's arrest. I gotta be ready for any move they make. So, yes, hell yes, shit's extreme. But that has fuckall to do with how I feel about Chelsea."

"You've got a bad feeling about Mancini and Zanetti?"

"You wouldn't? Zanetti's a mob boss. Mancini's whatever the hell he is, but no less tied to the mob. I don't know exactly how this shit works, but I'm thinking they're on edge wondering if my dad's gonna turn and rat them out. I don't see good things for my dad. But that's on him. He made those choices. But as far as I know, my mother's clean. I'm clean. And I don't want any fucking trouble."

"You know we've got your back."

"I know that. And I don't want to bring my father's shit down here and have any of you wrapped up in this."

"You love her."

Jesus.

"Yes, I love her. Christ, Logan, you said it yourself—I'm moving fast. What you didn't say was since you've known me I haven't invited a single woman to spend the night in my bed and I sure as hell don't sleep in theirs. Chelsea pulled that shit the first time we were together. She rolled out of my bed and left my ass lying there pissed as hell she was leaving. I didn't get it then. I should've been happy she was on board with a casual hook-up, but I was furious. Then days later I was still thinking about it. Lying in bed alone wondering why I'd been pissed but also why I was thinking about her at all. Why suddenly the thought of touching another woman that was not her made me sick. Wondering why her, what made her different, why couldn't I stop thinking about *her*. Then she let me in, just a tiny bit, and showed me a sliver of what she's hiding, and I understood why it was her. What made her different."

"She doesn't care about your money," he wrongly guessed.

"No, she doesn't. Actually, she couldn't care less about it. But that's not what makes her different. It's her determination and strength. It's her iron will to succeed. It's her ambition. The day I met Chelsea was the day I met the woman who would challenge me in every way. Chelsea doesn't settle. She sets her sights on something and makes it happen. *I need that*. I need to know the woman standing at my side is strong enough to fight life's battles with me. Chelsea will not only fight, but she'd battle to the death. She doesn't know any other way. The shit she's been through taught her that *nothing* comes easy. That's why I fell in love with her. That's how I know I want her to move in with me right now; today if possible. And that's why I'm going to do everything I can do to get her to say yes to marrying me as quickly as I can. And I don't give the first fuck if anyone thinks I'm moving too fast. I'm not a man prone to fucking around when I want something. I want Chelsea in my house, I want her to have my last name, and when she's ready I want her to carry my children."

Logan's gaze had gone from speculative to pensive.

"She's been through shit?"

I thought about how much information I wanted to divulge. If Chelsea hadn't shared about her past it wasn't my place to say anything.

"Yes. The kind of shit that could've broken her but instead it made her into a strong, determined woman. The kind of shit that you have firsthand knowledge of. Hers wasn't as bad, but I'm not sure there are various degrees of abuse. All of it is damaging."

"Her dad hit her?" Logan growled.

I didn't confirm. Not because I didn't trust Logan, but I'd given him all I was going to give.

"He say shit to her?"

Again, I didn't answer.

Logan blew out a breath, but none of the hardness left my friend's face.

"The man still alive?"

Unlike Logan's father who was dead, Chelsea's was alive and breathing.

"Yep."

"Are you gonna handle that?"

"Nope. Chelsea is."

I had all the faith in her that she was going to get to the rodeo in Omaha. And when she came out of the chute on the back of a bucking, twisting, jumping bull she was going to prove to herself she was never what her father said she was. If the man was there to witness it, all the better. But even if he wasn't, I sure as fuck would be.

"I'm pleased you found what you were looking for," Logan told me.

"Not as pleased as I am," I repeated his earlier words.

Logan chuckled and changed the subject.

"Dylan filled us in on Denny."

"Christ, that idiot's a douche bag. He grabbed one of the waitresses' asses. Chels rightfully lost her mind, but instead of getting me or Tony to toss him out, she did it."

"Heard she gave the asshole a titty twister."

I couldn't stop myself from smiling at the memory.

"I clocked him and Rod the minute they walked in. I didn't pay them much mind; that was my mistake. I know Denny's an asshole. I came out from the back and saw a commotion and it was like I knew Denny and Rod were causing trouble. I didn't think I'd hit their table and see Chels doing her best to tear his nipple off. But goddamn if she wasn't. He was howlin' in pain, and she was steadily twisting. When she let go, the stupid fuck lunged at her and found himself flat on his back. It was good luck Dylan had come in for a beer. Denny might've taken a swipe at me to save face, but he's not dumb enough to do it when I had backup."

"Do you think he's gonna cause trouble?"

"Denny's an asshole with a God complex, so who the hell knows. He wants to come at me, so be it. He thinks to fuck with Chels, I'll ruin him."

"I'll have a word with Ethan."

Ethan Lenox knew Denny well, hated him, and hated that the asshole worked at the same precinct he did.

"No need. I talked to Ethan this morning and gave him the heads up."

"What'd Ethan say?"

"He told me I should've called Denny's wife like I'd threatened. The problem with that is, Denny's wife is crazy and I didn't want my bar to be a crime scene. There's no guessing what she would've done, but I'm positive blood would've been shed, and I didn't want to have to close my bar for clean-up."

"You're not wrong."

I knew I wasn't. I'd met Denny's wife once and she had crazy eyes. The kind that said she'd stab you if you looked at her wrong. The two of them were a match made in hell.

21

Matt was going to be home any minute and I was running late.

Go figure.

I was running around the bedroom picking up my dirty clothes when there was a knock on the door. I shoved the clothes in the laundry hamper Matt had bought me—if that wasn't a hint, I didn't know what was—and dashed out of the bedroom.

Two weeks ago, I had officially moved in.

That was after Matt and I had our first fight. I wanted to pay half the mortgage and Matt wouldn't hear of it. That led to me reneging on our bet—and yes, he could make a bed with perfect corners in under two minutes. Matt had about lost his mind when I told him I wasn't moving in. Which in turn meant I lost mine when he told me I was. Thirty minutes later we came to an agreement; I would pay him what I was paying for my apartment, which was a few hundred dollars less than half the mortgage. Since I felt that he'd compromised from his initial argument that I was paying nothing, I gave in and agreed.

The next thirty minutes were spent arguing over utilities, which incidentally had been included in my apartment rent. Matt refused to allow me to pay half. So I made him a deal; he paid the utilities, I bought the groceries. I knew he was doing the mental math when it took him a few minutes of silence to agree. And he did with the caveat that he paid when we ordered in or went out. I sensed that this was nonnegotiable, and it didn't have to do with money per se, but it was Matt being the kind of man that paid for his girlfriend's dinner. I liked that he was the kind of man who wanted to do that. However, I was also the kind of woman who could and did take care of herself. There had to be a balance, and thankfully with Matt, I'd found that balance.

So, I'd moved in. I had a month-to-month lease and didn't have much to move. It took two trips with Matt's truck and mine. It was almost embarrassing to admit that the majority of my stuff was my riding gear. Matt had a huge walk-in closet and had reorganized to give me half; it was a generous gesture but only affirmed how little I had when my clothes only took up less than a fourth of what he'd given me.

Right as I made it to the door there was another knock.

I opened the door, and I froze.

I wasn't expecting anyone, therefore, I shouldn't have been shocked when a well-dressed woman was standing on the porch. But I was shocked.

It wasn't frequent that one or more of our friends showed up at our house unannounced, but it wasn't unheard of. However, a total stranger had never knocked. And by the way the woman was dressed, I knew she wasn't a neighbor. Matt's house was in a nice neighborhood, but it was firmly middle-class. This woman didn't scream money, she was far too elegant for that. She oozed money from her very existence.

"May I help you?' I asked.

"I'm looking for my son."

Even her voice sounded classy.

"Your son?"

"Matthew Kessler. Is he home?"

Well, hells bells, this is Matt's mom.

The mother who had been avoiding his calls now for a month and a half. Forget that I knew she came from a wealthy family—her husband only adding to that affluent lifestyle—this was Matt's mother. My boyfriend's mother who I was meeting for the first time, in filthy jeans and a t-shirt that I was sure was equally as dirty seeing as I'd just gotten home from training and had been more concerned about picking up the clothes I'd left scattered on the bedroom floor than taking a shower and getting ready to go to dinner.

Which was what I was running late for.

A date with Matt.

And now his mother was here.

Shit on a shingle.

"He's not here, but please come in."

"Are you sure? I wouldn't want to impose," she softly replied.

"Please, Mrs. Kessler, come in. It's no imposition at all." I stepped to the side and held open the door. "Matt should be home any minute. I know he'll be happy to see you."

Or at least I hoped he was happy. He sounded pretty damn upset the last time he left his mom a voice mail.

"Please, call me Ginny," she offered. "And you are?"

I felt my cheeks heat at my folly.

"Chelsea Sullens," I introduced myself and closed the

door. "Please sit down. Would you like something to drink? I'm afraid all we have is water and soda. Or I could make coffee if you'd like."

"A Pepsi would be wonderful if you have one."

"You're in luck. That's what Matt drinks."

Jeez, why am I smiling so big over a Pepsi?

I attempted to tone down my idiocy by rushing to the kitchen. Which only made me more of a fool, but I needed a moment to get my heart rate under control. I had never met a boyfriend's mother before. And it would be a gross understatement to say that meeting Matt's dad had been uncomfortable and meeting his sister disastrous. But I'd had Matt by my side, and my discomfort hadn't mattered when his was a hundred times worse than mine. Now, I was facing his mother by myself, and I didn't want to embarrass Matt.

I stopped at the fridge and found Ginny had followed me into the kitchen. So much for gathering my thoughts.

"How was your trip down to Georgia?" I lamely asked.

"It was fine, dear. Thank you for asking."

I pulled a Pepsi out and thought of something else to say. When I opened the cupboard to get down a glass, Ginny stopped me.

"No need to dirty a glass. The can is fine."

"Are you sure?"

"Yes, Chelsea."

I woodenly handed her the can not knowing what to do next. I heard the garage door go up and relief washed over me like a tidal wave.

Thank God, Matt was home.

"Matt's home," I chirped cheerfully.

I fought the urge to cover my mouth to prevent myself from saying any more words.

"Perhaps it would be a good idea for you to warn him I'm here," she suggested.

While her suggestion held validity, I didn't get the chance. The door opened and Matt walked in. The moment he saw his mother he rocked to a halt and his jaw clenched.

"How nice of you to call," he snapped.

"Matt," I whispered.

"Almost two months, over twenty phone calls, twice as many text messages, and five emails," he rattled off. "Not one message returned."

"I'm sorry, Matthew. I needed time."

"You don't say," he bit out sarcastically.

Ginny's gaze came to me and I felt sorry for the woman. She genuinely looked like she was struggling.

"Why don't you two go sit down?" I suggested.

"Chelsea knows, Mother. She knew everything before I took her with me to meet with Father and Roland."

"That's good you had Chelsea there with you. I'm sure the meeting was unpleasant."

"Are you joking?" he exploded. "Unpleasant. It was a nightmare and that was before Alessandra offered my girlfriend money to get me to move back to Connecticut. Then it turned ugly. And we haven't even gotten to the part where my sister told me she hated me."

All the color drained from Ginny's face, and she reached for the edge of the counter.

"My God," she breathed.

"Where were you?" Matt pushed. "Why weren't you there?"

Matt's mom looked gutted. I hated that for her, but more, I didn't like the pain I heard in my man's tone. I crossed the kitchen and wrapped my arms around Matt, tucking myself under his arm.

"I'm okay," he told me.

I nodded against his chest but didn't let go.

"Really, Chels, I'm okay, baby."

"Okay," I agreed, even though I knew he wasn't, and I didn't let go.

Matt's mom watched our exchange. Her face was still devoid of color, her expression wounded, her eyes sad.

"I always wanted that for you," Ginny said softly.

"I don't know what to say to that," Matt replied.

"There's nothing to say, Matthew, except I'm happy to see it."

An uncomfortable silence fell over the room. Ginny looked like she was trying to figure out how to salvage the reunion that had not started off well and Matt was silently waiting her out. If I hadn't been pressed to his side feeling his heart pound in his chest, I'd say he looked bored. But he was anything but. His muscles were strung tight and he was controlling his breathing, taking long, deep inhales and slowly exhaling. The quiet grew awkward and I was worried that if Ginny didn't start explaining herself soon, Matt would ask her to leave.

"I contacted the FBI and turned your father in." Ginny's whisper was barely above non-audible, but I knew Matt heard. I felt him suck in a breath—actually felt the air rush over my face— and I heard the gasp.

"Say that again," he demanded even though he didn't need his mother to repeat herself.

He'd heard her.

He'd felt her words to his core. I knew because he gave me his weight and my legs were struggling to keep us standing.

"I had no choice. Not when I found out how deep he was, how deep Alessandra had followed him down into the dregs. I couldn't save your dad, but I had to save my daughter."

"Jesus Christ."

Matt pulled away from me. The swiftness of his movement left me swaying to catch my balance.

"Jesus Christ," he repeated. "And you didn't think to call me?"

"No!" Ginny's denial was emphatic. She let go of the counter and squared her shoulders readying herself for the brunt of Matt's anger.

"No?"

"I didn't want you involved in any way, Matthew."

"Mom—"

"I've been married to your father for over four decades," Ginny strangely pointed out. "This has been going on for over half of our marriage. Imagine my embarrassment when I found out. Imagine my shame in not knowing that the father of my children is a frontman for the mob. Imagine my horror when I realized that my husband has allowed my daughter to become involved. I could not risk you becoming entangled in anything having to do with your father. I knew you were safe down here in Georgia. You were blissfully unaware, and I needed you to remain that way."

"Fucking hell!" Matt shouted and left the kitchen.

Did I follow him?

Let him cool off?

Take care of Ginny?

My eyes were bouncing back and forth between Matt's back and Ginny's grief-stricken form.

"Ginny?" I called. "Please come with me into the living room and sit down."

"You should go to him."

"I will as soon as I know you're sitting down." Matt's

mother looked like she was going to argue so I rushed on to tell her, "I would like to go check on Matt, but I can't do that until I know you're okay. Please, Ginny, I'm begging you to go into the living room and sit."

She stared at me for a moment, then thankfully she walked to the living room. As soon as her tailored slacks-covered rear-end hit the couch cushion I beelined it to the bedroom.

When I entered I found Matt pacing.

"What do you need from me?" I asked.

Matt didn't stop prowling around the room but his gaze cut to me. He looked like a pissed-off caged lion with a scowl so deep I was afraid his frown would be permanently etched onto his face.

"Can you believe that shit?" he spat.

"Yes."

"Yes?"

"I don't have a mother that loves me. So I can't know for sure, but I reckon that's what a mother who loves her son does."

"What?"

His large frame jerked to an abrupt halt. When his furious eyes zeroed in on me, I felt a tremble roll through me. I'd never seen another person so angry and that included my father before he'd turned me out with a leather strap.

"She was protecting you. That's what a mother is supposed to do, Matt. And she's right; if she would've told you, you would've flown to Connecticut immediately. You would've gotten involved. Then what? Those mob guys come after you? You confront your father? How does that help? Your mother did what she had to do to ensure your safety."

Matt's eyes closed and his head bowed.

"What am I supposed to do with this?"

"Are you angry with her for turning your dad in?"

"Fuck, no."

I didn't think he was, but it was good to have his confirmation.

"Then you take a moment to process the news that your mother loves you very much. Though I think you already knew that."

I hated, loathed, despised seeing my big strong man with his head tipped down. It was unnatural. It was all sorts of wrong. The sight of him in so much pain made my heart break.

"I love you, Matt. I wish there was something I could do to take away what you're feeling."

Matt stepped back and when the back of his legs hit the bed, he sat with his shoulders hunched forward.

I could take no more.

I made my way to the bed and when I was within reaching distance, his hands went to my hips and he yanked me between his open knees. His forehead went to my chest, his fingers dug in, his legs closed around my thighs, and he held onto me. My hands went around him, and I held on just as tightly.

We stayed like that for a long time.

Long enough for me to wonder what would've happened if my mom had loved me half as much as Ginny loved Matt. Would she have saved me from one of my dad's beatings? Would she have stepped in when he was yelling at me telling me I was worthless? Would she have gone with me when my dad kicked me out? Or given me money so I hadn't gone hungry?

We stayed like that long enough for the muscles in my arms to start burning.

But I didn't let go.

Long enough that I felt Matt relax.

"Thank you," he said without lifting his head.

"For what?"

"For this."

I love the way you hold me.

Matt raised his head and some of the redness had gone out of his face, but he still looked troubled. I unwrapped my arms, brought my hands to his face, and smoothed the grooves in his forehead with my thumbs.

"Everything's gonna be okay," I told him.

"How do you know?"

"Because it has to be."

He gave me a small, indulgent smile.

"I know everything will be okay because if your father pleads guilty, and your mother does whatever it is your mother's going to do, we'll still have each other. When your sister stops being a pain in your ass, and you leave Kessler Management behind, we'll still have each other. When things settle down and it's just you and me and TC and Balls Deep and my riding, we'll still have each other. No matter what, we have each other."

Matt's eyes drifted closed and when they opened, they were gentle.

"I want you to marry me," he whispered.

Thankfully he was still holding onto me, or my knees would've buckled.

"I know you do," I teased.

"Are you gonna marry me, Chels?"

"Are you asking me, or are you asking in preparation to ask, so you'll know the answer before you waste a proposal?"

I watched Matt's lips tip up into a smile. Having a mind of its own, my hand dropped to his cheek and my thumb traced the curve of his smile. Under my palm, I could feel the late-afternoon stubble. It wasn't profuse, but it would only take a day or two without shaving for him to grow a beard. I'd seen pictures of Matt and the guys in battle gear from when they were deployed. They all had thick beards. Matt had called it "going full native." Facial hair was something I could give or take. Matt looked hot with a beard, but he looked hot without one, too.

My mind had wandered to how Matt's beard would feel against my inner thighs when he turned his head and placed a kiss in my palm.

"Is my proposal allowed to be douchey?" he asked.

"How douchey?"

"Billboard?"

"No."

"Skywriting?"

"Hard no."

"A destination—"

"No."

Matt chuckled and my heart filled with happiness.

"Do I at least get to make it romantic? Candlelight, wine, soft music?"

I scrunched my nose.

Matt's burst of laughter bounced off the walls and reverberated through me.

It was then I finally smiled.

"No romance. No billboards, skywriting, or destination proposals. Got it. But fair warning. I'm not giving in on the ring. It's gonna be big, it's gonna make a statement, it's gonna border on the edge of too much. I'll make sure you have a band to wear when you ride, but when we're out and you've got your diamonds on your finger you will never forget you are mine."

I was a little nervous about what Matt's definition of too much was. I was certain our classifications on the matter wouldn't align. But I'd happily wear his ring even if it was a boulder on my finger.

"I don't need any reminders that I'm yours," I whispered.

"Refreshing."

"Matt—"

"There will be things I need to do," he said, cutting me off. "Things that I want to do to take care of you. Some of them will be small. Some of them douchey because I can, because I have the money. Some of them will be for you. Some will be for me. The diamonds I give you will be for me. I want to see them on the base of your finger and know that I put them there. But more than that, I want to see them and know they are there on your finger because you love me. Because you are my wife. Because I'm your husband."

I had no idea how I'd gotten so lucky, but I wasn't about to start questioning my good fortune now. I had no idea how this amazing man had fallen in love with me, and I wasn't dumb enough to ask him why he had. And because he did, because he could be open and patient with me, I wasn't afraid. Matt wouldn't allow me to fall in love with him only to take himself away. He wouldn't hurt me. He wouldn't abandon me.

But still, I wouldn't be me if I didn't give him sass.

"Will these diamonds cost more than a car?"

"Likely yes."

"Are we talking more than a Prius or Lincoln Navigator?"

"Somewhere in the middle."

I hid my shock and went on. "And when I need to do things for you, you'll let me?"

"Absolutely."

I had a feeling he was only saying that because he knew I wouldn't be able to afford to buy him anything that cost more than a luxury ride. But I let his quick acceptance slide.

"But just to say, baby, you giving me you is all I'll ever need. That's the best gift you will ever give me. Even after you give me children. They will be a blessing. But you will always be the gift."

It sucked that he was better at that than me. Matt always knew exactly what to say at exactly the right time. He was like a commando poet, and I was beginning to have an inferiority complex that he could be flowery and romantic, and I was terrible at it.

"Then, yes, I will marry you when you ask me."

"Jesus," he muttered, and his head fell forward.

Once again, his forehead was against my chest and his arms wrapped around my middle.

"And I'll give you children one day," I continued. "I'm teaching our girls they can be anything they want to be, and our boys will know that their momma will always protect them."

"Damn right," he growled.

"And I promise the only thing I'll ever ask you to give me is you. That's all I want. Just you. I love *you,* not the first-class rides, not the helicopters, not the diamonds. As long as you promise you know that, knock yourself out. Be as douchey as you wanna be, but I might give you shit if you start chartering yachts."

"But not jets?"

"Jets, too."

"What about a safari?"

Now that sounded like a badass vacation.

"Maybe after we have kids and they're old enough to enjoy it."

"You do know, we could go on more than one."

"Douchey," I mumbled.

Once again, my heart soared when Matt's laughter filled the room.

22

"Silas informed me you're selling your shares in Kessler."

We were in the formal living room. Chelsea was next to me on the couch, my mother across from us in one of the two chairs that had been arranged in front of the big picture window. I'd never sat in this room before. My ass had never sat on this couch and seeing as it was as hard as a stack of bricks, I wouldn't ever sit on it again. The family room was much more comfortable, the couch worn-in and soft. The recliner was overstuffed. But the layout wasn't conducive for a discussion when you wanted to look at the other person.

Chelsea had suggested the front room would be more comfortable than sitting at the dining room table. She was wrong. I was debating whether or not I was going to call goodwill and donate the couch when Chelsea's knee nudged mine.

Right, my mother.

"I am," I confirmed. "I retained Peterburg and Associates to represent me."

"Silas will be taking over for your father as CEO. The board approved the change."

Silas Lowman had been working for Kessler for twenty-plus years. He started as a financial advisor. Five years later he moved to wealth management and took over some of Kessler's highest-earning accounts. He'd made another move to his current role as chief operating officer about ten years ago. I was indifferent about the man just as I was about his move to CEO.

"I'm sure he'll do fine."

My mother's brows pinched together at my blasé attitude. But really, what had she expected? I was selling out. I wanted nothing to do with Kessler's management of the pile of shit my father had left in his wake. I wanted to wash my hands of all of it.

"I would like you to reconsider."

"Why?"

My mother's face smoothed and it struck me how at her age she was still very beautiful. Her beauty wasn't enhanced by injections and plastic surgery. She was aging but doing so gracefully. She still dressed the way she always had—classy but not extravagant. Her jewelry had always been understated and tasteful. Unlike her peers who I'd always found to be pretentious and on the bitchy side. They were all about flash and brazen, gaudy displays of wealth. My mother had never been like that, even though she could've outshined any of the women she associated with.

"Your grandfather started Kessler. I understand you never had a desire to be involved in the day-to-day operations. I knew when you were a child you were meant for bigger adventures. I knew you'd grow into a man who wouldn't find pleasure in managing other people's money. You needed a purpose. You needed to do something of value, make a difference. And I was correct, you grew into that man and then some. You've far exceeded any dream I could've had for you. But you are still a Kessler. And while right now that might be distasteful to you, it is still true.

"Your grandfather was a good man. He worked hard every day of his life. He did so with unmatched integrity. Kessler Management meant something to Branson. He understood the responsibility and duty he had to his clients. He understood the value of a dollar and how hard the people who trusted him with their money worked to earn it. He took that seriously. He appreciated his success and he learned from his failures."

An ache in my chest grew with every word my mother said about my grandfather. They were all true. My grandfather would die a thousand painful deaths if he'd been alive to witness what his son had done. How far my father had fallen.

All in the name of greed.

My father had hundreds of millions of dollars. He was not, and had never been, without money. He hadn't needed to work hard to make ends meet. He hadn't had to stress and wonder how he was going to feed his family. He'd never had to hustle to make a buck to put a roof over our heads. He was a goddamned multi-millionaire who lived in a mansion on an estate that ninety-nine percent of the world's population couldn't afford. He was the one percent. Yet that wasn't good enough for him.

Gluttonous bastard.

"I know you hate when people tell you Kessler is your birthright," my mother went on, and I felt my jaw clench. "But it is. It is your legacy. It is something you can give to your children. A reminder that a true Kessler is honest, hardworking, resilient. A true Kessler overcomes. Don't allow your father's shortcomings to rob your children of their great-grandfather. It will be all they have of him. His bequest to them through you. I am not asking you this because there's money to be made. The money is utterly worthless. But Branson Kessler was priceless."

Suddenly my emotions were all over the place. Or maybe it wasn't so suddenly. For weeks now I'd vacillated between anger and hurt. I was undecided if I hated my father, or I still loved him. One second, I was pissed at my mother for not returning my calls, but the next moment anger turned into concern.

I didn't want one thing to do with Kessler Management. Yet, I didn't want to give up my grandfather's company. I wanted it to remain in the family. Even if I didn't participate, a Kessler would still own shares. It would still remain in the Kessler family's control.

"I want Dad's shares," I told my mother. "I'll buy them for a dollar a share. I want Alessandra's, too. I'll give her full market value. And with her shares, I want her resignation."

Chelsea squeezed her hand on my thigh. I unclasped my hands and dropped one over hers. She immediately twisted her wrist and twined our fingers together. It wasn't lost on me that my mother had been watching Chelsea and me since we'd come out of my bedroom. And now with my mother's gaze studying our hands, I wondered what she was thinking. Given the chance, my mother would love Chelsea. Though, she'd likely need a stiff drink after she found out Chelsea rode broncs. And learning she also rode bulls might give my mother a heart attack. But once the shock wore off, my mother would see exactly what I saw in Chelsea.

Determination. Purpose. Grit. Integrity. Hard work. Commitment. Fortitude.

Chelsea was a Kessler.

All the good parts of who we were as a family.

I didn't need to let that set in. I didn't need to assess my feelings. I didn't need to reconcile my thoughts.

My heart had known long before my brain had caught up.

From the start, I knew who she was.

Chelsea wasn't born to be mine. She'd been born to do great things. She'd been forged through hardship. She'd been shaped into a strong, beautiful woman. I was simply the man who was lucky enough to stand by her side.

"I'll contact Peterburg and ask him to draft the documents," I continued. "I'll speak to Silas. I want the majority share, but I will not be offering any input. He knows the business, I do not. I also will not be participating in monthly meetings. I will review the minutes and vote on anything that I feel would move Grandfather's company in a direction I don't like. But I have a life down here and I have a full-time job."

"And you recently purchased a billiards room," my mother supplied.

"It's a bar and pool hall," I corrected. "But, yes, I did."

I wasn't surprised my mother knew about Balls Deep. She'd always made it her business to know what the family was doing. Which made how my father had kept his criminal activity a secret all the more surprising.

"How did you find out about Dad and Zanetti?"

My mother's posture immediately stiffened.

"I was having lunch with Sofia at Mancini's. She asked me if I'd seen the remodel on the building in White Plains. Obviously, I had no idea what she was speaking about, but she thought I did. Before I could ask her about it, she went on to tell me how pleased Arnie was that the business was booming. I thought she'd meant the restaurant business. She was not. And as she continued to speak about the profits and bonuses both Arnie and your father were receiving from Mr. Zanetti, I played along. I pretended I knew what she was talking about. I don't know why she'd never spoken to me about it before then, but she hadn't. That day, she was quite excited and talked and talked. I left lunch feeling sick to my stomach. I didn't want to believe your father was doing business with a man I very well knew was involved in organized crime."

My mother paused. Her eyes locked with mine and I saw the same disbelief and anger I felt staring back at me.

"I did not know, Matthew. He hid it very well. Layers deep under shell companies that I'd never heard of. He had accounts that I was not aware of. He hadn't used Mr. Huston in these business dealings, though even if he did, I'm uncertain Roland would've informed me."

My mom paused and looked over at Chelsea who'd been silent since we'd sat down.

"I should've known," my mother declared.

"How *would* you have known?" Chelsea inquired.

"Only a senseless woman doesn't keep track of her family's finances."

"I agree with you," Chelsea allowed. "However, she can only keep track of what she knows about. You are not responsible for Vernon's deceit. You are not a private investigator. You are a wife."

"Not for long," my mother countered.

I didn't have time to process how I felt about my parents' impending divorce before Chelsea continued.

"I'm not sure if at this juncture it's appropriate for me to offer you my condolences or my well-wishes of a life free of the man who cared so little about his family, he'd put them in harm's way."

My mother tensed before she smiled.

"Well-wishes are in order, dear. I've had more than a year to come to terms with the demise of my marriage. As it turns out, the man I am divorcing is not the same man I married. Though I'm sure that's the case in most divorces. In my heart, I separated from Vern the day the private investigator I hired—since you are correct, I am not one—brought me the evidence that laid out the life of a man I did not know. For more than half my marriage Vernon had been keeping secrets. Betrayals that cut deeply. I would've simply walked away had Mr. Zanetti not been involved. But I needed to protect my children. Alessandra's participation needed to be severed."

Alessandra.

The apple hadn't fallen far from the greed tree.

"Dad said you weren't returning my calls because you didn't believe I wasn't involved."

"That is ridiculous," my mother spat. "I knew you had nothing to do with your father's activities. I didn't return your calls because I wasn't ready to face you and tell you what I'd done."

"What exactly did you do?"

"I searched your father's office. Thirty years of my naïveté had made him complacent. Or perhaps he had always been brazen and I had simply been ignorant. Whichever the case, he had files in his desk. I found a contract for a two-million-dollar overhaul on the property Sophia had been speaking about. A property I hadn't known your father owned. That was when I knew she'd been telling the truth. Not only would I have noticed two million dollars leaving one of our accounts, but I would've had to approve an expenditure of that size. I checked the safe and found property deeds I hadn't known your father had purchased and bank statements on accounts I hadn't known he had. I made copies of everything and approached the FBI. Your father had been under investigation for years, but they didn't have enough to make an arrest."

"When the FBI questioned me, they didn't ask about Alessandra," I told my mom.

"Because nothing is in her name. It's not illegal to share a meal with a mob boss. It's not against the law to have lunch with degenerates and criminals."

"No, but collusion and conspiracy are," I pointed out.

My mother's shoulders slumped, an undignified pose I'd never seen her execute. My mother didn't hang her head. She didn't drop her gaze in shame.

"As part of the guilty plea your father has submitted to the court, he has sworn he acted alone. His testimony will be that you, Alessandra, and I had no knowledge of his criminal behavior. He's denied any dealings with Mr. Zanetti outside of the investment accounts he managed. The same with Arnie and Sofia."

"And the feds believed that load of shit?" I spat.

"Yes. The feds have the evidence I gave them, which implicates your father and one low-level mob man. Forgive me for not knowing the correct terminology. They have phone conversations between your father and this man making arrangements to pick up and drop off money. They have recordings of your father discussing gambling and about how he intends to launder the money. After years of being denied a warrant for a wiretap, as the sole owner of the cellular account, I gave my permission to the FBI to listen to those calls. They have photos of your father eating lunch with Mr. Zanetti but as your father has explained those lunches were to discuss legitimate business dealings. They have the names of the shell corporations and the property these companies own. Upon searching, they found stacks of currency. They have pictures of your sister meeting with a variety of unsavory characters but as your father swore to, Alessandra was there on Kessler's behalf to recruit new accounts and did not know who these men were prior to the business meetings."

Bullshit. All of it was total fucking shit.

"And you're okay with all of that? Zanetti and Mancini are dirty. Alessandra played a part. I'm not defending Dad. He's guilty, I'm glad he confessed. But the rest of it is shit!"

My mother gathered her composure and once again she was sitting upright with her shoulders back, posture perfect, regal, the way she'd always presented herself.

"Yes, Matthew, I am *okay* with all of that. As long as you and your sister are protected, I am *okay* with your father serving however long his sentence is determined to be in prison. I am okay with Mr. Zanetti, Arnie, and Sofia not being charged. I am okay with them walking free as long as their walk doesn't cross paths with my family. The alternative would be your father gives the FBI whatever information he has on Mr. Zanetti, and you and Alessandra will live the rest of your lives with a target on your back. That I find *that* unacceptable. That I will not allow. One day you will understand the love a parent has for their child. It will be then when you come to the understanding there is nothing you will not do to keep them safe."

My mother ended her explanation by looking at Chelsea.

I'd gotten what I needed from my mother, and since I wasn't ready to discuss her divorcing my father, and I was way over talking about my father, and I didn't want to think about the shit my sister had pulled, I decided I was done with the current conversation.

"I'm glad you're here, Mom. I should've told you that sooner."

Slowly my mother's gaze came back to me and just as slowly she smiled.

"Yes, well, I took some weeks to gather my wits before I could face you. I think I can forgive your poor manners. Just this once."

Next to me, Chelsea chuckled, and across from me, my mother winked.

"Now that all of the unpleasantness is out of the way," my mother started, "I want to hear all about how you two met."

Chelsea's body stiffened and her hand in mine twitched.

"I met Chelsea when she came to Triple Canopy for physical therapy."

"Oh, dear. How did you injure yourself?"

I looked at my lap and pinched my lips.

Here we go.

"I was bucked off a bull," she mumbled.

"A bull! What on earth were you doing on a bull? Good heavens, those beasts can kill you. You're lucky to be alive."

"Chelsea rides roughstock in the rodeo," I proudly announced.

"I don't know what that means."

"It means she rides bucking broncs."

"Good Lord, I think I need a brandy."

Called that one.

"And she rides bulls."

My mother's right hand came off of her lap. She covered her heart and very loudly announced, "Sweet mother of pearl. I think I'm having a heart attack."

Yep. Called that, too.

"She's excellent. You should see her ride."

"She most certainly is excellent," my mother agreed. "And thank you for the invitation, I think I'd very much like to watch a rodeo. I've never been." My mother's gaze roamed to Chelsea before she smiled. "Do you also like to ride horses?"

"Yes," Chelsea beamed. "I have two mares. Rebel's a retired barrel racer and Gypsy's a retired jumper. I board them just out of town at my trainer's ranch."

"Did Matthew tell you he's an accomplished rider?"

"Mom—"

"He didn't tell me, but we've ridden together, yes. If he'd told me how good he was I might not've bet him I could beat him in a race."

"Matthew. It's rude to show off."

"Mom, what she's not telling you is she's a champion barrel racer. I barely beat her. She's far better than I am."

Chelsea knocked me with her shoulder.

"That's not true. I'm not better than you."

"Baby, you are."

Chelsea shook her head and looked at my mom.

"He's just being nice."

"If there is ever a time when my son isn't nice to you, call me." My mother clapped her hands together and inquired, "Now, it's getting late. Should we go out or stay in for dinner?"

"You two should go out. Have some mother-son time."

"Nonsense. As much as I love spending time with my son, and he doesn't come visit me as much as he should, I'm much more interested in getting to know you."

"Oh. I'm...trust me, I'm not that interesting."

"I don't believe that to be correct. My son wouldn't have waited all these years to settle for an uninteresting woman. As I knew my son was destined to do great things, I also knew he was fated to find a woman who challenged him. Matthew does not do boring things. He does not remain still while the world spins around him. So, forgive me, Chelsea, but I do not believe you are anything less than extraordinary."

Yes.

That summed up Chelsea.

Extraordinary.

Remarkable in every way.

23

"Listen to me, Alessandra," Matt clipped over the phone. "You don't want this to turn nasty. I'm offering you half a million dollars for your five shares."

There was a pause and I nearly choked.

Five hundred thousand dollars for five shares.

"Market capitalization is not valued at six-hundred and fifty billion and you damn well know it."

Did he just say billion?

It had been three days since Ginny's visit. Four days until Athens. I had been training and working so many hours a day the only time I saw Matt was at Balls Deep. It was a Tuesday, and I was surprised Matt was home from TC early. Unfortunately, when he'd walked in he was on the phone with his sister and I was getting ready to walk out the door to go to work.

I was going to be late if I didn't leave now. However, Matt looked like he was ready to detonate so I didn't want to leave until I had a chance to talk to him.

"No shit you got the papers from Peterburg," he growled. "I figured as much when you called. My offer is nonnegotiable. Half a million and your resignation." There was a moment of silence, during which Matt's eyes got squintier and squintier. "Yes, Alessandra, I got the same call from Roland. I'm aware that Dad was sentenced and will spend the next ten years in jail. In my opinion he got off light, he was facing twenty. And yes, I know what his fine is. The good news is our mother is self-sufficient and has maintained her own money throughout their marriage and her lifestyle will not suffer. She does not want that monstrosity of a house, and if you paid even a little bit of attention, you'd know that she never liked it. She always preferred the cottage. So that's where she's going to live. If you have blown through the *massive* fortune you were generously given, I'm offering you five-hundred thousand dollars. I'm confident you won't go hungry."

Massive?

"Right. Fight me. I don't give a fuck. Silas is restructuring and I think by next week you'll find yourself jobless. When you come back and want to sell your shares, I'll give you fifty thousand for all five. Take it or leave it," Matt growled and shook his head. "Yeah, you've said that before. You can repeat it as many times as you want, but you forget, I hold all the cards. So pitch your fit, make all the threats you want, but there is not one single thing you can do to hurt me. However, I can ruin you."

Matt pulled his phone away from his ear and disconnected the call.

"Jesus, she's a bitch."

Did he think I was going to argue with him?

"Hey," I said softly.

"Hey." Matt blew out a breath and smiled. "Sorry to come in here yelling. She called when I was pulling into the driveway."

It was his house, he could yell the roof down if he wanted. Well, as long as he wasn't yelling at me, he could. Not that I thought he'd ever shout at me. Surprisingly we didn't argue. Which was a feat considering we were so much alike, and I was pretty much as stubborn as they came. Matt didn't even complain that I'd yet to catch on how to use a clothes hamper. He just picked up my clothes if he wanted them off the floor or waited for me to do it. And since Matt was damn near perfect, he didn't have any bad habits that annoyed me, though that was annoying in and of itself.

"What are you doing home early?"

"I asked Tony if he and Karen would cover the bar tonight so you could have the night off."

I spoke too soon.

"What?"

"You've been working your ass off at the bar and training," he said.

"Yeah, Matt. That's what I do. I work my ass off. I need to train but I also need a paycheck."

"You also need to rest and you haven't scheduled yourself a day off until the day we leave for Athens."

I felt it happen. My temper flared and my mouth ran away without me thinking what was coming out of it.

"So you took it upon yourself to give me the night off."

"Yep."

Yep?

Just yep?

"What the fuck? You don't get to do that. I have a job. And so help me God, if you tell me you own the bar and can do whatever you want to do, I'll quit."

Matt clamped his mouth shut and my eyes turned into slits as I stared at his lips.

He *was* going to tell me he can do whatever he wants.

That was freaking infuriating.

"Baby, you're killing yourself."

"No, I'm not. To take days off I have to make them up before I leave."

"Okay, how about this? I want to spend more than a few hours a night with you. I want to see you when you're not dead on your feet and falling face-first into bed. I want—"

"This isn't about what you want, Matt."

His upper body jerked back like I'd struck him.

"It's not?"

"No, it's about what I have to do to survive. I have to work to pay my bills. I need money for gas and food to go to Athens. You know I don't have a sponsor this year, which means I pay all my entrance fees. I pay to replace old gear. I pay for everything. But beyond that, I made a commitment. I don't get to shirk my responsibilities because my boyfriend's my boss."

"Yeah, baby, you also made a commitment, *to us*. A relationship is about what you want, what I want, and what both of us need. And what I want isn't so much about me but about what I want for you. You cannot perform at your best if you're dog-ass tired. You won't be on your game if you're running on three hours' sleep a night. And I say this with all honesty, I want you riding your best in Athens. I want you to score the points you need. But fuck, Chelsea, I don't want you getting hurt."

He was wrong: I was running on *four* hours' worth of sleep. But I was used to it.

"I don't like you going behind my back."

"And I don't like you not taking the time to ice your muscles before you rush home to change and leave for the bar."

How did he know I wasn't icing down my shoulder for as long as I should?

"What? You're not gonna ask how I know?"

I didn't appreciate his sarcasm but more, I didn't like how easily he could read me.

I scratched that onto the list of annoying bad habits Matt had right under him making decisions without consulting me first. And while I was at it, I might as well add that Matt being my boss meant he could change my schedule without my permission.

"Three nights in a row I've watched you wince when you move your arm," he told me instead of waiting for my answer.

Which was good because I'd decided I wasn't speaking to him.

"You need an early night. You need to sleep. And you need to rest your shoulder."

He was right, but I wasn't going to admit how tired I was.

"I came home from work early, so I can take you to dinner. Then I want to take you somewhere and show you something. It's likely going to make your head pop off and spin around in circles, but I'm showing you anyway. When we're done, I'll bring you home, give you a rubdown, and get you into bed before three in the damn morning. You'll be rested and ready to train tomorrow."

That sounded divine. Yet, I was still pissed and I didn't want him to show me anything that would piss me off further.

"Chels, this is me looking out for you. Trade places with me, baby, and tell me if you were watching me burn out and you had the means to stop it you wouldn't."

"I'm not burning out," I denied. "I'm used to this."

"I know you are," he muttered.

"Why do you say that like it's a bad thing? I work hard. It's who I am."

"You work *damn* hard," he corrected. "I know you're used to working an eight-hour shift after training for nine hours. And three or four hours of the nine is spent on the back of an animal jerking your body around and throwing you to the ground. I'm telling you this because I love you, but your body needs a rest."

My insides froze.

How many times had I heard that?

It normally came right before someone told me I was stupid.

"Chels?"

"It's not your business," I told him.

"Wrong. Everything about you is my business."

No, it wasn't. It couldn't be.

Do you even like riding bulls, or is it all about showing TJ up? You're reckless, and you're gonna kill yourself. Todd's angry words played in my mind.

Then I heard Ty. *At some point, you're gonna have to ask yourself what it's worth.*

"Chelsea," Matt snapped.

"It's worth it," I told him.

"What is?"

"The work. The training. It's all worth it. I'm not reckless."

"I never said you were."

I was having an argument in my head that Matt wasn't a part of, but now that I'd started, I couldn't stop.

"I love riding."

"I know you do," Matt told me softly.

"It's not about proving my dad wrong; it's about proving myself right."

Matt said nothing but he didn't take his eyes off of me. They were full of love and concern.

And for some reason that settled me. Matt wasn't losing his patience. He wasn't getting irritated at my single-mindedness to accomplish my goal. He wanted me to take care of myself. He was worried about me being hurt.

Why wasn't I as worried as he was about my safety?

Stupid, silly pride. I couldn't admit I was tired. I couldn't admit I needed a night off. I was so hellbent on proving I could do everything on my own, with no one's help, that I was willing to jeopardize my safety.

Stupid.

So, so, stupid.

"Every time I climb in the chute I feel a surge of adrenaline," I confessed.

"I bet you do."

"But that's not why I do it. That's not the rush I'm chasing. It's the battle I crave. Each time I climb up the rungs I go to battle. When I'm in the chute, war wages. And the moment I nod my head and that gate opens I'm forced to face my weaknesses. I'm free to acknowledge I have no control. I have no choice but to hold on and ride."

"What weaknesses are you battling, Chels?"

"Fear."

"Fear?"

I heard the shock in Matt's tone and went on to explain.

"I know my dad thinks I wanted to ride because I'm a stupid girl with a stupid dream thinking I can keep up with the boys. But that is not why I asked Mr. Coleman to put me on a bull. It was because I was afraid. I was turning a barrel on this little pony we had. Jackassing around doing something I shouldn't have been doing. Especially on Rosy. She wasn't trained and when I yanked on her reins to cut the barrel, she tripped and landed on me. It was the first time I'd fallen off a horse. It was the first time I'd been hurt. So I started thinking if it hurt that bad to be crushed by a pony how bad would it hurt if my horse tripped? And the fear started. Then it multiplied. Then my next two races I pulled back because I was too afraid to ride like I always had."

I'd been so lost in the memory I didn't realize Matt had crossed the room until he pried my hands apart and held on to them.

"I didn't want to be afraid, and I couldn't ask my dad for help. I couldn't ask my brothers, so I went to Mr. Coleman. He told me I had to face my fear head-on. He told me to get out of the saddle and conquer something scarier. So when I got back on my horse I knew I had nothing to be scared of. He put me bareback on a bronc. An old gelding that still had some kick in him. I was tossed off in two seconds flat, but the fire was lit. I loved it, I wanted to do it again. Every day I went to the Coleman Ranch. I'd finally gotten up my nerve to try a bull when TJ caught me and told on me."

"Mr. Coleman sounds like a smart man," Matt said.

"He was. After my dad kicked me out, Mr. Coleman let me stay at the ranch. In exchange for room and board, I had to work. Mr. Coleman worked from sun up to sundown. No breaks. He taught me about hard work. He also taught me the satisfaction of seeing a project to completion."

This was the part I needed Matt to understand.

This was vitally important if our relationship was going to last.

"I appreciate you looking out for me. And you're right, I am tired. You were also right when you said it was dangerous for me to ride when I'm exhausted. But I need you to really hear me when I tell you that I have to work. It is important to me. It makes me who I am. It's not about the money. It's about the accomplishment. It's about knowing that I've finished what I've started. It's the pride I feel when I put in the work. To you, Balls Deep is a bar. To me, it's more than that. It's success."

"I hear you." His hands slid up my forearms and farther still until they were sliding over my biceps. "I promise you; I heard every single word you said."

I slumped forward and placed my head on his chest. I was bone-tired and had no desire to eat before I crawled into bed.

"Thank you."

"Can we compromise?" I fought back the groan but couldn't stop my body from going rock solid. "Baby, I said I heard you."

"What do you want to compromise about?" I reluctantly asked.

"The week leading up to a rodeo, you limit your hours at the bar. A few hours a night, just to run in and check on things. You can make up the hours when you get back, or don't. You're salaried and the manager. You make the schedule. You have good employees, use them. You need to be focused on training. That's what's important."

"Would you be telling this to your manager if she wasn't your girlfriend?"

"Fuck, yes."

Damn. I believed him. Matt was that kind of guy.

"Okay," I agreed. "Seven days before a competition I'll limit my hours."

"Thank you," Matt breathed.

I lifted my head off his chest and was shocked at the relief I saw.

"I'm sorry I went behind your back and talked to Tony. When you accepted the job, I promised you I wouldn't interfere. I broke that promise but I hope you understand I did it because I was scared you were going to hurt yourself."

"I know you and that's why I'm no longer mad. So how about we order in, laze on the couch, and not go see what you want to show me that you admitted will make my head pop off and spin around?"

Matt's lips twisted before he smiled.

And standing there I realized how much I'd missed spending time with him. I also saw how tired he was.

"Before you agree to laze on the couch with me, can we compromise about something else?"

"Sure. But first, you have to agree if we order in and laze on the couch you forfeit your right to freak the fuck out later and acknowledge you're giving up any objections you could've had if you went to see what I wanted to show you."

I was too tired to attempt to decipher what the hell he was talking about.

"Consider this my acknowledgment."

A wide triumphant smile formed on Matt's handsome face. It was the victory I saw that scared me. Maybe I should've rethought my easy agreement.

"What are we compromising about?"

"You only come to the bar two nights a week."

"Chels—"

"I know during the season, when I'm training, we're going to have to find time to see each other. I know me even saying that is selfish. But it's only for three months. So, I'm asking you to bear with me. You're burning yourself out, too. You're working all day at TC then coming straight to the bar and staying with me until closing. It's too much. I love seeing you. So the compromise is, if you want to stay until close please only do it two nights a week. If you want to come in after work, have a beer, eat dinner with me, limit your time to a few hours, then come home and rest."

"Your dreams are not selfish," he forcefully corrected.

Of course, that was the part he'd pick out to comment on.

"Matt—"

"Say it, Chelsea. Tell me you understand that your dreams are not selfish."

Whoa.

I blinked at the vehemence of his tone.

"I understand."

"Promise?"

I brought my hands up and rested them on his forearms.

"Yes, I promise."

"Yes, I'll compromise. Through the season, I'll be there every night to have dinner with you, but I'll only stay until closing on Friday and Saturday nights."

It was my turn to smile wide and victorious.

The victory wasn't because I'd gotten what I wanted. It was because we were killing it at this compromise business.

"You pick dinner," I told him. "I'm gonna go change into my pjs."

"In a minute."

"Matt, I'm—"

His mouth dropped down and his lips brushed mine and my protest died. I loved it when he did the lip brush. It was the prelude to the good stuff, though any time I felt Matt's lips against mine it was good. So maybe I'd been hasty. The lip brush was the sweet before he stole my breath and made me tremble. It was the soft and gentle he gave me before he plundered and took. Not that he could actually steal something I gave freely.

"Go change, Chels, or dinner will be delayed."

I felt a shiver roll down my spine.

"Dinner can wait."

Matt picked me up, dropped me on the couch, came down over me, and dinner was delayed.

It was later, but not late. After we ate tomato soup and grilled cheese and watched two episodes of old-school *Fear Factor,* we were now in bed, I was happily tucked to Matt's side, and my eyes were drifting closed.

Then a memory hit, and my eyes popped open.

"Remember when we were getting ready to get on the helicopter and George caught us making out?"

"Yeah."

"You said something to me. What did you say?"

Matt's big body under mine began to shake.

"*Presto amore mio, così posso darti il primo orgasmo su un elicottero.*"

"What does that mean in English?"

Matt's shaking turned into a full-on belly laugh. His hilarity was so great he'd rolled into me, shoved his face in my neck, and roared with laughter.

"What's so funny?"

"I'm shocked it took you so long to ask," he said, still laughing.

"Well? What did you say?"

"You asked when we were going to get onto the helicopter."

I didn't understand. Why was that funny?

"That's what you said?"

"No," he sputtered. "I told you, soon so I could give you your first orgasm on a helicopter."

"Please tell me George doesn't speak..." I trailed off.

"Italian," Matt supplied.

"Please tell me George doesn't speak Italian."

"George is good at kissing ass. I'm positive he knows how to do that in a variety of languages."

"Matthew!" I snapped and tried to slap his chest.

My hand was captured by his and he rolled, taking me to my back. His face was still in the crook of my neck, he was still laughing, but I didn't find anything funny.

"Baby, you will never see him again. What do you care?"

Good point.

"Well," I huffed. "You didn't give me an orgasm on my first ever helicopter ride. Now I feel cheated."

"Sorry, Chels, I'll hook you up the next time we go up."

The next time.

"I don't think I should have to wait that long," I told him.

Matt bared his teeth and gave me a gentle love bite before he licked the sting away.

"I want your mouth on my cock while I eat you, baby. Climb up."

Matt rolled to his back and didn't make me wait.

I came before he did. Then I crawled down his big body, rode him reverse, and we came together.

24

The arena was packed.

The vibe said there was a good time to be had.

People were packed into the stands—old and young alike. Cowboy hats and ball caps. Boots and tennis shoes.

The air vibrated with adrenaline.

Chelsea's focus was intense. Even as she explained what was going on she was fixed on her goal.

An eight-second ride.

Dylan was at my side as I showed the official the pass Chelsea had given me. I hadn't seen her in over an hour. She and Ty had gone off, leaving me and Dylan in the stands. According to the schedule, bull riding was the last event and I estimated I had less than thirty minutes to see her before she needed me out of the way so she could get her head where she needed it to be.

"Chelsea's with Ty in the traps," the man told me then pointed to the area behind the bucking chutes.

"Thanks."

"This shit is wild," Dylan muttered.

He was not wrong.

But the knot in my gut had prevented me from fully appreciating the excitement going on around me.

I caught sight of Chelsea as two cowboys made their approach with big smiles. With great effort, I tamped down the urge to quicken my pace.

"There she is," one of the men drawled.

Chelsea turned to look at the man. A slow, beautiful grin formed, and I was immediately taken in.

She was beautiful, sure. Her cowboy getup, complete with sexy-as-all-fuck red chaps, cowboy hat, and beat-up boots added to that beauty. But it was her smile. She was in her element. Happy, excited, ready to kick some ass. And that was beyond beautiful.

"Damn, if it isn't Sam Henry out in the wild," Chelsea returned. "Heard a rumor you were here."

"Couldn't miss my girl's first ride back."

His girl? What the fuck?

"Easy," Dylan mumbled.

"You're so full of shit. You're here for the points." Chelsea laughed. "Where's Darlene?"

"Where she always is. In the stands waitin' to cheer on her man."

"Hey, Palmer," Chelsea greeted the other man.

"Chels. Good to see you back."

Ty gave Chelsea a nudge and pointed at me and Dylan.

"Matt. Dylan. Good timing," Chelsea beamed. "This is Palmer and Sam."

When I was done shaking the men's hands, I moved to Chelsea and slid my arm around her back while Dylan was introducing himself.

"Ty, good to see you."

The other man grinned and shook his head.

"Matt, good to see you," he greeted. "Ready to watch your woman kick ass?"

"Absolutely."

"You got five minutes, then I need her back. They're loading up now."

The knot in my gut grew.

"Where'd you draw?" I asked.

"Twelfth. And I'm riding Smoke Wagon."

"Goddamn," Palmer grumbled. "He's a motherfucker, Chels. Spins hard right straight outta the gates. Watch your hand and keep it high."

Chelsea nodded.

"If you can dismount left," Sam added. "Palmer's correct, he favors his right side."

"Saw that. Last night we watched the highlights."

I listened as Chelsea offered wisdom about the bulls the other two men were gonna ride and something struck me. Something I wondered if Chelsea understood. These two men fully accepted her as one of their own. Sam had teased her and called her a girl, but that was not how they viewed Chelsea. She was a cowboy, just like they were. These men did not share her father's point of view. Chelsea wasn't a stupid girl with a stupid dream. She was their equal.

Yet, the knot in the pit of my stomach didn't loosen.

"It was good to meet you, Matt. Dylan, you, too. I'm gonna go get ready." Palmer paused and turned to Chelsea. "Ride strong, Roughy."

"Ride strong," she returned.

I noticed people were clearing out of the area and I took that as my cue to go back to my seat. I was about to say goodbye when Sam stepped closer with a hard expression on his face.

"If that stupid fuck gives you trouble, you find me. No

bullshit, Chels. He so much as gives you a dirty look, I wanna know."

I felt Dylan move closer to me as my body turned to stone. Every muscle coiled tight, readying to fight.

"Come again?" I growled.

Chelsea jolted beside me and pushed her small hand into my stomach right where the knot of unease had turned into a ball of fury.

"Goddammit," Ty bit out. "She hasn't seen the roster, you asshole."

"What? Who are you talking about?" Chelsea's tone was hard and full of contempt.

"Shit, Ty," Sam started. "I thought she knew."

"Knew what?"

"Nothing. There's not a damn thing you need to know. Head in the game, cowboy."

I agreed. Chelsea needed her head filled with nothing but her ride. But *I* damn well needed to know what the hell was going on.

"Tyler—"

"She's last in the chute, Ty. How'd you plan from keeping it from her?" Sam asked.

There seemed to be a standoff and the longer it went on the harder Chelsea started to shake.

"Someone better tell her what the hell's going on," I demanded.

"TJ's here," she whispered. "He's riding. That's why you didn't want me looking at the roster."

"Fuck," Ty grunted.

Fuck was right.

Chelsea's brother being there was not good. It would throw her off her game and bring up bad memories for her.

The desire to get her the hell out of the arena was overwhelming. One slip-up and she could be seriously injured. One wrong move on the back of a two-thousand-pound animal could be deadly.

But she'd hate that. She'd be pissed at me and angry with herself if she didn't ride.

Grow a pair, asshole.

Time to suck it up and give her what she needs.

I pulled Chelsea in front of me, lowered my face, and hated every word I forced myself to say.

"Suck it up. Right now, baby, suck it up and lock it down."

Chelsea blinked and I went on.

"You belong here, and you know you do. You *know* it, Chels. You have earned this. So, lock it the fuck down, and get ready."

She stared at me with a blank expression and I leaned in closer.

"You got a battle to wage, baby. A war to fight. Clear your head and ready yourself to win."

It took only a moment for the fog to recede and determination to shine in her eyes.

"I got this."

"Yeah, you do."

Chelsea closed the distance and pressed a hard kiss on my mouth before she stepped back and straightened her cowboy hat.

"Ride strong." She tipped her chin to Sam.

"You, too, Roughy. Show these twats how a real cowboy rides."

Without another word, Chelsea turned and strutted. Shoulders back, head high, each step full of resolve.

Goddamn magnificent.

"What number is he?" I asked Sam as soon as Chelsea and Ty were gone.

"He's number ten. Fourth out."

I nodded and asked, "Is he stupid enough to say something to her?"

"Here? Before a ride, in front of everyone? Hell, no. He tried that once and found himself an ass beating out back. No one talks shit to our girl. And if they do, she shuts it down, then the rest of us teach a lesson in manners."

More proof Chelsea had been accepted.

Yet, that fury was still bubbling.

"You'll let me know if her brother needs a refresher in manners."

It wasn't a question, but Sam answered anyway.

"We'll do, hoss. Enjoy watching your woman."

Dylan and I were nearing the stands when he asked, "You gonna fill me in on what the fuck that was about?"

I scanned the area looking for anyone that looked like Chelsea. If her brother was riding, I had a feeling at least her father would be here and maybe her other brother, Russ.

I gave Dylan an abbreviated rundown. Needing him in the know in case something went down, but also, needing to preserve Chelsea's privacy. When I was done, we'd found our seats. Dylan's knee was bouncing, and rage was rolling off my friend.

"Stupid fucks," he snarled.

"They are that," I agreed.

"What the hell possesses a man to behave like that?"

"Won't call him or her brothers men," I told him.

"You're right about that."

I sat back and waited for the main event to start.

The first three riders didn't last more than three seconds, and I felt the muscles in my neck tense.

"You look like you're ready to come out of your skin," Dylan joked.

"I feel like I am."

"Damn, brother, you get jittery like this when you faced down tangos?" He laughed.

Hell, no.

"Tonight, I'm not the one wearing Kevlar. My woman is. I'm not the one putting my life in danger, my woman is."

"True story," Dylan muttered.

Chelsea's brother was loading in the chute, and Metallica's "Enter Sandman" was blaring as the announcer introduced TJ Sullens. I was watching the asshole get ready when movement to my right captured my attention. An older man stood and was cheering loudly.

What were the chances that was Chelsea's father?

Out of the hundreds of seats in the arena was it possible it was my lucky day and the asshole was sitting one row in front of me? I glanced at the younger man still sitting. I had him in profile, but his gaze was on the man in the chute and he was wired.

Russ.

Hell, yeah, it was my lucky day.

The gate opened and I watched TJ ride. It might've been a dickhead thing to do but I was waiting for his ass to be tossed off and trampled.

A few moments later my wish came true, or the first part of it did; TJ was tossed off. The bullfighter rushed to his aid to distract the bull as TJ got to his feet and ripped off his helmet and jogged to the rails.

I looked at the clock. Seven-point-forty-four seconds. No points.

I couldn't stop the smile from forming.

"Dammit!" the older man shouted. "Damn. It."

"It was a good ride, Dad." The younger man clapped him on the shoulder.

"Not good enough!"

Yeah, that had to be Chelsea's father.

"Heard your daughter's riding tonight, too, Trevor."

"Don't got no daughter, Clive."

Motherfucker.

"Chelsea—"

"Don't got no daughter."

No, motherfucker, you do not.

"Jesus," Dylan clipped.

I tore my gaze from Trevor Sullens and did what I told Chelsea to do—locked my anger down.

I kept my eyes on the next rider and waited.

By the time the rider before Chelsea was trotting out of the ring only two riders had points on the board.

"Ladies and gentlemen!" the announcer's voice boomed.

Imagine Dragon's "Thunder" played in the background and I shot to my feet.

Christ, the song was perfect. Every word was Chelsea.

I felt the thump of the bass hit my chest, adrenaline bled into my veins, and fear ricocheted through me.

"Your last cowboy's about to go," the announcer continued. "Chelsea Sullens out of Hinesville, Georgia."

The cheers from the crowd were deafening. My gaze went around the arena but quickly went back to the chute. Chelsea's back was to me. Her hat had been replaced with a helmet and a Kevlar vest covered the blue-and-white plaid shirt. I watched her gesture to her rope man and look over at Ty. His mouth was moving, then he leaned away and Chelsea went back to wrapping her hand.

"Breathe, brother."

I'd breathe in eight seconds.

"After last year's season was cut short with a broken shoulder and twelve broken ribs, we're happy to have her back. This is Chelsea's second season on the pro circuit. Tonight she's riding Smoke Wagon, a five-year old bull, with two hundred bucks on him, but he's only been ridden nine times. Let's see if Chelsea's gonna be number ten."

Fucking hell, only nine riders had stayed on him for points.

I watched Chelsea shoot her hips forward and my heart dropped to my gut. Her head nodded, the gate flew open, and my world tilted.

Smoke Wagon came out with a vengeance and spun hard right like Palmer had predicted.

Seconds ticked by and the crowd roared.

I didn't breathe.

The bull bucked, reared, twisted, and Chelsea held on.

I didn't breathe.

Seconds felt like hours as I watched my woman's body get tossed around like a ragdoll.

But she held on.

"C'mon!" the announcer yelled. "Come on, Chelsea. Come on."

I still wasn't fucking breathing.

I wasn't sure if I even had a pulse.

Smoke Wagon twisted right, his back hoofs were off the dirt, I saw Chelsea's ass start to slide, her spur digging deep in an effort to stop herself from falling off.

"Hold on, Chels!" I shouted.

The buzzer sounded.

The buzzer.

Chelsea was still riding.

"Hell, yeah!"

Then suddenly her body was flying. She hit the dirt, her right shoulder slamming down hard, the bull's hoof slamming down harder less than a foot from her head.

"Get up, baby," I whispered.

The bullfighters waved their hands, jumped around, and yelled trying everything they could to get the bull's attention as Chelsea scrambled to her feet and ran at a full sprint back to the chute. In one jump she was halfway up the rails.

"That's how you ride a bull!" the announcer shouted. "And boy did she make it look good. Chelsea's gonna put eighty-seven and a half points up on the board. Bringing her ahead of Sam Henry. Chelsea Sullens takes Athens."

"Fuck, yeah!" Dylan yelled. "She did it."

He slapped me on the back and I felt myself breathe.

But I hadn't taken my eyes off my woman.

Her helmet was off, she was holding it high above her head, and she was looking out into the crowd smiling.

Hundreds of people were cheering for her.

Fear turned into pride.

Chelsea Sullens was one badass cowboy.

Though the next time her name was announced she would be Chelsea Kessler.

That was for goddamn sure.

25

I was pretty sure there was nothing that could bring me down from the high I was riding. Not even the ache in my shoulder. Not even Ty coming at me with ice packs after I was done with my interview. Not even him wrapping an ace bandage around my chest and shoulder to keep the cold packs where he wanted.

Ty had gone to go find Matt and Dylan while I was packing my gear with shaky hands. I knew from experience I needed to eat before I crashed. The adrenaline dump was coming, the unfortunate part of riding a rush so high I felt like I was flying.

I was so totally focused on folding my chaps I hadn't heard his approach. Which was unlucky because I was unprepared to hear my brother's voice.

"Good ride."

All these years and it still hurt. TJ didn't even need to hurl insults. Just the sound of his voice felt like I'd been punched.

"I was hoping you'd be here."

I lifted my gaze and clapped my eyes on my brother. I tried to think when the last time I saw him in person was and I couldn't remember—maybe five, six years.

Not long enough.

"Yeah, you were? Why? So you could tell me how stubborn I am? How stupid? So you could gloat when you scored and I didn't? Oh. Wait." I paused and pushed away from the table. "I know, you were hoping I was here so you could remind me I'm a worthless piece of shit."

"I never said you were a worthless piece of shit," TJ corrected.

"Oh, you're right. You and Russ just stood there while Dad told me I was worthless. The same way you stood by and watched Dad beat my ass for fucking Barrett even though you knew it wasn't the truth. But then, you and Russ watched that a lot and never stepped in."

"Chels—"

"Don't, TJ," I cut in. "There's nothing you have to say that I want to hear."

"I want to—"

"What the fuck's going on here?" my father's voice boomed, and I flinched.

"Dad—"

"Let's go, boy," my dad demanded.

Boy? Damn, some things never change.

I glanced at my father and a whole slew of bad memories invaded my mind. Memories that normally threatened to hurl me back to a time when I'd cower and cry for him to stop hitting me. But looking at the old man now standing in front of me I wasn't afraid of him. He hadn't aged well, deep wrinkles marred the area around his eyes. His beard was gray and unkempt. His clothes uncared for. He looked like shit. He was once a handsome man. It was good to see his outside was now as ugly as his temper.

I didn't spare Russ a glance, I couldn't. He was the one who had hurt me the most. And not because he'd tattled on me the most, earning me my father's ire. At one time he and I had been close. Then he turned on me. Without warning. Without reason. Without provocation. One day he was my big brother, the next he was the devil and made it his mission to be just as nasty as TJ and our dad.

A thought struck me. This was what I'd waited for. This moment was what I'd worked my ass off to get. My father and brothers watching me ride. For years all I'd wanted was the chance to prove to them I was good enough. I was better than what they said. I'd prayed the day would come.

And now it was here.

All three of them standing in front of me.

I'd won. I'd beat TJ.

There was no denying I was better.

And it was utterly meaningless.

"All of you go."

I went back to folding my chaps. I wanted them gone before Ty brought Matt and Dylan out back. I didn't want the confrontation. I didn't want to waste another minute of my life thinking about them.

"Don't you tell me what to do," my father scoffed.

The same mean, gruff voice he'd used on me a million times no longer made my insides shrivel.

"On second thought, maybe you should stay," I said conversationally. "While I pack up you can explain to me where your life went so wrong you turned into a complete asshole."

I grabbed my rope and picked up my wire brush and started to clean the rosin off.

"What'd you say to me, girl?"

"You see, I had a motherfucker for a daddy." I continued to brush my rope as I spoke. "He took his hand to me more times than I can count. He beat me bloody with a leather belt. I had two brothers who did nothing to save me from that pain. I had a brother who lied about me. A brother who called me names. A mother who was mostly comatose. But I'm not an asshole. So I figure something had to have happened to make you such a miserable fuck, and whatever that something is has gotta be bigger than having a motherfucker for a daddy."

"I'll strap you bloody right here."

My father took a step closer. I dropped my wire brush and snapped the long rope in my hand.

"No, you won't," I returned. "You think to touch me, it will be me strapping your ass this time."

"Stop, Dad!" Russ shouted.

TJ swept his arm out, trying to push me behind him. I stumbled. Matt walked around the corner.

Bad timing.

Matt took off in an all-out run, I rushed around the table trying to head him off, and my father caught me by my hair. My neck snapped back, pain radiated down my shoulder and back, and I came to a jarring halt.

Russ moved fast and grabbed our father, lifting the old man clean off his feet. Unfortunately, that meant I was with my dad when Russ tossed him to the side, so I tumbled down, too.

Before I could scramble to my feet, I was in the air and cradled in Dylan's arms.

Oh, no.

Matt.

Dylan was moving back to get clear of the fight that was no doubt getting ready to break out.

"Put me down."

"Let Matt handle this."

"No, Dylan. Put me down."

"He wants you safe."

Matt had my father up on his feet, holding him by the scrunched-up material of his shirt.

"You like hitting women?" Matt asked and gave my father a violent shake. "Huh, asshole? You like hitting your daughter?"

"She's not my daughter," my father spat.

That worked out well for me. I didn't want to claim the dick as my father.

"Yeah, I heard you say that shit back in the arena. Right before Chelsea wiped the floor with your son. Tell me, you piece of shit, did you choke on your words? Did they taste good coming back up? Did it burn your gut when you watched her accomplish everything you said she wouldn't?"

Shockingly, my brothers hadn't moved in to protect our father. Or maybe it wasn't shocking. All my life I thought they just didn't like me and that was why they'd never stepped in to help me. It turns out they were just cowards.

"She's not my goddamn daughter."

Matt let my dad go with a shove and his gaze sliced through my brothers.

"Pathetic."

"*Please*, let me down, Dylan."

As soon as my boots touched the dirt I took off running. I hit Matt's side, burrowed under his shoulder, and wrapped my arms around him.

"They're worthless, sweetheart. All of them. Don't waste your time."

"I don't know which one of you is the bigger pile of dog shit. The old man for beating his daughter or the two of you for not helping your little sister. You stood by and watched. You knew what was happening and neither one of you did a fucking thing to help her."

"For the last goddamn time, she is not my *fucking* daughter!" my father roared.

"Well, thank God for that because I don't want to be yours!" I shouted back.

"Dad. Let's go," Russ gritted out.

"Funny, your daddy said something similar when your momma told him she was pregnant with you."

What was my dad talking about? He didn't want me? Well, no shit.

Matt's arm got tight around me, and I pressed closer.

"He packed her shit up, drove her back out to the ranch, and dropped her ass off on my porch knocked up."

Wait.

What?

"What?"

"Enough, Dad! Let's go," TJ interjected.

"Didn't want you then. Don't want you now. Didn't want her either. The only good part about having her back was there was dinner on the table when me and my boys got in."

Trevor wasn't my dad?

"Did you know?" I asked Russ.

"Yeah, Dad told me when I was about ten. I wasn't old enough to remember when she left."

About ten.

That was around the time he'd turned on me.

Trevor told Russ I wasn't his daughter and Russ stopped being my brother.

"And you? When did you find out?"

"I always knew," TJ admitted. "I remember her leaving. We didn't see or hear from her for a little over a year. When she came back, she was pregnant."

"She left you?" I whispered.

"Walked out the door and didn't come back until some guy dropped her off."

Some guy.

My father.

I wanted to feel something. Maybe feel sad for my brothers that our mom had left them. Maybe feel angry on their behalf that their mother would leave her sons.

But I couldn't.

I felt nothing.

I tipped my head back and looked at Matt.

"I'd like to go home now."

My voice sounded strange, like a robot, a hollowed-out shell of a person.

"Take her. I'll pack her gear."

Ty.

I couldn't even drum up enough emotion to be embarrassed that Ty had a front-row seat to the Jerry Springer episode that was my life.

Trevor Sullens, you are not the father.

Trevor wasn't my father.

"Where's Mom now?" I asked.

"Dead," Trevor spat.

"Dead?" I wheezed.

"She died. Two years ago, Chelsea. Liver cancer."

My mother died two years ago, and I hadn't known.

My father wasn't my father.

My brothers hated me because I was the bastard child their mother had brought home after she'd abandoned them.

My mother was dead.
I'd been wrong. Something could bring me down.
I was no longer flying high.
I was sinking to the bottom.

26

Chelsea was asleep in the back seat of my truck. I'd forced her to stay awake long enough for me to drive through a fast-food place and make her eat something before she passed out.

"Want me to find him?" Dylan asked.

He was asking about Chelsea's biological father.

"I'm not sure. The asshole left her before she was born. That right there sums up the kind of man he is. She had an asshole raise her. I'm not sure I'm all fired up about introducing her to the one who abandoned her."

"Trevor could be lying."

I'd already thought about that.

"He's telling the truth. You saw him; he hates Chelsea. He taught his sons to hate her. I'd bet he loved his wife and when she left it tore him apart. He took her back and used Chelsea to punish her for her infidelity."

"That scene was jacked-up. I hated it happened at all, but damn if they didn't trample over her win."

Dylan was correct—it was jacked-up. It was also a long

time coming. Secrets that had been kept from her for far too long.

I glanced in my rearview mirror and I drew in a breath through my nose to calm my anger. Chelsea lying across the bench seat. Hands tucked under her cheek, knees curled up, my jacket balled under her head was not how she should've been spending the night of her win. We should've been out celebrating. We should've been out at a bar, her friends congratulating her. She should've been laughing and happy.

But instead, she was emotionally wrecked.

"You never said, did she like the house?" Dylan asked.

"She doesn't know yet."

"I thought you were taking her to see it the day you left early."

"I was going to. But to say she was unhappy I'd fucked with her schedule wouldn't be a fair assessment. After we talked about it, she admitted she was exhausted and needed sleep. So, we made a deal."

"What kind of deal?"

"The kind where she doesn't get to have a shit hemorrhage since she passed on her opportunity to see her surprise before I gave it to her."

"That worked out well for you," he noted.

"Yeah, it did."

I wasn't worried Chelsea wouldn't like the house; it was perfect. Not too big, but not small. It sat on forty acres and already had a six-stall barn. Some improvements needed to be done, but Chelsea and I would do them. And none of the improvements would impede Chelsea from bringing her girls home and that was the whole reason I bought the house. I wanted her to have access to her horses anytime she wanted. Once Gypsy and Rebel were settled, we'd put the other four stalls to use.

The rest of the drive was spent with Dylan doing what he could to keep my mind occupied. Talk of work had led to Hadley's pregnancy which led to the slew of babies that had been born. Without meaning to my mind wandered to Chelsea and me adding to the family. Which made me think about my family and the bullshit my sister was pulling. She'd refused to sell me her shares in Kessler, which in the grand scheme of things wasn't the end of the world. She only owned five percent and since no one on the board was particularly fond of her, there wasn't much trouble she could cause. I just wanted her gone. As of next week, she'd no longer be an employee. Silas had drafted her termination letter and with Kessler legal council's approval, it would be delivered to her on Monday.

My dad had two days left to get his affairs in order before he turned himself in. A better son would've gone to visit him before he went to prison. I found I was not a better son. I was a son who was still pissed as fuck at his father. Last night my mother had called to inform me she'd served my father with the divorce papers, and he'd agreed to sign them. I was now a thirty-six-year-old child of divorce. And the only reason that bothered me was that despite what my mother had said, I knew she was in pain. Right now that pain was laced with anger but soon that anger would dissipate and forty-plus years of marriage would be gone. I hated that for her, and I didn't like how Alessandra was behaving. My mother had reported that my sister was mad at her for leaving our father and felt that we all should be standing by him.

Of course, Alessandra felt that way—not out of loyalty but greed. She stood to lose the most out of my father's incarceration. She no longer had daddy's protection and money. It was gone. My father's fines wouldn't wipe him out, but he'd lose quarters of his wealth. Which meant, Alessandra would lose a lot of money when it came time to inherit her share of our father's fortune. Or I should say, inherit, period. I didn't want and would not take any money my father intended to leave me. It was all Alessandra's.

We were pulling into my driveway when I asked, "On Monday would you mind pulling my sister's financials?"

"Sure. You looking for anything in particular?"

"Overall net worth. How much cash she has on hand, debt, and bank accounts. I wanna know where she keeps her money."

"Done," Dylan returned.

And I knew it would be done. He'd have the information I wanted before I poured my first cup of coffee Monday morning. That was Dylan. He was good at collecting intel, but he was a better friend.

"Appreciate it."

I didn't bother pulling my truck into the garage and killed the ignition.

"We're home?" Chelsea's sleepy voice came from behind me.

Dylan turned in his seat and smiled at my woman.

"Shit time for you, Chels. So I didn't get a chance to tell you congratulations on your win. I also didn't get to properly tell you how badass it was watching you ride. Just to say, you forget to invite me to your next rodeo I'm gonna be pissed."

"Thanks, Dylan."

"I'm serious, Chelsea, you were great out there."

"Quit flirting with my woman and get out of my truck," I grumbled.

"Worried I'll steal her away?"

"Yeah. Sure. I'm so scared I'm quaking."

"Got a good look at your woman in those chaps, brother. I might—"

The palm of my hand landed on the center of his chest with a thud and Dylan sucked in a breath.

"Damn. I was joking."

"I know you were. That's why you don't have a bloody lip."

"Your propensity for violence is appalling," Dylan said with an impressively straight face.

"My violent tendencies are growing by the second," I warned.

I heard Chelsea chuckle; it wasn't a laugh, just the tease of one, but after the night she'd had I'd take it.

"Lean your head back."

Chelsea was standing in front of me naked with her back against the shower spray. My hands were in her hair massaging in the conditioner.

She tilted her head under the water and sighed.

"That feels good," she moaned.

"Good."

"So does this."

She wiggled against my erection resting on her stomach. My jaw clenched and my cock throbbed.

"Ignore it."

"Kinda hard to ignore."

"Try."

Her eyes opened and she smiled.

So damn strong.

"Now why would I do something stupid like that?"

Any other time, I'd agree with her. There was never a

good time to waste a perfectly good hard-on. However, I was doing my best to take care of her, and fucking her against the wall of the shower wasn't part of my plan.

Clearly, Chelsea had other plans. One of her hands cupped my balls and the other fisted my cock. Slowly, her hand started stroking between us.

"Chels, baby..." My words died and turned into a moan when her thumb swept the head of my cock.

"I love that you're taking care of me," she started.

Her fist tightened and stroked harder.

"Then let me do that."

"You always take care of me."

I fucking loved that she thought that but if she didn't stop jerking me off, I was going to come.

"You always give me what I need even when I didn't know I needed it," she continued.

Her hand on my balls was doing amazing things.

My hands in her hair tightened.

"Tell me what you need right now, Chels. Anything and it's yours," I grunted.

"I need you to be you. Be my Matt. The man who made me believe I was beautiful. The man who makes me feel sexy and loved."

"You are loved," I insisted. "You're so beautiful when I look at you I'm amazed you're mine."

Chelsea's lips started to tip up but before she could fully commit to the smile my mouth was on hers. At the first glide of her tongue on mine warmth spread. I slowly deepened the kiss, teasing her until she was moaning into my mouth. Her hand pumping my cock was an exercise of control. When I was edging toward climax, I broke the kiss and pulled my hips back. When she released her grip on my cock I went to my knees.

The shower wasn't small, nor was it big. The one at the new house had much more room. I smiled as I lifted her leg over my shoulder.

"Back against the wall," I demanded.

I felt Chelsea shift and lowered my head. Unlike our kiss, I didn't slowly tease. I devoured her pussy. My thumbs spread her pussy lips apart, my tongue stabbed into her wet opening, and I ate. I licked, sucked, grazed my teeth over the sensitive skin until she was grinding into my face.

I hooked her knee and stood, taking her with me until I was standing. She automatically wrapped one leg around my waist and circled my neck with her arms.

"Guide me in."

My teeth ground together when she dropped one arm and found my cock. The tip of my cock slipped through her wetness and in one hard thrust I was fully inside of her.

Heaven.

"Lift your tit," I grunted.

I lowered my head and captured her nipple.

"Yes."

Chelsea's moan reverberated around the small space and I sucked harder.

"Other one."

Her hand moved to her other breast and she lifted it to my mouth like an offering. A gift I would never refuse.

"Harder," she panted.

I drove my cock deeper.

"Harder, honey. All I want to feel is you."

I shifted her leg around, her ankles locked, my hands went to her ass, and my fingertips dug into the soft skin over hard muscle. Chelsea's thighs tightened and she used her strength to match my thrusts.

"Harder," she demanded.

One of her hands slid up and she fisted my hair until my scalp tingled.

"I fuck you any harder, baby, you won't be walking tomorrow."

And that was the goddamned truth.

"I don't want to walk. Harder, honey."

There was a nagging thought in the back of my mind. The knowledge she was using sex as a way to not feel the pain. Yet, I told her I would give her anything she needed. And that included fucking her against the wall when all I wanted to do was wrap her up in my arms and take her to bed.

Later.

Now I'd give her what she wanted, including my foul mouth I knew she got off on.

"You want me to fuck you harder, baby? Reach down and toy with your clit and I'll give you what you want."

Chelsea let go of my hair and reached between us. Her hips jolted and her eyes went unfocused.

"That's it, Chels," I encouraged. "Faster, baby."

I felt her hand working between us. Her fingertips grazed my shaft and my pounding became punishing. Each drive brutal. Every thrust deep.

My head dropped to her shoulder; the feel of her slick warm pussy was so good I had to close my eyes to fight off my orgasm. The feel of her pressed tightly against me felt so good the last of my control slipped.

"Hold on tight, baby."

Her thighs tightened.

"Tighter, Chels. Hold on."

I used my grip on her ass to slam her down on my cock as I drove up.

"Every inch of you is sexy as fuck," I groaned. "All of you

so fucking beautiful. Strong and sweet. But goddamn, you taking my cock, nothing sexier. Christ, you're hot and tight. So fucking wet with just my mouth I can't drink you down fast enough."

"Matthew."

"You're gonna make me come, Chels. I'm ready, baby."

"Yes," she breathed.

"You feel too fucking good. I can't hold it back," I warned.

Her hand between us lost its rhythm. Her pussy rippled around my cock, and I was gone.

"Fuck." I drove hard and planted my cock deep. "Can you feel that?"

With every rope of come that shot out, my cock throbbed.

"Yes," she hissed.

"That's what you do to me."

I was lost in the sensations of Chelsea's orgasm spasming around my shaft, prolonging mine until I swayed and had to readjust my hands so I didn't drop her.

I lifted my head and watched the rest of her climax. If it felt as good as it looked it was a damn good one.

Once some of the haze left her eyes I leaned forward and kissed her forehead.

"I love you, Chels."

"I love you, too, Matt."

Damn, I love hearing her say that.

She was not the first woman to tell me she loved me. But she was the first who meant it. She was the first woman I'd ever said those words to. And she'd be the only woman to ever hear them.

"Do you think you can stand?"

"No."

"Then hold on so I can get us out of here and dried off."

I reached behind me and turned off the water.

"You can't hold me and dry us off."

"Watch me."

I stepped out of the shower, grabbed a towel, and very clumsily with great difficulty I dried us off.

Well, not completely. When I dropped Chelsea on the bed, water still dotted her legs. But it was good enough. Since she'd moved in, we now had a spare set of sheets and I changed them in the morning.

27

Every muscle in my body ached. It was a good ache, the best kind of throbbing. Except for my shoulder. I was pretty sure when I fell on my father—no, not my father, Trevor—I'd pulled something. There was still a twinge of pain in my neck, but it was my shoulder that hurt. And the rough shower sex hadn't helped, though I wasn't feeling any pain during, and I'd never tell Matt how badly it hurt now. He'd probably get out of bed and demand we go to the emergency room. There was nothing they could do for a tear or a strain. I knew the protocol—rest.

I felt Matt's hand still on my hip and the pectoral muscle under my cheek tensed. Which in turn made me tense up.

"How are you feeling?"

How was I feeling? That was an interesting question. I'd gone from the highest of highs to the lowest of lows in the space of an hour. I'd gone from the feeling of accomplishment and pride to overwhelming grief. Anger mixed with shock. Heartache and fury mingled, leaving me numb.

"I don't know how to answer that," I told him. "In a weird way, I'm almost relieved Trevor's not my father. I know that sounds strange and it shouldn't make a difference. He did what he did and it makes no difference if I'm biologically his or not but I'm still relieved I don't share blood with him. I'm not sure how I feel about my brothers, but I do like knowing why they hated me. It doesn't excuse how they treated me. They did what they did, but a small part of me can empathize with them."

Matt's hand on my hip slid down to my bare ass and he pulled me tighter against his side.

"They do not deserve your empathy," he rumbled.

I loved the way Matt wanted to protect me, even from my mind understanding why my brothers had treated me like shit.

"Our mother left them," I reminded Matt. "Who knows what would've happened if she hadn't gotten pregnant with me? Maybe she would've stayed gone forever. TJ said he remembers her leaving. That had to be terrible for him. He had to have been about seven. One day his mom was there and then she was gone. I'm sure Dad...Trevor didn't help him deal with his pain. So I'm not excusing his behavior but I was raised by Trevor; I know the kind of father he is. He wasn't just an asshole to me. He was hard on the boys, too. Though he cut them way more slack than he did me. And I finally know why Russ turned on me. I always wondered why. What I did to make him go from my brother, my playmate, to a complete dick. Now I know. It was never me. It was nothing I did. I wasn't a perfect child but even if I had been, Trevor, TJ, and Russ still would've hated me."

The more I thought about why my brothers behaved the way they did, the reason why Trevor disliked me so much the more the feeling of unworthiness lifted. Their anger wasn't about me. I was the reminder that my mother had left. I was the byproduct of her infidelity. Trevor was prouder than any man should be. His prideful demeanor was off the charts. He would hate his wife leaving him. I wasn't sure if he ever loved my mother, but it would be a hit to his ego. On top of that, her sleeping with another man and getting pregnant would send him over the edge.

"I'm sorry your mother's gone," Matt whispered.

And that was the grief. The crushing sorrow.

I tucked in closer to Matt needing to soak up his warmth. I needed to feel his strong arms wrapped around me, reminding me I was in our bed, I was safe, I was now cared for.

"You know, the day I turned eighteen as I was walking away from that house, I swore to myself she was dead to me. Out of all of them, she'd hurt me the most. And not because she sat on the couch and watched me leave. Because she was my mother. Not a mommy who kissed bruises. Not a mom who cuddled and tucked me in. Not my teacher, not my friend, not anything. The woman cooked my meals, did my laundry until I was old enough to do it myself, and she kept the house clean. She did literally nothing else. She never asked how school was, if I had a crush on a boy. She didn't explain what my period was. Never touched on the topic of sex and birth control. She was a live-in maid so I can't mourn the loss of a woman I barely knew. But I can mourn what I never had and will now never have. I will never have a mother and that is eating away at me. There was some small part of me that had been waiting for her to find me, to explain why she'd been the way she was, to beg me to forgive her and tell me she loved me. That's gone. That's what I can't wrap my head around. I will never know why she was the way she was. How she could leave her boys, why she left them, if she'd planned on coming back for them."

"Chels," Matt groaned. "Fuck, baby."

"I don't want Dylan to find my real father," I told him.

"What?"

I hadn't been asleep in the back seat. I'd laid there awake for a long time pretending to be, so I didn't have to talk about what had happened. I'd needed time alone in my head to sort through my feelings. Not that it had helped; by the time I had drifted off to sleep I was no closer to sorting anything out but at least when I'd woken up I was no longer fuming mad and the shaking had stopped.

"I heard you two talking about it. I didn't mean to eavesdrop, but I was awake."

Matt's body turned to stone under mine.

"I heard Dylan ask you if I liked the house," I admitted. "Though, since the current trauma is taking up all my mental capacity, I'm choosing not to think about it. I know the deal was since I didn't go look at what I now know is the house I don't get to freak out. And since I made that deal, I'll keep my word. But I feel like I need to explain to you that buying a house isn't a surprise. Buying me flowers is a surprise. Buying me a pair of shoes is a surprise. You buying yourself a new house, one I hope I'm invited to move into with you, is way bigger than a surprise."

"I didn't buy myself a house," he denied.

"I heard—"

"I bought *you* a house. I bought *us* a home. I bought you a place for you to have your horses with you. A place where one day you can teach our children to ride. A home for you to cuddle your babies, kiss their bruises, and ask our daughters about how their days were. A home for us to raise our family. I bought us a *home*, not a sterile estate, not a big, lonely mansion. A home for us to fill with love and happiness. A place where our children will know they are always safe. A refuge. Though, you'll need to explain something else to our daughters."

"What do I need to explain to our daughters?" I croaked out through my tears.

"While they will always be safe to be anything and anyone they choose to be, their boyfriends will not be. You'll need to make it clear that once upon a time their daddy used to be a sniper and there will never come a day when I'll need more than one shot to bring down my prey. I hear one cross word directed at my babies or be it one touch I find to be inappropriate I'm heading to my safe."

"I'll be sure to explain that."

"Clearly. So there is no doubt."

"They'll be crystal clear on the topic of their daddy being a badass former SEAL with a propensity for violence against anyone who does them wrong. I'll also explain you're a tad bit crazy and overprotective."

"That last part's a good idea, baby. It'll help minimize the complaining if they're forewarned that they won't be dating until they're eighteen."

At eighteen I was kicked out of my house, making me homeless.

And there I was now, tucked close to the man I loved discussing our daughters not being allowed to date until they reached majority. They would never know the pain of rejection. They'd know love and safety. They'd never doubt their mother's love. They'd never wonder if their dad loved them.

Night and day.

Worlds apart.

And that was it. The cycle would be broken, I'd make sure of it. It was done. There was nothing any of them could do to me. The hurt had been delivered. The pain had been caused. The wounds had healed over.

My life was not about proving someone wrong. I was worth so much more than that. It wasn't about staying on the back of a bull for eight seconds. It was about triumph, success, hard work, and I didn't need to cause myself physical damage to achieve my dreams.

What's it worth?

That was what Ty had asked me.

The new question was slightly different, but the answer was the same.

What was *I* worth?

Everything.

Matthew had taught me that.

"Do you want to go see your new house tomorrow?"

My new house.

Geez, he said that like it was no big deal.

I wanted to call it douchey. But what it was, was the kindest, most generous thing anyone had ever done for me. So it was far from douchey and bordered romantic.

"I don't want to sound ungrateful, but can we wait?"

Matt gave me a squeeze and said, "We can do anything you want to do."

I knew down to my soul he meant that.

"It's just that today was great then it sucked. Tomorrow I want to spend the day with just you and me. I want to lock the door, turn off the phone, and make the day all about us. I want to celebrate my win with you. I want to put distance between the shit with my family and something new, and special, and wonderful. I don't want our family home tainted with the memory of Trevor. I need the day with you, feeling safe and loved. Then I'll be ready to face the world."

Matt rolled me to my back, lifted his hands to palm my cheeks, and held my eyes captive.

"You are the strongest woman I know. Those fuckers keep trying to knock you down, but they can't. You go to your knees and get right back up. Fuckin' hell, baby, that strength is so beautiful. But, Chels, this isn't them knocking you down. This is me taking care of you. Don't bury the hurt, it needs to come out. I need you to trust I won't let you fall."

"I know you'd never let me fall."

"Then please let go and let out the hurt."

Man, oh, man. Matt loved me.

Yep. He loved me like crazy.

"Matt, honey, I've been letting go of the hurt for months. Every day you take care of me and every day a little more of the pain slips away. Tonight, before you showed up, I was facing down three men that had made my life hell and I was thinking about how badly I wanted that standoff, how I'd dreamed of proving to them how good I was.

"But I realized it was all for nothing. I didn't need to prove anything. Not to myself and certainly not to them. They are meaningless. My win tonight was *mine* and mine alone. *I* won the battle. *I* fought the war and came out victorious. That won't happen every time I ride; it won't even happen half the time. But I learned an eight-second ride doesn't mean victory. Conquering my fear does. I'm not afraid to love you. I'm not afraid you'll leave me. I'm not afraid to have a family. I won."

I brought my hands up and mirrored him holding onto my face and brought him closer.

"So, yes, Matt, I know. I believe you'll never let me fall because since the day I met you you've been holding me up. Let's relax and celebrate tomorrow. Take a few days, then go see our new home. And if it's over three bedrooms, you're sporting for a housekeeper twice a month, Richy-rich."

Matt grinned down at me.

I knew then it was over three bedrooms.

"How about we start celebrating tonight?"

My nipples tingled and a shiver rolled through me.

"Works for me."

"I wanna watch you suck me off."

Another shiver.

"Works for me."

"I know it does, because you know I love playing with your pussy while I watch you work my cock."

He was right. I did know that. I also loved it when I got to watch Matt watching me. His eyes got dark and hungry. And that always meant good things for me.

"You gonna let go of me so I can get down to pleasuring my man?"

His eyes flared, and since he was so close, I also got to feel his heart rate tick up a notch.

"Yeah, right after you tell me you love me."

"I love you, Matt."

"I love you."

Then he let go of my face and I took my time exploring his neck, chest, and abs before I took his thickness in my mouth and got down to business.

Damn, it felt good to be a winner.

28

I was topping off the travel mug Chelsea had handed me before I left for work this morning when Dylan walked into the break room.

"Report's on your desk," he told me.

Just like I knew it would be.

"Find anything interesting?"

"I found a lot of things interesting. But first I feel compelled to warn you you're gonna catch a load of shit today."

I gathered that when I turned my phone on this morning and my text messages and voice mails blew up. Just like Chelsea had wanted, we'd turned off our phones. We also hadn't answered the door the three times someone knocked. It had been annoying as fuck when the doorbell started ringing between pounds, which was a good indication it had been Quinn. Though Hadley would also be a good bet. We hadn't answered. Instead, we'd laid in bed and laughed our asses off until the noise stopped. Then I'd given my woman another orgasm.

That had been our day. Orgasms. Lots and lots of

orgasms. So many of them we'd fallen asleep before ten and neither of us had moved a muscle all night. I knew because I'd woken up with Chelsea still on top of me. Exactly how she'd fallen asleep after riding me so wild even I was shocked at the filthy things she was telling me she wanted me to do to her.

This morning before I rolled out of bed I assured her we would be trying out everything she'd suggested. She'd claimed temporary insanity by way of too many orgasms and dehydration. She was probably right about the dehydration though I still wasn't giving her a pass. I loved her ass too much to pass up the chance to take it—which she'd begged me to do last night. The only reason it hadn't happened was that I didn't have lube. Better believe I was stopping to get some tonight before I went home.

"Whatever it is you're thinking about, please for the love of God stop," Dylan grouched.

"Huh?"

"Dude, your face just went all funny, and not that I'm looking but I think you have a stiffy. I know I'm good-looking, love you like a brother, but even still, I don't swing your way."

"If you're not looking then how the hell do you know my dick's hard?"

"Yeah, so, I think I'll come back later," Logan choked out.

"That was not what it sounded like," Dylan said.

Which only made it worse.

"Right," Logan drawled.

"Matt's the one with his dick hard," Dylan complained.

"And...I think I'll wait to get coffee." Luke chuckled.

Perfect.

My day started with my woman's warm, naked body on

top of mine after a celebratory sex marathon and had slid straight to hell.

"I don't want to know whose dick is hard," Luke started.

"Apparently, Matt's popped wood and Dylan's admiring the oak," Logan supplied.

"Can we stop talking about my cock?"

"Jesus, I leave for two weeks, and the place turns into Pornhub." Trey walked in with an empty coffee mug. "Why are we talking about Matt's cock? Did he break it off yesterday? Addy and I stopped by but after hearing what sounded like the animal kingdom being played out live-action style in Matt's living room we didn't knock. And, brother, I hope those sounds were coming from your woman. Either that or she was taking your—"

"You're done," I cut him off.

"Oh, c'mon, I was just getting to the good part."

"No, you weren't," I returned. "You were gonna piss me off."

"Is it possible to piss off a man who's spent the last twenty-four hours locked in his house playing *Here Kitty Kitty*?" Dylan asked.

"And that, brother, is why you don't have a woman." Luke laughed. "You're playing *Here Kitty Kitty* while the men are playing *King of the Jungle*."

Welp. That went downhill fast.

"What can I say, playing with—"

"Nice," a very feminine voice hissed.

We all turned in unison to find Sawyer standing in the doorway.

Fuck.

"Hey, Sawyer, sorry," I started.

Before I could finish, she waved her hand and smiled at me.

"Stopped by your house yesterday to congratulate Chels. The two of you sounded like you were celebrating just fine, so I didn't bother knocking."

My life was now complete. I could die knowing that Trey and Addy *and* Sawyer heard me having sex with my woman.

I said nothing because I wasn't sure there was anything I could say to make the situation less uncomfortable. I supposed I could've thanked her for not interrupting but that seemed a little rude. I could've apologized but I wasn't sorry I was celebrating with my woman. So I kept my trap shut and prayed everyone else did, too.

An awkward silence fell and I took that as my leave.

"I'm getting back to work," I said even though I hadn't actually done any work yet.

"Oh, please, don't stop on my account. I'll just get my coffee so Dylan can finish telling you all about what he likes playing with," Sawyer said very sarcastically.

The problem was, it hid none of the hurt that washed over her features. My gaze went to Dylan and his face was set in stone. There were very few times I'd seen the man mad. He was normally happy-go-lucky. But right then I wasn't sure if he wanted to toss Sawyer over his shoulder and take her someplace private to work out the very obvious tension between them. Or if he was just going to bolt and get as far away from her as he could. Either way, he looked a little scary and a whole lot feral.

"You wanna play, Sawyer?" Dylan ground out.

I bit back my groan.

Wrong play, brother.

"I think I'll pass."

"No, Sawyer, I'm asking if you wanna continue to play this passive-aggressive game you've got going on."

"Dylan," Luke warned.

"I'm not—"

"Yes, you are. You come in here, and it's unfortunate what you overheard. We should've been more careful about who could hear us. It was uncool, I'll give you that. But you trying to throw my words in my face, seriously uncool."

"It's uncool I heard but not uncool what you were saying?" she spat.

"We'll leave," Logan said. "Give you two some privacy."

"No thanks. The last time I was alone with him he forgot my name."

"What?" Dylan asked.

Now, there were times when you knew someone was asking to buy time to come up with a lie. Then there were times when the person was genuinely stupefied. Dylan was the latter. He had no idea what Sawyer was talking about.

"Don't do that," she hissed. "Don't you *dare* pretend you don't know what I'm talking about."

"Sawyer, I have no idea—"

"Oh, so you know my name now. But you called me *Felicity* when you were inside of me."

Dylan looked like he'd been struck. All of the color bleached from his face and he swayed back.

"How...What?"

The hurt on Sawyer's face was painful to witness.

"We should go," I suggested.

"Right." Sawyer gave a sad smile. "With all the playing you do why would I think I'd be remotely memorable?"

With that, she left the room.

There was a long bout of silence before Luke broke it.

"You slept with Sawyer?"

The muscle in Dylan's cheek jumped but he didn't answer.

There had to be an explanation. Dylan played the field,

but he was not an asshole. He wouldn't fuck Sawyer then screw her over. As far as I saw he was friendly with the women I knew he'd been with. He was a lot like I was before I met Chelsea. Always casual but he didn't jack women around.

"Who's Felicity?"

Logan's question jerked Dylan out of his stupor, but the pain etched in his face was worse than what Sawyer's had been.

"My wife."

After he dropped that bomb, Dylan left, giving none of us time to recover.

"Dylan has a wife?" I mumbled. "How the hell is that possible?"

I glanced between my three friends. They each had identical looks of shock but also disappointment.

I'd been to Dylan's house. He lived alone. No woman was living there with him. No wife had ever accompanied him to one of the many barbeques I'd attended with him. He'd never talked about a wife, or any woman for that matter. And further from that, Dylan was not *That Guy.* I didn't believe for a second he'd cheat on any woman, most especially the woman he'd married.

With that thought in mind, I turned and ran down the hall. Something was wrong. But when I got to the lobby I saw Dylan's Jeep tearing out of the parking lot.

"Is something wrong?" Lauren asked from behind the reception desk. "Dylan came running through here like there was a fire."

Fuck, yeah, something was wrong.

"Everything's good."

"Is Dylan—"

"He's fine."

Not stupid by a long shot, Lauren eyed me with suspicion.

"If you say so," she muttered and went back to looking at her computer.

I knew she'd grill Logan later. I didn't envy the man, but I knew he wouldn't tell her about what Dylan had said. Not even under torture would Logan give up a secret. I knew that as fact, seeing as I'd been a POW with him and had heard every second of the torture he'd endured. Not a single secret had passed his lips.

It was nearing four o'clock when I had a chance to finally look at the report Dylan had put together. He'd been thorough. And my sister was more of a twit than I thought. She was in debt up to her eyeballs and broke. She didn't just spend money like it was going out of style, she also had made a slew of bad investments. Investments that my father would've never allowed her to make if he'd known. Which meant she'd gone behind his back and used a different broker.

How in the hell had she blown through a ten-million-dollar inheritance? Four million was still managed by Kessler but that would cover her debt. It was mind boggling that a person could spend six million dollars and have nothing to show for it. And why hadn't my father stopped her from cashing in her investments?

Jesus.

I was reading an investor presentation from a coffee company my sister had invested in—and lost her ass on—when my phone rang.

Addy's name flashed on the screen, and I picked up.

"Hey, Addy."

"Hey, Matt. I was wondering if Chelsea was in there with you?"

"In my office?"

"Yeah. We're waiting for her in the gym. She was supposed to be here twenty minutes ago. We figured she was waylaid."

"Chels is coming into TC today?"

"Yeah. I called her a while ago and asked her if she wasn't busy to come in and help us go through scholarship applications. She said she'd be in at three-thirty."

I had no idea Chelsea had planned on coming to TC. This morning before I'd left for work she'd handed me a to-go mug of coffee and told me she was going back to bed and sleeping the rest of the day. After that she'd stumbled back to the bedroom like a zombie. I hadn't called to check in because I'd hoped she was still in bed sleeping.

"Did you try calling her?" I asked.

"Obviously. She hasn't answered. That's why I figured she was in there with you and busy. Your door was closed and the last time I walked in—"

"How many times have you tried calling her?"

An ugly thought of her in a ditch on the side of the road filtered through my mind.

"Three times."

"I'll call you back."

"Matt, I didn't mean to worry you. She's probably running late and doesn't want to pick her phone up while she's driving."

"I'll call you back."

"Okay, Matt," Addy whispered.

I pushed back from my desk and scrolled to Chelsea's

name as I walked down the hall. It rang several times then I was sent to voice mail.

What the fuck?

I got to Dylan's door and dialed again.

The same thing happened. It rang, then voice mail.

Dylan's office was still empty, so I called him and got the same.

Fucking voice mail.

"Dylan, when you get this, call me. It's important."

I disconnected and jogged to the lobby. Luke was at Lauren's desk and stopped me before I could get out the door.

"Yo! Where are you going?"

"I've gotta run home real quick."

"Everything okay?"

It would be if you stopped talking to me.

"I'm sure it will be."

I made it across the lot and got to my truck when Luke caught up to me.

He slid into the passenger side and waited until I backed out before he asked, "What's going on?"

"I don't know. Chelsea was supposed to be here twenty minutes ago to meet with Addy. She tried calling Chelsea three times, no answer. I called her twice and was sent to voice mail."

"Did you ask Dylan—"

"He's not in his office."

Luke pulled his phone out. He'd connected a call and a second later Dylan's voice mail filled the cab. Luke repeated the process three more times before Dylan picked up.

"Yeah."

"We need you at the office."

"Why?" he slurred.

"Are you drunk?"

"Nope."

"You're fucking drunk, Dylan. What the fuck?"

"What do you need? I can do it from here."

"Are you sober enough to do it?" Luke angrily clipped.

"Just tell me what the fuck you need."

"Track Chelsea's phone."

"She okay?"

Suddenly Dylan didn't sound so inebriated.

"Precautionary. Call me back."

Luke hung up and I drove.

"I'm sure it's nothing," Luke said.

"Yep," I lied.

A ball in my gut had already knotted.

Chelsea would not send me to voice mail. She wouldn't not show up to meet her friends.

Something was wrong.

The question was, how big was that something?

29

The house was empty.

Chelsea's Ram was in the garage, her purse was on the counter, but her person and cell phone were not in the house.

Luke was in the garage searching for...what? What was Luke searching for? A clue about where Chelsea had gone?

I glanced around the bedroom floor. Yesterday's clothes were still in a pile. She'd slept naked but had put on one of my shirts to make coffee.

Which one? What color?

Think, goddammit.

My eyes landed on my ratty old Iron Maiden tee that should've been tossed out a decade ago. That was what Chelsea had been wearing.

She'd gotten up, got dressed, then what?

Where would she go without her purse? How far would she get on foot? Why wouldn't she have driven?

I pulled my phone out of my back pocket and called Dylan.

"Is she there?"

"No. I need Ty Lowen's number. He's Chelsea's trainer. He owns a ranch out—"

"Got it. Ready?"

It was good to know my friend could sober the hell up quickly in the middle of a crisis.

Is this a crisis?

Fuck.

"Text it to me. Any luck tracking her phone?"

"No. Signal's offline."

"How the hell is that possible? She sent me to voice mail."

"Could be she turned off her phone or is now in a dead zone."

Jesus Christ.

Dead zone.

My chin dipped down and my eyes landed on Chelsea's boots. I ruthlessly shoved the word *dead* out of my brain and stared at those damn boots.

"What about her phone records? Who has she talked to this morning?"

"I'm working on that now. Give me five minutes and I'll call you back. Does she have onboard GPS in her truck? I could track that."

"Her truck's in the garage. Purse is here, too."

"Did she go for a run?"

Damn. Why hadn't I thought of that?

I went to the walk-in and flicked on the light. Her running shoes were on the floor where she'd kicked them off. I looked around and cataloged the rest of her footwear. Boots, boots, and more boots. Sandals, flip-flops, and another pair of sneakers. I'd watched her unpack, and I did so thinking she didn't have much. What was missing? I took another look, slower this time. Then it hit me. She had one pair of tan-colored suede ankle boots. That was what was missing.

"She's not out for a run," I answered.

"You don't have cameras at your house," Dylan told me something I very well knew. "I'm checking your neighbors to see if someone on your block has a Ring or cameras. Closest traffic cam to your house is ten miles away. I have facial rec running but so far nothing."

Nothing.

Fuck, that was exactly what I had. Nothing to go on. Not a single clue where Chelsea had gone.

"I need to call Ty," I told him.

I disconnected and pulled up the text Dylan sent.

Two rings and Ty answered, "Ty Lowen."

"Ty. Matt. Have you seen or heard from Chelsea today?"

"No. She's taking the week off. Is everything okay?"

"Yeah," I lied, not wanting to worry Chelsea's friend. "Just do me a favor and call me if you hear from her. Or hear of anyone seeing her."

There was a beat of silence before Ty responded.

"You two fighting?"

"Hell, no!" I clipped. "She was supposed to meet up with some friends and hasn't shown up. Her phone's off and her truck is still in the garage."

"Did she call one of those ride share places or a taxi? A few months back, maybe six, she had to replace the alternator."

"I'll check. Thanks. Call me if you hear anything."

"Will do."

I shoved my phone in my pocket and took a breath.

I was fucking up, big time. I was letting panic overtake thought. I needed to calm the hell down and use my brain.

This was what I did. This was what I'd spent years training for.

I did not freak out and panic. I detached and observed. I was precise in my examination of my surroundings. I planned. I used my patience and skill to my advantage. I didn't go into any situation with fear, ever.

I inhaled slowly and exhaled even slower.

No Chelsea.

Where would she go? Who would she go with? Why wouldn't she answer her phone?

"Nothing's out of place in the garage or backyard. I checked all the windows and doors, except for in here. No tampering," Luke said from the doorway.

"I need to start her truck. Ty said she had the alternator replaced a few months ago. Dylan's running her phone records now. Maybe she called an Uber to come pick her up?"

But even as I said the words, I didn't believe them. Chelsea wouldn't have called an Uber. She would've called me. And if not me, she would've called one of her girls to come pick her up. Though, she hadn't called me to tell me she was coming into Triple Canopy. She hadn't called me all day. I thought it was because she was sleeping off our Sunday celebratory marathon.

Had I done something to hurt her? Said something that would make her leave me? I looked around the bedroom. No, all of her stuff was still there. Her purse was on the counter. And Chelsea would never walk out on me. When I pissed her off, she called me on it.

"I'll check her truck," Luke said. "Do you want to stay here and wait and see if she shows up, or go back to TC and wait for her there?"

My friend was being careful with his words. But the

deep lines creasing his forehead told the real story. He didn't believe Chelsea had called for a ride, either. He didn't believe she walked out of our house for a leisurely stroll around the block.

Luke knew the same as I did, something was wrong.

By the time Luke and I got back to TC, Dylan was waiting for us in the conference room. As was Trey, Logan, and Brady.

"Carter and Nick left ten minutes ago," Trey started. "They're driving the routes between here and your house. Jason's driving out to Ty's."

"I called Ty. He hasn't seen her."

"Jason wants to drive the route," Logan carefully added.

They were searching for accidents.

Fuck.

"I put a call in to Jackson," Logan continued. "He's keeping an ear out."

Jackson Clark was a firefighter. His station would get a call out if there was a wreck that required an ambulance.

It was a damn good thing my friends were thinking straight because as the minutes ticked by I couldn't pull my shit together.

Some fucking operator I am.

"Got her phone records," Dylan announced and slid a printout across the table. "This is the last week. I can go back further if we need."

I felt no shame in violating Chelsea's privacy as I scanned the paper.

"I marked the numbers of everyone we know. Addy, Hadley, all of the women are highlighted."

In the last week, ten numbers that had no ties to TC had called her.

"Have you traced the other numbers?"

"I've two left," Dylan told me. "Five are telemarketers' cloning numbers. One's a livestock feed company. One's a company that makes custom ropes. One belongs to Karen Harris."

"Karen's a waitress at Balls Deep."

"I'll call Karen," Logan offered. "And drive out to the bar."

Yep. I'd lost my touch. Actually, I was losing my fucking mind. Why hadn't I thought about Balls Deep?

The bar and Ty's place. Where else did she frequent? Her friends' houses and TC. She was a homebody. She worked, she trained, she spent time with those she was closest to.

Luke's phone beeped and I watched him look down and read his text.

"Shiloh called Echo and Phoenix. Even though Chels isn't officially reported missing, Shiloh put some feelers out. They're keeping an eye out."

Officially reported missing.

My chest started to burn.

I could no longer keep the denial at bay.

"Call Ethan. I wanna know where Denny and Rod are," I growled.

"You don't think—"

I cut Trey off and said, "I think that motherfucker threatened me right before I kicked his ass out of my bar. I think he's a douche bag who wouldn't mind fucking with me and would have no issue using Chelsea to do it."

"Goddamn, Matt, you think he's stupid enough to snatch her?" Trey asked.

"The asshole is stupid—period. I don't know what he'd do. Chelsea made him look like a punk when she attempted to rip his nipple off. Karen slapped the shit out of him in a bar full of people, and I put him on his ass. And the asshole threatened me. I'd bet he'd love nothing more than showing up at my house, putting Chels in cuffs, and taking her down to the station. You know as well as I do, he could drag out a booking for hours. That'd be hours of her sitting there before she'd get to call someone. Hours of me worried about her."

"Now that I could see him doing," Trey admitted. "I'll call Ethan."

"One of the numbers belongs to Russ Sullens," Dylan stated. "The other belongs to Trevor Sullens Junior."

Red-hot rage slithered down my spine.

"The call to TJ lasted ten minutes. That's the last call."

I glanced back down at the list of calls. Addy had called at two-oh-eight, the conversation lasted eighteen minutes. That was when Addy had asked Chels to come to TC. Chelsea was home and fine at two-twenty-six. TJ's call came in at two-fifty-five and lasted ten minutes. That call disconnected at three-oh-five. To make the twenty-minute drive to get to TC by three-thirty she'd have to leave the house by three-ten.

"Track TJ's phone," I clipped. "I wanna know if he's still in Georgia or if he went back to Omaha. Russ, too."

Dylan's eyes narrowed as he tapped on his keyboard. Then I watched as the muscles in his neck pulsed.

He lifted his eyes and I braced.

"Hinesville. Liberty Inn off East Oglethorpe Highway and—"

"Across from the Chevy dealership," I interjected. "I know it."

"Get me a room number and find Russ, too!" I shouted over my shoulder as I ran from the room.

Why the hell was TJ fifteen minutes from my house?

I had my phone up to my ear calling Chelsea again. When it went straight to voice mail, I disconnected.

"Where are you going?" Trey yelled from behind me.

"Going to talk to TJ."

"Fuck!"

I didn't wait for Trey to shut the passenger side door before I reversed out of the parking spot.

I didn't make conversation as I broke every traffic law from TC to the Liberty Inn. It wasn't until I was pulling into the parking lot when Trey asked, "How are we playing this?"

Great question.

"Any way we need to."

"You gonna fill me in on why Chelsea's brother would harm her?"

"No time."

I parked and cut the engine.

"Room three-sixteen," Trey told me and jumped out of my truck, ready to take my back in an unknown situation with no intel as to why I believed TJ would want to harm Chelsea.

Trust.

Straight up, no questions asked, trust.

I took the stairs two at a time up to the third floor.

"How big is this fucker?" Trey's voice was steady even though we'd run up three flights of stairs.

"My height. Slim but strong."

"Easy day," Trey muttered as I found the room.

I pounded on the door and stayed in the line of sight of the peephole, not giving one fuck that if TJ checked, he'd see me. Trey stood to my right. He'd be the surprise TJ didn't see coming.

TJ opened the door. Before he could get in a word I planted my hand in the middle of his chest and shoved him back in. Trey followed and closed the door behind us. I felt Trey move around me to clear the room. Not that there was much to clear—the room was empty except for us—but Trey would check the head.

"What the fuck?" TJ shouted.

I cut right to it. "Where's Chelsea?"

"Chelsea?"

"Yeah, asshole, your sister. Where is she?"

"How the hell would I know?"

"Clear," Trey called from the back of the room. "No struggle."

My heart slammed in my chest and my gaze zeroed in on my target.

"Why'd you call her?"

TJ jerked back and the asshole I'd seen the other night crept in. His body language screamed dickhead, his posture turned aggressive, and his fists clenched.

"None of your fucking business," he snapped. "Get the hell out of my room."

"See, it is my business. Chelsea made it clear the other night she wanted nothing to do with you, your dick of a brother, or that motherfucker who abused her. So why'd you call her?"

"It's none—"

My patience snapped. My hand went around TJ's throat and by the time I'd pushed him back to the wall his face was bright red and his arms were flailing in an attempt to break my hold.

Good luck, fucker.

"Listen closely, TJ. I'm gonna let you go and you're gonna tell me exactly what you and Chelsea talked about. Then you're gonna tell me where Russ is and why he called her."

A sickening, gargling sound came from TJ and I smiled.

"Hurts, doesn't it?" I snarled in his face.

"Brother, he won't be able to talk if you kill him," Trey warned.

I loosened my grasp just enough to allow some oxygen to fill his lungs.

"I wonder if your sister felt this kind of pain when your father was beating her. I wonder if she had a hard time breathing when he took a leather strap to her until she was bloody. I wonder how *she* felt knowing her two brothers didn't fucking protect her from that monster."

"I didn't..." he gurgled.

"No, asshole, you didn't," I spat. "You didn't do one fucking thing to protect my woman. You let that dick beat on her. You watched it happen. You told her she was a piece of shit. You made her feel worthless. Now, tell me why you called her."

I released TJ's throat and stepped back.

He immediately fell to his knees and dragged in a lungful of air. After several attempts, he coughed and sputtered.

"Christ, you think he needs CPR?" Trey muttered.

"I wouldn't piss on this asshole if he was on fire. CPR is out of the question."

"Buck up, idiot, and breathe." Trey shook his head.

"Hurry the fuck up!" I demanded.

TJ clumsily got to his feet and leaned against the wall. His face was still a nice shade of ashen and his throat was bright red. He'd wear my mark for days. A perverse thrill washed over me. I liked knowing every time TJ caught sight of his neck, he'd remember my hand around it. He'd remember what it felt like to have his oxygen cut off, he'd remember what it felt like to have his life literally in my hand.

"You don't understand." TJ coughed again. "You don't know what it was like."

"You know what I hate almost as much as a fucker who takes their hands to a woman? A man who makes excuses. I don't give a shit how it was. Why'd you call her?"

"He didn't just beat *her*," TJ whined. "She didn't even have it the worst."

Someplace deep, *very deep*, a small, microscopic part of me felt bad for TJ. I had not grown up in a home where I was hit. My father had never raised his hand to me or said an unkind word. He'd never been anything but supportive and encouraging. Maybe I was being unfair to Chelsea's brothers and maybe if she wasn't mine—wasn't the woman I loved more than anything—I would've been able to find some compassion. I couldn't say for certain, but I would like to think I was man enough to step up and take whatever abuse was aimed at my sister like Logan had. His father had abused him and his mother, but Logan was able to save his sisters from their father.

TJ and Russ had not done shit for Chelsea. Not only that, but they'd added to her pain.

So, no, I couldn't drum up compassion even if it would've been the right thing to do.

"Why'd you call her?" I whispered.

TJ scowled but didn't answer.

"Chelsea's missing. You were the last person to speak to her. So, I hope you understand, though I don't give a fuck if you do, I don't give a shit what happened to you. I want to know why you called her and what you spoke about."

"My sister's—"

"I suggest you tell him what he wants to know," Trey interjected. "I wouldn't if I could, but I won't be able to control him if you don't start talking."

"I called to apologize."

I couldn't help it, I blinked in surprise. That was not why I thought he'd called her.

"I wanted to explain to her why I was such a dick. I wanted to tell her about Mom dying. I asked her to meet me."

Whoa. What?

"What'd she say?"

"She told me that she was sorry about what happened to me and sorry to hear about Mom dying but she wanted nothing to do with any of us."

There it was; Chelsea could find the compassion for her abusers that I couldn't.

"How'd the call end?"

"She asked me never to contact her again and to pass the information along to Russ."

"And where is Russ?"

"Back home in Omaha. He's married. Has two daughters. He needed to get home."

A nauseating thought flooded my mind. Chelsea had nieces. Two girls that might be getting abused like she had. Would she bolt and go to Omaha to check on them?

"Did you tell her that Russ has daughters?"

"Yeah. I told her Russ wanted her to meet them and his wife."

My temper flared to life but before I could lash out Trey stepped in.

"What else are you leaving out?"

"Nothing. That was the whole conversation. She said no

to meeting me and told me she didn't want anything to do with us."

"Did she ask you if Russ hit his daughters? If your dad was around them? Anything that would make you believe she'd go to Omaha?" Trey took over questioning TJ, asking the same questions I was thinking.

The benefit of having your brother at your back.

"She didn't ask, but he doesn't. Russ's wife made him go to counseling before they got married. Anger management, too. Russ doesn't spend a lot of time with our dad. Neither do I. Only when I ride. And since Athens was my last rodeo, that time spent with him will be next to zero."

"You knew she'd be there," I accused.

"I did. I wanted to see her. I didn't think it would end the way it did. I didn't want my dad to see her. But I wanted to watch her—in person. Watching your baby sister on YouTube isn't the same as watching her live. I had to see it, just once. She's fuckin' amazing out there. Better than Russ or I ever was."

I thought back to all the conversations I'd had with her about how meaningless her brothers had made her feel. How hard she'd worked to prove them wrong. Then I remembered her coming to the realization there had never been anything to prove; she'd never been what they told her she was.

I hoped like hell TJ was telling the truth and Chelsea's nieces were well cared for. I hoped that Russ could be the type of man who broke the cycle.

But like Chelsea, I was done.

"Respect her wishes and don't ever contact her again."

I watched belligerence infuse the other man's demeanor before he managed to lock it down.

Maybe there was hope for the asshole.

"You'll take care of her."

Better than you fuckwits ever did.

"Until my dying breath."

I jerked my chin and Trey followed me out the door.

We were nearing my truck when I tossed my keys at Trey.

"I need you to drive."

He nabbed them out of the air and jogged to the driver's side.

When we got in and he started the engine, an overwhelming fear came over me.

"I need you to promise me something."

"Anything." No hesitation from Trey. He'd promise me anything and he'd keep that promise.

"Promise me you'll take care of Chelsea."

"You know I will. But—"

"If something happens, I need to know you'll take care of her."

It had been years. Not since our last mission that damaged Luke's eyesight, left Trey's face scarred and almost without a limb, that I'd allowed myself to slip into the dark, cold, calculating mindset. But I felt it, the moment I detached from the humanity I fought so hard to find. Not even when my friends' women had been in danger had I allowed myself to go back there.

"We're going to find her."

"Promise."

"Matt."

I turned and looked at my friend and watched him flinch.

He saw it.

He'd been by my side enough times to recognize the

darkness. He'd seen it in himself, in me, in Logan, Luke, Carter, and the rest of the men we'd served with.

"No matter what, I promise to take care of Chelsea."

There was a beat of silence then Trey asked, "Where to?"

"Denny."

30

Matt was going to be pissed.

No, he was going to breathe fire and wreak vengeance like the world had never seen when he found me.

And that scared me more than the two days I'd been sitting in this room.

Two whole days.

I could not say my accommodations were not comfortable. I was after all being held captive in a ridiculously obscene freaking mansion. Though it was not Matt's parents' estate, and I didn't actually know where I was, just that I'd been flown on a private jet to get here. I'd been blindfolded after the plane landed and it hadn't been taken off until I was in the foyer of a monstrosity larger than the Kessler house.

I'd been treated to four-course meals and offered expensive wine. I'd showered in a luxurious bathroom and had been given clean clothes that were way more costly than anything I would buy myself.

I'd been kidnapped.

I'd been doing nothing but sitting around for two days.

Matt on the other hand was freaking the fuck out; that I was sure about. Further from that, I was worried he was plotting murder.

I didn't know if he'd been notified about where I was or what these people wanted from him, but I knew he'd still be planning. I knew he'd be looking for me.

I had no idea who had or why I'd been taken. But the private jet and mansion were glaring indications these people knew Matt and he had something they wanted.

My first guess would be the Zanetti guy—head honcho mobster. My second guess would be Mancini—the restaurant owner slash mob guy. Maybe Matt's dad had something they wanted, and they were going to use Matt—well, me—to make Matt get it for them.

I'd spent the first twenty-four hours scared out of my mind. I'd cried and begged to be let go. I'd shook and trembled with fear. I cowered away from everyone who'd come near me. But that fear had morphed into fury.

I was so freaking angry I was being used against Matt my vision blurred with it.

I knew that was why I'd been taken.

And I knew I needed to contain my fury and wait for Matt. I had no choice but to wait. I was locked in a room, only taken out to eat, then escorted back. The place was swimming with scarily big men, all armed. I watched out the window and there were even guards that patrolled the garden beneath the window.

The door swung open and my usual escort scowled at me.

Listen, buddy, if you don't want me here, let me go, don't give me dirty looks.

"Dinner."

"I'm not hungry."

"Dinner," he repeated.

His hand brushed his suit jacket to the side showing me the gun at his hip.

Yep, still armed.

Damn.

"I'd like to make a phone call."

"Dinner."

I walked across the room and asked, "Do you know any other words besides dinner?"

"Do you know how to keep your mouth shut and follow directions?"

"Nope," I told him honestly.

"I do not like mouthy bitches."

"I don't like assholes who order me around and threaten me with guns."

I was pushing my luck and I knew it, when his hand shot out and grabbed my arm.

"Keep your mouth shut and follow directions."

To no avail, I tried to yank my arm free.

"Keep your hands to yourself and don't touch me," I hissed.

"This will go easier for all of us if you go back to being silent."

Easier? What did I care if I made his job harder? He was holding me captive.

"You think this is easy? You kidnapped me."

"I did not," he grunted. "Kidnap you."

"Oh, you're right. Forgive me, you're just the one holding me hostage. Why? What did I do to you? What do you want?"

The man's face turned a shade of magenta, and I knew I'd pushed too far.

With a violent shake that sent agony through my shoulder, he pulled me close.

"Don't talk. Don't fight. Do what you're told and this will be over soon."

That was what I was afraid of.

This was going to end, and when it did, either I'd be dead or Matt would've rained hellfire down, or both. And if Matt rained fire he could get in trouble, or worse, get killed. And I knew he wouldn't be alone. Luke, Trey, Logan, Carter, Dylan, and Brady would be with him. All of my friends' men would be in harm's way. They'd come to rescue me. They'd help Matt. They'd be in danger.

"Listen. I was thinking. I promise, I swear I'll do whatever you want but let me call my boyfriend and let him know I'm okay. I'll tell him I went on vacation and I'll be home in a few weeks."

The guy gave me a look that told me he knew Matt would never buy that lie.

"Okay, fine. I'll tell him I want to break up. That I'm leaving him and not to look for me."

The guy tilted his head and gave me a new look that conveyed how stupid he thought I was.

Matt would never believe that either.

"Please," I begged. "Please let me go. Matt has to be worried, which is going to make him angry."

"No doubt," he agreed.

"He's going to find me, and when he does there will be..." I trailed off, not knowing what there would be.

Blood. Carnage. Death. Jail time.

Oh, God.

"No doubt there will be something," the man muttered. "Just keep quiet."

"Your funeral."

"It won't be mine, but it will be someone's."

My insides froze. My skin caught fire. And I reacted without thinking.

I swung my left fist and connected with the man's jaw. He released my arm and I attacked. I punched and kicked. Everything happened in a haze of fury. The implication that Matt or I would be the ones to die had sent me into a fit of rage. If I was going to die, I would not do it quietly. If they meant harm to Matt, I would not be silent. I would fight to the death. I would fight until...

The wind was knocked out of me when my back hit the wall, momentarily making me lose my train of thought.

Both of my hands were pinned above my head, my legs were trapped with no way to kick.

"Stop!"

The man's face was right in mine. So close, the tip of his nose brushed mine.

I opened my mouth to scream but something made me stop.

Why wasn't he hurting me? He was bigger, way bigger. Why hadn't he hit me?

"Stop it, Chelsea!" He shoved his torso deeper into mine. "You keep quiet, and you and Matt walk out of this alive. You pull that shit with anyone else, you're dead and Matt lives out the rest of his life behind bars. That's if Zanetti doesn't kill him first."

Zanetti.

I'd been right.

"You've got a few hours left before this ends. Don't fuck up now. You hear me?"

"And when this ends, Matt's alive?"

He pulled back and stared at me.

"Yes."

"Then I hear you."

"No matter what you see or hear. Keep quiet."

"Why didn't you hurt me?"

It was a stupid question, but I had to know. For some reason, I wanted to trust what this guy was telling me, but I was afraid that my mind was playing a trick—and it was wishful thinking. Or he was trying to get me to let my guard down so he could hurt me later.

But there was something in his eyes. Remorse, maybe? Guilt? I hadn't seen it earlier. But thinking back over the last forty-eight hours, only this man had come to my room. When I ate, he stood behind me. When I was done, he walked me back.

Was he guarding me, or was he protecting me?

He hadn't let any of the other men near me, even when they'd said they'd take me back to the room after I ate. He simply shook his head and grabbed my arm, making me follow. I'd thought that maybe he was the boss. But maybe not.

"Quiet, Chelsea, before I change my mind."

His growled words held no heat.

I knew when a man was getting ready to strike.

I knew what hatred in a man's eyes looked like.

And I'd felt the rage and anger emanating from a man before he unleashed his wrath.

This man before me didn't have it in him to hit an innocent woman.

I'd bet my life on it.

"You won't change your mind," I told him. "But I'll stay

quiet and won't cause trouble no matter what I hear or see. But know this—if you're lying to me, if you're trying to trick me, and something happens to Matt or my friends, you better pray I'm dead after this. Because I will hunt you down and kill you."

"I believe that, Chelsea," he muttered and stepped back. "Wait for me to take you down."

I watched as he walked into the en suite bathroom. I waited for him to return, no longer looking disheveled.

He was at the door when he asked, "Ready?"

"Yes."

"Matt's a lucky man," he said so softly I barely heard.

But I had.

Who the hell was this man?

I was using my fork to push around the duck breast on my plate when it happened. I heard high heels clicking on the marble before I saw her.

Alessandra.

Every nasty word and threat she'd hurled at Matt flew through my brain in a rapid-fire montage of bitchiness.

Make all the threats you want, but there is not one single thing you can do to hurt me.

Matt had said that to his sister.

And she'd found the one thing that could hurt him.

She'd done the one thing that would bring her brother to his knees. The only thing. She'd taken me.

What a C-U-Next-Tuesday.

A well-dressed older man walked in behind her, and a shiver went down my spine. He looked like a shady character out of *Goodfellas*.

All of the guards bustled around like God himself had descended from heaven.

"Is everything in place?"

"Yes, Mr. Zanetti," one of the men answered.

"Roland Huston has been neutralized?"

"Yes," the same man answered.

Alessandra was glaring daggers at me. My tongue itched to lash out. My palms twitched to smack the shit out of her.

She'd never know how lucky she was to have a brother like Matt. A good, kind man, that had she not been so nasty would've stood by her. He would've never allowed anything bad to harm her. But instead, she was a greedy, manipulative bitch.

"Do you have something to say, Chelsea?" she crooned sweetly.

There was so much I wanted to say. But I'd rather go home safely to Matt, so instead, I replied with a simple, "No."

"It is rather fitting that my weak brother would find himself a weak woman."

Mr. Zanetti's gaze came to mine and I did my best to be something I was not: fragile and weak. I slumped my shoulders and made myself look as docile as possible.

With his perusal complete, he dismissed me and went back to questioning his men.

"The house has been searched? As have the safes?"

"Yes."

"Good. All that's left is for my bride to collect her money." Zanetti smiled. "And of course our guest will need to be disposed of. Alessandra. Make your call and send your brother a picture of her. We need to be on our way."

There was a lot to process.

First, I was the guest that needed to be disposed of.

Second, it seemed that Vern's attorney had already been disposed of. And third, Alessandra was Zanetti's bride. As in, they'd gotten married?

That was gross on so many levels. The biggest being the man was a mob boss, just down from that was he was older than her father.

Gross!

Alessandra opened her clutch and pulled out her phone. With a devious smile that would make the devil proud she called her brother.

She put the phone up to her ear but didn't take her bitch eyes off of me.

"Yes, Matthew, I realize this isn't a good time for you." There was a pause. "It would seem the ball is now in *my* court. So here are your choices. Buy my five shares for ten million or give me yours plus Dad's fifty-one and we'll call it an even trade for Miss Sullens."

Ten million dollars?

Or all of the shares in Kessler.

No, *no*, no.

I dropped the fork that I was still holding and I felt a hand graze my arm.

A brief touch.

A reminder to stay quiet.

"Of course, you may. She's sitting right here enjoying her dinner. Let me put her on."

"Speaker," Zanetti grunted as Alessandra lowered the phone.

"Say hello," Alessandra demanded.

"Chels?" Matt's voice echoed in the big room.

The sound bounced off the walls, ricocheted, and slammed straight into my chest.

"Hey, sweetheart."

"Are you okay?"

I pinched my lips and felt my sinuses clog.

No, I was not okay. It didn't matter if Matt gave Alessandra the money or the shares, I was going to be disposed of. And then Matt would be. What about Ginny? Did Alessandra plan on taking out her mother, too? Did she know that it was Ginny who turned in Vern?

"Chels, baby?" Matt called.

"I'm fine."

"Are you hurt?"

"No."

"That's good, baby, hang tight."

"Don't give her—"

I didn't get to finish telling him not to give her the money before the whole house was plunged into darkness and chaos ensued.

I was grabbed from behind and plucked out of the chair, right on up over the back of it. The movement happened so quickly I forgot to struggle.

Then I remembered and my guard's mouth lowered to my ear.

"This is when you stay silent, Chelsea," he growled.

"What's—"

"You'll be out of here soon. All you have to do is be quiet and do not run."

I'll be out of here soon?

"There's like twenty guards," I hissed.

"There's eighteen. Easy day."

Easy day?

I'd heard Matt and the guys say that. It was some sort of SEAL motto. Something they said to each other when something was absolutely not easy.

There was a bang, the sound so piercing I covered my

ears. The man twisted, shoved me to the floor, and covered my body with his.

When I got my breath back I whispered, "So you're a friendly?"

"As friendly as I dare to be without Matt putting a bullet between my eyes."

31

"Say hello," my sister snottily demanded.

My own fucking family had taken my woman.

My blood.

My sister had plotted and schemed. The bitch had married Zanetti. I wasn't sure which one of those two assholes was getting more out of the deal. My sister getting the manpower she needed to pull off the kidnapping or Zanetti ensuring my sister couldn't testify against him. Either way, they'd fucked up. That marriage was their downfall. It was the first piece of the puzzle we needed. Once Dylan had found the marriage certificate everything else had fallen into place.

There was a stretch of silence before I called, "Chels?"

"Hey, sweetheart." I heard the tremble in her voice and I vowed to put a bullet in Zanetti's heart.

"Confirmation." Trey's voice in my earpiece reminded me my team was listening

"Are you okay?" I asked, looking down the sight of my scope and counting the men in the room with Chelsea.

"Charge set," Logan told me through the comms.

"Chels, baby?" I prompted.

"I'm fine."

"Are you hurt?"

"Lights out in, three..." Carter started the countdown.

"No."

"That's good, baby, hang tight."

"One." Carter finished and the street went dark.

"Don't give her—"

I didn't hear the rest of what she was going to say.

In a split second, I adjusted my Armasight to night vision, the sight picture changing to black and white as I tracked a man running across the backyard toward the house.

"Engaging," I warned and took the shot.

A second man came into view and I pulled the trigger.

The recoil of my AXMC felt familiar, like old times. And I felt another mark slash across my soul. Two pulls of the trigger, two men dead.

"Standby."

A moment after Logan's notice, a large explosion rocked the house.

There were quieter means of entry. We could've silently maneuvered into the house, but we were relying on chaos. There were six of us and nineteen—now seventeen heavily armed men, a mob boss, and my sister.

My fucking sister.

We needed the men scrambling. Luke and I would pick off the ones who ran out the back, the entry team would clear the house. Trey's sole mission was to nab Chelsea and get her out.

"Two out the side." Two snaps came from my left, then Luke called his hits. "Down."

Four down, fifteen to go.

There was a volley of gunfire in the house and I fought to keep my heartbeat steady.

Cold.

Emotionless.

Chelsea needed me impassive and detached.

My rifle and my scope—that was what I'd been reduced to.

Emotions could wait.

The gunfire stopped and I asked, "Status?"

One by one, the men called in their shots.

Ten more down. Five left.

"Trey, you got eyes on the package?"

"Negative."

"You have a friendly in there," Dylan warned.

"What the fuck?" Carter barked. "How did we not know that?"

That was a fuck-up. No, worse than a fuck-up, a total clusterfuck.

Our mission had been approved by the FBI.

"DEA just called in," Dylan continued. "FBI didn't share the takedown. They were planning their own. They've got a man inside and they're pissed as fuck."

Not my problem.

"Well, they might have a dead agent," Carter returned. "Upstairs clear."

Goddammit.

"Code phrase?" Logan asked.

"Indigo violet," Dylan told him and I hoped the agent was alive to use it.

"Two going for the back," Logan cautioned. "That's your overwatch one."

I put my crosshairs on the back door and didn't have to wait long for Zanetti and my sister to appear.

With a slow, even pull of my trigger, a bullet left the chamber and a millisecond later pierced Zanetti's heart. I adjusted and took the second shot. Alessandra dropped to her knees, her hands going to my carefully placed shoulder shot, and she wailed in pain.

My sister would never know how lucky she was. She would never know the restraint it had taken for me not to put a bullet through her heart. She'd never understand the only reason I'd left her breathing was because I loved my mother. Better her daughter in prison than six feet under.

"Two non-lethal," Logan panted. "Cuffed and down."

"Where the fuck is Chelsea?" I growled.

My control was slipping. I could feel it waning as the minutes ticked. It was only by a miracle I'd been able to lock my fear down for the last forty-eight hours. It was only because my brothers had a constant refrain reminding me Chelsea needed me clear-headed. It was only because I knew I couldn't live the rest of my life without her that I'd been able to remain cold.

But the longer it took to find her the harder it became to stop myself from rushing into the house to find her.

Trust.

I had to trust Trey to find her, and my team had to trust me to watch their backs.

"On your knees!" Trey shouted.

There was a muffled commotion through my comms and I couldn't stop myself from lifting my cheek off the buttstock of my rifle to listen.

"Get the fuck away from her. Knees, motherfucker, now!"

"Luke, the field is yours," I called in and stood, picking up my rifle as I went.

I swung the heavy rifle over my shoulder. The sling

caught, and I jumped off the gazebo I'd used as a sniper perch and ran across the backyard, ignoring the dead bodies and my sobbing sister.

"Entering. Back door," I notified the team as I pulled my night vision goggles down from my helmet then reached for my Sig in my thigh holster. "Location?"

"Chef's kitchen."

West side of the house, far corner.

I'd memorized the layout of the house, same as the entry team had. Plans changed in field, each of us knew the role of the other men. We could be moved around and still be effective.

I made it to the door and Chelsea was standing with her hands waving in front of a man in a suit. The man was struggling to push her behind him, but Chelsea was having none of it.

"Behind me, Chelsea," the man demanded.

"Don't shoot him," she pleaded.

"Get on your fucking knees. Chelsea, come to me!" Trey shouted.

The room was pitch black. The man could not see us, though he could see the IR illuminators our goggles needed to work in complete darkness. Night vision only amplified light, it didn't allow you to see in total blackout conditions. So when the man's head turned in my direction, he wasn't seeing me he was seeing a dot. He knew someone new had entered the room and his efforts to get Chelsea behind him intensified.

"We need the lights," I told Dylan through the comms.

"In three," he returned and counted down.

I pushed my goggles back up as the hum of the fridge filled the room. Thankfully the overhead lights in the chef's kitchen were off and didn't leave us momentarily blinded.

Just the soft glow of the under-cabinet lights illuminated the room.

The man looked at me, recognition filled his eyes, and he breathed a sigh of relief.

"Go on, Chelsea, you're safe," he told her.

I didn't have time to brace before Chelsea flew across the room and jumped.

I caught her around the middle as her legs wrapped around my hips and she shoved her face in my neck.

Not the most tactically sound maneuver but Chelsea was in my arms and Trey would cover us. I turned my back to the scene playing out and moved out of the room when Chelsea's head came up and her legs started to unwrap.

"Don't shoot him!" she yelled.

"Code phrase," Trey demanded.

The man said nothing. He stood perfectly still.

"Sixteen dead, two cuffed," Trey told him. "Code phrase?"

Still nothing.

If this was the agent, he wouldn't blow his cover.

"Zanetti's dead," I informed him. "What's the code phrase?"

Anger swept over the man, and I lifted my Sig. Barrel dead center to the man's chest. If I was wrong and the guy wasn't DEA but worked for Zanetti and was pissed I killed his boss, he'd find a bullet through his chest, too. My aim was just as good at close range than it was at five-hundred meters.

"Fuck. Months of living and breathing with scum for nothing," he hissed. "Indigo violet."

Zanetti was dead. That wasn't nothing. But then I hadn't been the one building a case against him.

Trey lowered his weapon. I did not.

"If there's a single scratch on my woman, I'm holding you responsible."

I shoved my Sig back in my thigh rig and wrapped my arms around Chelsea.

"Ready to go home?" I asked.

Chelsea didn't answer. Instead, she asked, "Are you okay?"

"I am now."

"Okay, then let me down."

My arms wrapped tighter, and I frowned at her request.

"Just for a second. Please."

I set her on her feet, and when I did, she grabbed my hand and pulled me toward the agent.

"What's your name?" she asked. "Or are you not allowed to tell me?"

The man's smile was indulgent when he said, "Tim."

"Thank you, Tim."

"There's no reason to thank me," he returned. "I scared—"

"Thank you, Tim," Chelsea said firmly.

"You're welcome, Chelsea."

Her hand in mine loosened and she turned to look up at me.

"If I didn't already have a great dislike for ostentatious mansions, spending two days in this place would've done it. I hope your mom's new house is small and cozy or we're not visiting her."

My lips twitched and I muttered, "Noted."

"Thank you for coming to get me."

Slayed.

My armor fell away and all the emotions I'd buried came rushing to the surface. Relief so vicious I felt it sting my eyes.

"Chels." I could get no more past the clog in my throat.

"Let's go home."

Home.

I nodded and Chelsea hopped back up and wrapped her arms around my shoulders.

"I want to be carried out," she announced. "Like a queen who's been rescued by her king."

Trey barked out a laugh and, in my ear, I heard the other men's echoing laughter.

"Aw. Isn't that sweet?" Carter cooed.

"The king has saved the day," Logan added.

"Jesus." Luke chuckled. "Brother, you're never living that down."

Luke was right but I couldn't give two shits the team would razz me for years to come.

My Queen was alive and safe in my arms.

32

For once I was dressed and ready on time.

It was Matt who was running late.

He was still in the shower and our friends were due to arrive in twenty minutes.

I hopped up on the granite top of the double sink vanity, looked through the clear glass door, and watched Matt soap up his body.

When his hand roamed down his chest, over his abs, and down farther between his legs I felt my nipples pebble. One of his soapy hands wrapped around his cock and slid up and down.

"I thought more than two strokes meant you were playing with it, not washing it."

"Thought I'd give you something to watch."

Maybe this wasn't a good idea.

"Stop playing with yourself and tell me what happened with Denny."

Matt let go of his dick and rinsed the shampoo out of his hair.

"He dropped the complaint."

Thank God.

In Matt's attempt to find me that first day I was missing, he'd had a chat with Denny, the asshole who'd threatened him at the bar. The chat had disintegrated into a fight when Denny had taunted Matt, telling him he might know where I was. Obviously, Denny had been lying but at the time Matt hadn't known that. Denny being the asshole he was, pressed charges and wanted Matt arrested for assault. Which led to Karen going down to the station and making a formal complaint against Denny.

"Did he say why?"

"No. But Ethan told me Denny's wife is on a tear. Someone filled her in on what happened. So, my guess is she told him to drop the charges, or she'd leave him."

I was no longer one to look a gift horse in the mouth.

Denny had dropped the charges.

The end.

"Well, that's good. I've heard conjugal visits suck."

"Oh, yeah?" Matt laughed. "You know a lot of married couples banging behind bars?"

Matt paused then said, "That'd be an awesome name for a club, Banging Behind Bars."

I groaned my reply, "Yeah, a strip club, maybe."

"I wonder what the profit margins are for a gentlemen's club."

"Please tell me you're joking. I'm not managing your strip club."

Matt was still laughing when he shut off the water.

"Grab me a towel, would you?"

I jumped off the vanity and pulled a nice, warm fluffy towel off my new towel warmer that was in my brand-new bathroom.

Well, it was brand-new to me since we'd only moved in

two days ago. And I knew the towel warmer was new because Matt had it installed the day the house closed which was a week ago.

The shower door opened and I held out the towel.

"At your service, my lord," I teased.

Instead of taking the towel Matt grabbed my hand and yanked me forward.

I collided with his wet body and his mouth dropped to mine.

I got the lip brush I loved so much right before his tongue invaded my mouth. By the time he was done plundering, more than just my shirt was wet.

"Damn, I love your mouth."

I smiled against his lips. I knew he did, he told me all the time.

"How long do we have?"

"Not enough time," I told him, knowing where his mind had gone.

"Quickie?"

"Not even you can pull one off in five minutes."

"Bet?"

"Sure, but you leave me hanging I get three tonight and you get none."

"Three?"

"Worried?" I teased.

His gaze dropped to my bare legs, then up to the hem of my dress, and he smiled.

"Hands on the vanity, Chels."

A tremor slid through me as I turned and made my way back to the vanity.

I felt Matt's hand on my ass and the material of my dress slid up and over my hips. His other hand went between my legs and he cupped me there.

"Have I told you today how beautiful you are?"

"Yes," I whispered.

His fingers pushed the crotch of my panties to the side and his knuckles grazed my clit.

Warmth bloomed and excitement flooded.

"I love you, baby."

His gruff, hunger-filled voice swept through me.

I lifted my head and found Matt's gaze in the mirror. So much love shone in his eyes I lost track of what he was doing between my legs.

Love he freely gave every day.

Love that had gotten me through being kidnapped and the nightmares that followed.

Love that made those same nightmares go away. I was safe and cared for and I knew Matt would always come for me.

Love that made me feel beautiful.

Love that showed me I was stronger than I'd given myself credit for.

I love you I thought. But instead of saying the words, I held his eyes.

I silently told him everything I wanted him to know.

I knew when he heard it. His face softened, his fingers at my hips dug in, and a rumble emanated from his chest.

Matt's chest pressed against my back and his mouth dropped to my ear.

"Hold on tight."

"I always do."

"Hold tight, baby."

God, I loved the way he growled in my ear.

"Always, Matthew."

The tip of his cock skimmed over my clit and my hips jerked in response.

"I'm never letting go," I warned him. "Never, honey."

With a single thrust, his cock filled me.

Three minutes later with his thumb on my clit and his teeth grazing my neck I moaned my orgasm. Three strokes later he groaned his.

"How long do you think she'll get?" Addy asked.

I looked away from the barn that Matt and Trey had disappeared into and turned toward my friend.

Addy was asking about Alessandra. She was alive, but that was what Matt had intended. As much as I hated the woman I was happy he hadn't had to do more than injure her. He'd explained he'd left her breathing because he knew his mother would be devastated if her daughter had died. I believed that was part of the reason. But he also hadn't killed her because, no matter what she'd done, she was still his sister. And I understood that. Admired it. Matt was a good man—he valued life, understood the grave implications of taking one—even when that life had been spent doing bad things. I wasn't the only one who'd had nightmares after he'd rescued me. Mine had lasted a week. A month later his were finally starting to subside. I figured I'd gotten over mine as quickly as I had because I always knew Matt was searching for me. I'd known he would find me, and as scary as that time had been, I knew Matt was coming.

I had to sit and wait. Matt had to take lives. None of the guys had talked about it with me. No one had told me who'd done what. And I would never ask them to share. They'd all made sacrifices for me that day. Whether they'd pulled the trigger or not. The house had been heavily guarded with mob enforcers; every man who'd come for me had risked his life.

I was beyond grateful.

Addy picked up her iced tea and pulled me back to the conversation.

"Matt said it depends on if she makes a deal."

"That mob guy's dead," Hadley stated. "What exactly does she think she has to make a deal?"

"She has nothing," I explained. "And the DEA had an undercover agent in Zanetti's crew. He was there when Alessandra asked Zanetti to have me kidnapped. It was her idea. And he was there when Zanetti's men came to the house to take me. She's screwed. She has nothing to bargain with unless she has something on Mancini. But Matt's dad said she doesn't have anything, and through his new attorney, has tried to tell her to plead guilty."

I was surprised when Matt told me he wanted to fly to New York to visit his father. But when he explained he wanted to tell his father to tell Alessandra to plead guilty I thought I understood—a Kessler doesn't make excuses. I'd been wrong. Matt didn't want me to have to go through a trial. He didn't want me to have to relive the nightmare.

He needn't have worried. Not only was I strong enough to testify, I wanted to.

Alessandra hadn't broken me. She hadn't ruined her brother.

Matt and I were stronger than ever.

In our new home, starting our new lives.

"What the hell are they doing?" Shiloh laughed and pointed at the barn.

Our backyard was full of people.

All of our friends were there—a housewarming party,

sans gifts. That was Matt's decree, but I seconded the thought.

Their presence was the only gift we needed.

Matt was on the back of Rebel and my baby didn't look happy. She was stubborn like her momma and would let Matt groom her, but she'd dig her hoofs in if he tried to walk her with a lead. And he'd never ridden her.

Gypsy came happily prancing out with Trey up in a saddle.

"Does he know how to ride?" I asked Addy.

"No clue, but I guess we're gonna find out." She giggled.

"You're living dangerously," I called out to Matt.

"Danger's my middle name."

I rolled my eyes at his predictable comeback.

"I'll remind you of that when she bucks you off."

"Come here."

Just then Rebel decided to sidestep and started to neigh.

"That's your cue to dismount."

Matt swung his leg over the saddle horn and in the blink of an eye his boots were on the ground.

"I don't think I've ever seen him move that fast," Quinn muttered.

"Smart." I continued to yell across the yard.

"C'mere."

I pushed back from the table and made my way across the patio and hit the grassy area that surrounded the back of the house.

When I hit the gravel that made up the rest of the backyard leading to the barn I asked, "Why do you have the horses out?"

"Will you turn Rebel out for me?" he strangely asked instead of answering.

He handed me the reins and walked to the gate.

Rebel liked me and only me, so she easily followed.

"Why'd you ride her out if you were going to put her in the paddock?"

"Because she wouldn't move. I pulled and she backed up. I offered her a treat and she knocked it out of my hand. The only way to get her to move was to get on her. And I know she only walked out of the barn was because she needed room to buck."

That was probably a fair assessment.

"And Trey? Why'd you saddle Gypsy?"

"He's never been on a horse." Matt shrugged. "And Gypsy loves everyone."

Okay, that was fair. But I still didn't understand why he was moving the girls.

"Why are you putting them in the paddock?" I asked and let Rebel loose.

"How do I get off?" Trey asked.

"Swing your leg over and jump," I told him.

"Just jump?" he asked with wide eyes.

How was it possible this man had been a big, bad, tough Navy SEAL but he looked scared to jump off of a horse?

"Yes, just jump. She won't move."

But on the off chance she did, I slid my fingers into her bridle.

Trey's dismount was clumsy and ungraceful but when his feet were back on the ground he smiled.

"I totally nailed that," he gloated.

I patted Gypsy's rump and she ran through the gate.

Matt closed it and held his hand up. "Wait right here. Don't move."

"Why are you being weird?"

"Just don't move."

Before I could confirm I wouldn't move, he ran back into the barn.

Yes, ran, like a weirdo.

A few moments later he came back out.

My breath whooshed out of my lungs.

Behind him was a beautiful dapple-gray quarter horse.

"Oh my God!" I covered my mouth and did my best not to jump up and down like an excited ten-year-old.

But seriously.

Matt bought us a horse.

And not just any horse—a beautiful gray with magnificent dappling.

Matt brought her around and that was when I noticed something was dangling from her halter.

The afternoon light caught and the largest diamond I'd ever seen sparkled.

"Marry me?"

I tore my eyes off the ring and looked up at Matt.

"You bought a horse," I accused.

"Marry me, Chelsea."

"You bought us a house and a horse."

"Say yes, and we'll fill that house with—"

"Yes."

Matt smiled and said, "I'm afraid to ask which you like better, your horse or your diamond."

"Don't ask," I warned.

"Refreshing," he muttered.

"Will you stop saying that and kiss me?" I demanded.

Matt's arm went around my waist and he hauled me flush to his chest. When his lips were a hair's breadth away, he whispered, "I should be jealous. You just wanna ride your new man."

Um. Maybe.

"Wanna know his name?" he asked, still whispering against my lips.

The vibrations made me tingle all over.

I nodded.

"Trigger."

When he closed the scant distance and kissed me, I was laughing.

Matt had never tasted so good.

Chelsea was out on Trigger.

It was his name that had sealed the deal between him and a four-year-old with an impressive pedigree.

"Has she decided what she's gonna do?" Luke asked.

He was asking about Chelsea and if she'd made a decision about competing.

"She says she's done. Her shoulder's not a hundred percent and the specialist she went to told her even with extensive therapy it's unlikely she'll ever have full rotation."

"Damn," Luke muttered.

He knew a thing or two about career-ending injuries.

"How's she doing?"

Chelsea had once again proved her strength. She got the news, she weighed her options, then she'd made her decision.

That was it.

"She's magnificent."

"Spoken like a lovesick sap," Luke teased and poured another round of shots.

"No," Logan snorted. "Spoken like a king."

The men around the table broke out in gales of laughter.

I glanced at Luke, then at Logan, Carter, Dylan, and finally Trey.

My brothers.

My family.

I was a lucky man.

Then I picked up my shot glass and tossed it back...like a motherfucking king.

33

Dylan

There was a knock on the door, and I knew.

I wasn't sure how I knew but I did.

My reprieve was over.

I was actually surprised it had taken them this long. Though with Chelsea getting kidnapped and Matt's sister in the hospital under arrest recovering from a gunshot wound, I shouldn't have been. Logan, Trey, and Luke would give Matt time to take care of his woman before they roped him into cornering me and demanding answers.

I knew because I would've done the same. There was no way that if one of them dropped a bomb I would've let them get away with that shit.

And the reality was, they hadn't given me a month. They'd given me a long time; they just hadn't known it.

Up until what happened in the break room, my secrets had been mine.

But then, Sawyer had dropped a bomb of her own and I felt like my world had imploded.

Worse than imploded, it had completely crumbled to burning rubble.

Sweet Sawyer.

How in the hell had I fucked up so badly?

Oh, right, I was piss-ass drunk, that was how I'd fucked up. The one night a year I allowed myself to lose control and feel the full weight of a loss that still scorched my soul.

The one fucking night, and that was when Sawyer decided to make her approach. The one fucking night when I'd been so trashed that until she brought it up, I had no recollection of it. And even then, I only remembered bits and pieces. I remembered seeing her at the bar, we had a friendly conversation. I was one drink away from having to call a taxi when she offered to drive me home.

And there was my fuck-up. I should've said no and left. I should've gotten my ass home and finished drinking myself stupid alone like I always did. But, fuck, I didn't want to be alone, I wanted to talk to Sawyer, not cry over my dead wife. I wanted to keep hearing her laugh, but more, I wanted to continue to make her laugh. To feel something on that goddamn night besides pain and grief.

It was the single most selfish thing I'd ever done in my life.

I didn't remember Sawyer bringing me home. I didn't remember having sex with her, though I was sure we did. Not only was the woman insanely sexy, but she was also funny to boot. And I sure as hell didn't remember calling her Felicity. That was something I was positive I'd never done before, though, in all the years since she'd been gone, I'd never been with a woman on that day. Not that I was attempting to make an excuse for the inexcusable.

The pain and devastation in her eyes had killed.

Goddamn, I was a fucking prick!

Sweet, pretty, funny Sawyer.

There was another knock accompanied by the doorbell.

"Be right there!"

Up next is Sawyer and Dylan in Conquered.

Grab your copy now.

ALSO BY RILEY EDWARDS

Riley Edwards

www.RileyEdwardsRomance.com

Takeback

Dangerous Love

Dangerous Rescue

Dangerous Games

Gemini Group

Nixon's Promise

Jameson's Salvation

Weston's Treasure

Alec's Dream

Chasin's Surrender

Holden's Resurrection

Jonny's Redemption

Red Team - Susan Stoker Universe

Nightstalker

Protecting Olivia

Redeeming Violet

Recovering Ivy

Rescuing Erin

The Gold Team - Susan Stoker Universe

Brooks

Thaddeus

Kyle

Maximus

Declan

Blue Team - Susan Stoker Universe

Owen

Gabe

Myles

Kevin

The 707 Freedom Series

Free

Freeing Jasper

Finally Free

Freedom

The Next Generation (707 spinoff)

Saving Meadow

Chasing Honor

Finding Mercy

Claiming Tuesday

Adoring Delaney

Keeping Quinn

Taking Liberty

Triple Canopy

Damaged

Flawed

Imperfect

Tarnished

Tainted

Conquered

The Collective

Unbroken

Trust

Standalone

Romancing Rayne

Falling for the Delta Co-written with Susan Stoker

BE A REBEL

Riley Edwards is a USA Today and WSJ bestselling author, wife, and military mom. Riley was born and raised in Los Angeles but now resides on the east coast with her fantastic husband and children.

Riley writes heart-stopping romance with sexy alpha heroes and even stronger heroines. Riley's favorite genres to write are romantic suspense and military romance.

Don't forget to sign up for Riley's newsletter and never miss another release, sale, or exclusive bonus material.

Rebels Newsletter

Facebook Fan Group

www.rileyedwardsromance.com

facebook.com/Novelist.Riley.Edwards
instagram.com/rileyedwardsromance
bookbub.com/authors/riley-edwards
amazon.com/author/rileyedwards

ACKNOWLEDGMENTS

To all of you – the readers: Thank you for picking up this book and giving me a few hours of your time. Whether this is the first book of mine you've read or you've been with me from the beginning, thank you for your support. It is because of you I have the coolest job in the world.

Made in United States
Orlando, FL
31 January 2023